Into the Distance

Brenda MacKenzie

© Brenda MacKenzie 2015

Brenda MacKenzie has asserted her rights under the Copyright, Design and Patents Act, 1988, to be identified as the author of this work.

First published in 2015 by Endeavour Press Ltd.

This edition published in 2015 by Createspace.

For Keith, with everlasting happy memories

Chapter One

High up on the ship's hurricane deck Leonie Grant leaned over the rail, enthralled by the pageant on the quay. Grey November fog threatened to engulf the crowds yet failed to quench enthusiasm as spectators roared '*Bon voyage!*' and waved Union Jacks at the troops who waited to board the SS *Britannic* bound for Australia.

She jammed her velvet hat down over her ears and focussed her Bulls-Eye camera. A prism swam in her eyes; scarlet, blue and green of uniforms; the glitter of campaign medals, steel scabbards and helmets; as if a richly embroidered carpet covered up the grime. Briefly her mind turned to science as she wished there was such a thing as coloured film now, in 1900, to capture the scene. She steadied her hands and clicked the shutter as the military band struck up the poignant chords of *The Girl I Left Behind Me*.

As the sounds swelled into the air she glanced at the dozen or so other passengers all intent on the scene below. Who might they be? Were they, like her, embarked on a journey into the unknown, or well-seasoned travellers? The music ceased and

Leonie turned to her aunt, who stood stiffly at her side. 'Isn't this a wonder?'

Beneath Ruth Fox's hat veil Leonie caught a brief flicker of response. It quenched her hope that Aunt could put aside grief as she herself determined to do. In an effort to instil warmth into the pale face she mouthed above the roaring crowd, 'What an adventure!' and slid an arm about her aunt's thin waist.

This was what she'd always craved; independence, a chance to travel and explore places around the globe. She dropped her arm to adjust the camera strap around her neck. Together, the two women gazed down at the cavalry horses now being led towards the ramp and down into the ship's hold. Leonie gave a start as Ruth suddenly spoke.

'How fortuitous,' her aunt's tone was measured despite the tumult, 'I understand we shall witness an historic event in Sydney.'

'The Inauguration of the New Commonwealth, ma'am,' an elderly civilian nearby interjected. 'These men represent our Queen.' He bowed to Mrs Fox. 'An elite corps specially selected, just returned from the South African campaign.' He pointed down to the quay. 'Look ladies, there go the 7th Hussars.'

Leonie watched the troop march briskly forward, spurs rattling on the cobblestones. A flurry of movement caught her eye as one of the cavalry horses balked at the ramp, its ears turned back with fright. She stared as the creature reared, dragged free from its handler and lunged dangerously near the edge of the quay. A woman's scream pierced the air. The horse uttered a frantic neigh, its breath clouding the soldier who grappled with the reins. A hush fell over the crowd.

Suddenly a civilian about to board leapt forward grabbed the reins and dragged the horse to safety. He pressed his face to the horse's head and murmured into its ear. Impressed, Leonie saw the man run a hand down the horse's steaming flanks until it grew calm, before helping to ease it back in line.

A burst of clapping echoed in the chill air.

'Wasn't he brave?' Leonie released her aunt's arm as a sliver of sunshine lit the rescuer's bare head. Her trained eye registered fair hair and alert features as she quickly snapped a picture and, leaning over the rail as far as her tight stays allowed, she saw him cast his satchel over a shoulder, pick up a panama hat, and stride towards the ship, ready to climb the gangplank.

As if conscious of attention he looked up to the few passengers on the hurricane deck and raised his hat. She waved and right then decided she must meet this fellow traveller.

Ruth Fox's voice broke in and the moment was spoiled. 'Do be careful, don't lean out too far.' Little puffs of air escaped her veil to drift away.

'Don't worry Aunt, it's perfectly safe.' She stood straight as the familiar mixture of affection and impatience flew in. Aunt treated her as a child even though she'd attained her majority. Yet compassion for her fretful relative underlined Leonie's query, 'Oh, I hope you aren't terribly cold?'

Ruth removed gloved hands from her fur muff and rubbed them together. 'Well I must say it's too uncomfortable to stand here much longer.' Irritation chipped her words. 'Do you have to fiddle with that camera?'

A tightening in Leonie's throat threatened a quick retort but she was determined not to let cross words sour the occasion. As she rewound the little knob she insisted, 'I must record this historic scene; it's something special to write about to folk back home.'

Dense smoke belched from the two massive yellow and black striped funnels and swirled about the quay. Her lungs filled with acrid smells and she was gripped with a sense of unreality. A blast from the ship's siren made her jump. It was finally real. The SS *Britannic*, pride of the White Star Line, would be their home for the next six weeks.

A lone military cornet piped a lament and down below she saw white handkerchiefs scattered like snow amongst the scarlet flags. Commands were bellowed between ship and shore as each contingent of troops marched forward to embark. Leonie stood with her aunt and the small party of civilian passengers all tapping their feet to allay the cold. Muffled hoots sounded farewells from vessels in the harbour as orders were shouted and gangplanks rumbled away. 'Look! They're casting off the ropes,' she said.

Engines vibrated along the planks and up through their thin soled boots. A gentle breeze stirred hat feathers, ribbons and furs. The tension all about was palpable, a unanimous indrawn breath as Leonie watched the gap between the ship and the dock slowly widen to leave a dark grey 'V' in the ship's wake.

'We're off!' the cry rang out.

She took Ruth's arm and felt a quiver run through it. 'We'll be all right, I'm sure,' she said and gave it a gentle squeeze. Did she fancy the smile on that sad face?

'Come, we'll go to our cabin and prepare for luncheon.'

'You go ahead, Aunt. I'll follow soon; just want to take a few more snaps.' She saw her expression tighten beneath her veil.

'Very well, be careful you don't catch a chill…'

With half a mind to rush after her, Leonie watched as her aunt stepped over the swaying deck and was soon lost to view down the companionway. As she cradled the Bulls-Eye camera, Uncle's gift for her 21st birthday, enthusiasm fired her thoughts. Women were gaining equality in Australia and this was what she wanted – to make a career of her hobby. Camera film came before spending her small allowance on replacing threadbare clothes.

Aunt Ruth was unaware that whilst her husband the Reverend did the rounds of his parish, Leonie regularly visited Barkers photographic studio in Exeter. Here, for a small fee, she'd studied the techniques of this expanding profession. Secrecy was forced upon her; having no wish to provoke a row with Aunt.

A shadow slipped over her mind for dear departed Uncle Bertram. What anguish must it be for his widow to lose a dear husband and suffer the shock of finding them both bereft of home and subsistence? Leonie sensed something else laid beneath her aunt's bereavement, something that made her twitchy. She told herself it must be anxiety for her re-union with her brother Sebastian after all these years. Once more she resolved to be kind to her aunt during this long, cramped voyage together. What if they *were* like two hens cooped in a hen house?

She eased her cold feet in the outgrown boots as slowly the English shore slipped from view, and peered until the last speck of land vanished while fog closed all about them like a protective womb. Then she turned and made for the nearest companionway, and was unprepared when the ship heaved on entering deeper waters, so she stumbled and missed a step.

'May I?' A young man stood at the bottom and extended his hand.

Leonie gave a start. She recognised the fair-haired man as the one who'd saved the horse. Perversely, as if to deny the spark of interest she felt, she flicked his hand away.

'Thank you, but *I'm* not likely to plunge overboard, am I?' Her light-hearted remark tripped out and too late she knew it sounded churlish.

The fellow dropped his hand, inclined his head and continued on his way.

Not a good start to get to know her fellow passengers; and stepping back onto the deck she took deep breaths to clear her head.

***

As Leonie entered the dining saloon she saw that swivel armchairs flanked twelve long tables and were bolted to the floor. Magnificent crystal fittings flooded the saloon with the new electric light. Save for the rise and fall of the horizon glimpsed through port holes, she decided this could be a superior hotel on land.

A babble of conversation filled the saloon and whisked away her reverie about that young man.

'Do come and join us!'

Leonie made her way to her aunt, seated between two elderly sisters, and soon they were all doing justice to roast lamb followed by lemon pudding. She was pleased to see her aunt tucking into her food after weeks of making a pretence of eating. It had been a difficult time eking out their money, living on cheap cuts.

Those army officers free from duty were dispersed at various tables in the dining saloon. Leonie was thinking it social injustice that the other ranks were catered for in their own lower deck quarters. Resolved to make amends to the young man she'd earlier rebuffed, she spotted him further down the saloon and hoped that freedom on board ship dispensed with the need for formal introductions.

Several officers shook hands with her and then a serious looking somewhat older officer at a nearby table caught her eye. There was something vaguely familiar about him. Leonie frowned, unable to place him, and then her attention was quickly taken by other passengers; a diamond merchant, taking samples of stones to Sydney for the new wealthy entrepreneurs and other civilians who would disembark at Port Said. Leonie moved about the saloon on her aunt's arm stopping for a few words here and there. The young man had disappeared.

Ruth murmured in her ear, 'I'm going to our cabin to lie down for a while. No, you stay, dear, and make acquaintance,' she added. 'I'm just a little weary.'

'Hello.' A young lady from another table touched Leonie's arm. 'Selina Rogers. I'm travelling with Miss Gibson as her secretary.'

Leonie guessed Selina was near her own age. Tall, of slim build, dark-haired with olive skin, she looked almost foreign. Her long nose and lively brown eyes were level with Leonie's own.

'Leonie Grant, I'm travelling with my aunt.' She pointed out Ruth now taking leave of new acquaintances.

'Saw you taking snaps,' Selina said with a grin. 'Me – I've never learned. You must show me your photographs some time.'

'Be careful – I can be a bore with it but I'm set on making a career from my camera.' Leonie was intrigued by this lively young woman, confident they would become friends. She'd noted the easy way Selina chatted with young ship's officers and heard her ask,

'Shall we be bolted down like these chairs when the sea cuts up rough?'

'It's a choice between that or being chained in the hold,' was the sailor's response.

Selina suggested excusing themselves from the others. 'Let's go exploring, shall we?'

'Yes let's; this is my first time at sea – what an amazing ship.'

'So what prompts your journey?' Selina asked as they left the saloon.

'My aunt received an invitation to live with her brother in Australia. He emigrated a quarter century ago and waited until he's in a position to suggest we join him.'

'Does it mean you've left England for good?' Selina shook her head. 'That's a brave step if you don't mind me saying.'

Leonie found herself divulging personal facts. 'When my uncle, the Reverend Fox, died six months ago we lost the tenancy of our home and my aunt had no means of support. I was offered work as a shop assistant in Selfridge's store – a live-in job – but I couldn't support us both on the wages. It seemed like Fate when my Uncle Sebastian's invitation arrived.' She frowned. 'I'm still set on finding employment; how about you, how did you manage it?'

'Luck; I trained as a typewriter at a Ladies College in London; always longed to travel and here I am. Miss Gibson's the perfect employer; she writes pieces based on her travels for magazines back home. I typewrite them for her.' Selina's smile broadened. 'I'm so pleased we'll share this voyage.'

'I am, too.'

'How about taking a stroll around the promenade deck? Don't know about you, but I've a need to walk off that meal.'

'Good idea. I'm sure my aunt will be pleased to rest without me barging about the cabin. By the way, doesn't the clatter of typewriter keys set up a racket in yours?'

'We've come to an arrangement. When Bobby – that's Miss Gibson – is writing up her notes I'll amuse myself elsewhere. Usually before dinner I'll do my typewriting. That's when Bobby will be in the Lounge Bar; she can't abide the machine's clatter.'

Leonie nodded. 'Sounds like a good plan.' She smiled, unable to imagine her aunt entering any kind of bar.

'Most publishers wouldn't accept anything typewritten,' Selina explained as they linked arms and edged along the sloping deck. They both took deep breaths of salty air.

'Not looked upon as polite, you see. Bobby explained a ship's motion is not conducive to legible handwriting so they had to back down.'

'How modern you sound. I'd love to be able to typewrite.'

'I'll teach you sometime,' Selina's offer came quickly. 'It'll be fun. Maybe we can do a swap; I'm certain you'd be a dab hand with needle and thread and I'm hopeless.'

'You've spotted my darned stockings?' Leonie's giggle fetched Selina's smile.

'I can't abide waste myself. I'm not one to squander what Bobby pays me. The fact is,' Selina divulged, 'I intend to remain single for quite a while. The world is opening up for us females. Women already have the franchise in Australia, y'know.'

'I'm all for that; not for me, stuck in a staid marriage. I'm determined to make a go of things in Australia.'

'Then we have much in common. Oh look, there's that reporter.'

It took a few moments for Leonie to register this. She stared in the direction Selina pointed and saw the young horse rescuer, as she'd come to think of him, writing in a notepad. 'You know him then?'

'No, but Bobby got into conversation when we boarded. He's a scribbler for the *News of the World*. It's rife with dubious stories and sordid acts. I'd be wary of him if I were you.'

They drew back and observed him. Leonie's interest was spiked. 'Impressive how he saved that horse on the quay, don't you think?'

'Yes but reporters have to be resourceful, part of their training I suppose.'

'Come on. I'd like to meet him.'

'Well,' Selina arched her brows, 'a girl after my own heart.'

Leonie hid a smile; though not averse to the idea of innocent flirtation her interest lay in the young man's occupation. Whether the young reporter was alerted Leonie couldn't tell. Snapping his notebook shut, their quarry walked away. The two young women halted and stared after him as he reached the vertical ladder which led to the poop deck and climbed up fast.

Disappointed, Leonie reflected her friend's mood. 'After scandal, do you think?'

Selina's expression was complicit as she took Leonie's arm. 'Definitely keep an eye on that fellow.'

The incident served to draw them close as, pushing thoughts of the reporter from her mind, Leonie fell into step with her new friend as they continued their promenade.

***

What a mercy, Ruth Fox reflected as she made her way to their cabin, to have engaged that nice young man at Thomas Cook's travel agency. He'd secured a passage for them on this ship when all other ships were requisitioned as troop carriers for the South African war.

'The SS *Britannic* has been commissioned to transport an elite deputation of troops to Australia,' he'd explained pedantically, 'in recognition of that country's contribution to the war. Fortunately there are some berths available for a dozen passengers.

You, madam,' he remarked, 'will be able to participate in celebrations in Australia to mark the new twentieth century.'

Ruth's head throbbed. A great wave of weariness flooded her brain. All those weeks vacating the home she'd shared with dear Bertram and selling off their belongings to supplement meagre savings. At least Leonie had been caring, taking on responsibilities for practical matters.

A constant fear nagged the back of her brain. Bertram had shielded her from concerns about Leonie but now, cast adrift on the open sea, they had finally caught up with her. What if Leonie had inherited traits…? But surely the signs would have been clear by now? Leonie was twenty one years of age and it would be impossible to monitor her all the time.

Ruth's brows furrowed. It was a constant worry that Leonie often lacked decorum and she prayed the dear child would soon be settled in a conventional marriage.

She sighed deeply and fingered the gold locket at her neck which held her husband's portrait, as she fought years of anxieties which disturbed her peace of mind. She must be strong and reveal terrible secrets to Sebastian. Her spirits quaked. Not all her secrets! How thankful she'd been that he'd already emigrated all those years ago when that nasty *News of the World* published its lurid account of the event.

Seated on a stool before the small mahogany washstand and mirror that served as a dressing table, Ruth wore just her chemise, for the ship's radiators pumped out constant warmth. She picked up her hair brush and began to sweep back her long dark hair, speckled with grey, now loosened from pins. She must put her trust in the Lord.

Although tiny, the cabin provided adequate space for the two of them and she approved the facilities which were fitted out in the most ingenious way; cupboards with hanging rails either side of two iron framed bunks left enough room for their cabin trunks. An electric bell, a brand new device, made it a simple matter to summon the stewardess.

As she gazed into the mirror restful thoughts of her dear brother Sebastian, who waited for them in Australia, fetched a smile. She wondered how all these years might have changed him. A picture flew into her mind, for his reckless nature had never ceased to give her qualms. Once again, she recalled his promise almost a quarter century before.

'*You wait. I'll send money for your passage, Ruthie,*' he'd declared. '*Soon as I've made my fortune!*'

What a chance, and such perfect timing. Replacing the hair brush Ruth moved to her bunk and lay down. She reached into an inner pocket of her travelling case, extracted his letter and for the umpteenth time took in his every word.

'*My Dearest Sister. During all these years in this distant continent I have resisted the urge to write you, fearing I may build up hopes that could never be realized.*

'*I accept that my long silence must seem cruel but this was never my intention. I pray that this tardy brother of yours still has a small place in your heart. I have waited until I was in a position to invite you, and now being in sound financial circumstances, I implore you to consider leaving the Old Country and coming to settle over here. And what of our dear dead sister's child? I pray she would accompany you.*'

Ruth's hands clamped together as her mind grew fuzzy, unable to focus on dreadful secrets. Once in Australia she must unburden herself to Sebastian. Cocooned in the warm bed and lulled by the steady throb of engines, her brain slipped its shackles and she fell into a deep sleep.

***

Turbulent seas made for a disturbing night when the ship rounded the Bay of Biscay and many passengers were laid low in their quarters.

In an agony of sea sickness Ruth Fox writhed on the hard iron bed. Leonie plied her with Dr William's Little Pink Pills, recommended for the purpose, to no helpful effect. Even Lottie, their sturdy stewardess, failed to make her aunt comfortable with a hot water bottle pressed to her stomach.

'I've never seen her so ill.' Leonie's concern seemed to fill the cabin.

'Never you fret, miss. I'll be on call whenever you want. There's always some gets sea sickness bad, but they always recover fit as a fiddle in a day or so.'

After a sleepless night Leonie stood and stretched her stiff body. Ruth had fallen into a noisy slumber, no longer twisting and turning and tying the sheet into knots. Relieved, Leonie drew on her dressing robe, placed her feet in slippers, and crept as quietly as she could from the cabin.

'Lottie, are you there?'

The curtain over the stewardess's cubby hole was whisked back and Lottie, already dressed in her black uniform, looked out. 'Morning Miss Leonie, how is Mrs Fox, miss?'

'She's fallen asleep. I'm going to get dressed. I need a breath of fresh air.'

'I'll be listening out, don't you worry, miss.'

Back in their cabin Ruth hadn't stirred. Leonie dressed quickly, thankful to be one of the lucky ones untroubled by sea sickness. The ship had a will of its own, a heavy rolling motion, so it took an age to stab each toe inside her stockings, draw them up and attach them to suspenders on her stays. It took even longer to pull on her outgrown boots. She grasped the washstand for support and adjusted her garments. Throwing her khaki serge cape over a heavy skirt and high necked wool blouse, she decided this would be her regime; up very early to take breakfast in the saloon, certain Aunt would prefer breakfast on her own in the cabin. This at least would afford them a little space for privacy at the start of the day. She would make allowances for her aunt's difficult behaviour and do nothing to upset her.

Chapter Two

Except for the staff hovering behind the buffet, the saloon was deserted. Leonie studied the generous display but with a thought for her digestion chose a light meal of stewed prunes, a few cuts of ham, two slices of toast and a pot of tea. She took a seat near to one of the port holes, glad that the heavy white china plates were anchored to the table and likewise the dishes and condiments which rattled but remained in place.

The port hole gave glimpses of furious dark waves dashing against the hull as the ship dipped and rose and for a few moments she sat entranced before turning her attention to the food, surprised to find a good appetite. Despite the tea swishing around the cup she managed to drink enough to complete her meal.

Leonie took a deep breath as concern for her aunt filled her thoughts. Not just her present sickness, but her mental state. It was a puzzle; her aunt's agitation told her there was something wrong. Feeling restless she stood, drew her cape tight about her shoulders and pulled the hood of her cloak down over her head. Fresh air would help to clear her head.

A notice attached to the saloon exit bade people '*Do not venture outside onto the deck for your own safety*'.

Suddenly a beam of sunlight shone through the port hole and rolled over the floor like a slick of butter. Good, Leonie decided, the storm had abated. She got up and heaved open the iron door and gasped, quite unprepared as a powerful gust instantly doubled her up. The sea darkened as solid clouds obliterated the sun and salty brine slapped her face like a wet rag. Panic leapt in her throat, for the heaving ship seemed set on dragging away under her feet. Stunned by the mighty roar and pummelled by the wind, she reached behind and scrabbled for the iron door handle. Then, just as the full force of nature threatened to propel her over the slippery deck and into the depths, the door gave way.

'Here, grab my hand!' a voice rasped.

Her hand was gripped in a vice as she was yanked back inside the saloon and heard the heavy door clang shut behind her.

'Daft thing to do,' a curt voice reprimanded. 'Oh, it's you?' His mouth twitched as he took in her state. 'And certain about to plunge overboard, I'd say.'

Cross and bedraggled, Leonie saw the young reporter gazing down at her. Mortified, she stuttered, 'Thank you. Serves me right for…' She managed a smile through cold lips. 'Yesterday – I didn't mean…' Her teeth wouldn't stop chattering.

'Sorry we've had to meet like this.' The young man grinned. 'So, when you're dried out how about meeting me back here for a hot drink? I think you owe me that, don't you?'

Leonie nodded and pushed wet hair off her face. 'I must fly and change into dry things but yes, I'd like that.'

'I'll wait here then.'

It surprised her as she dashed away that they hadn't introduced each other as protocol would have demanded back home. Her pulse quickened at the thought. As she made her way crab-like towards the cabin she caught whiffs of disinfectant and nauseous smells of vomit. Holding her breath she reached their cabin, thankful to find her aunt still slept.

Casting the sodden cloak over a hot radiator, she stared into the looking glass. Though slightly freckled, her straight nose and defined cheekbones were not features she'd exchange for one of the pretty doll-like faces portrayed in women's magazines. The elements had coloured her cheeks and brightened her eyes and, smiling, she took one of the hair brushes laid out on a lace cloth and applied it vigorously to her hair, then twisted it into a loose knot at her neck. At five and a half feet she was hardly a giant, as her aunt eyeing her would sometimes imply. Leonie ran a hand down her waist to reassure herself of the gentle feminine curves as thoughts of the young reporter filled her mind; his quick reactions, cultured voice and the boyish grin seemed at odds with his occupation, she reflected. Did he really dig up nasty stories? Well, she'd soon be able to size him up. With a crocheted shawl about her shoulders she crept from the cabin.

Leonie re-entered the saloon, which was still mostly deserted. She caught sight of the reporter as he raised an arm in greeting and, balancing each step across the swaying floor, she made her way to him.

'How are you now?'

'Very well thanks to you. It was silly of me…'

His eyebrows lifted. 'How about we introduce ourselves first, eh?' He held a chair steady for Leonie to sit.

'Leonie Grant; I'm off to Australia with my aunt, Mrs Fox – please call me Leonie.'

'Adam Mallory; reporter for *News of the World* and delighted to make your acquaintance. Now, what would you like me to order?'

'A hot chocolate, please,' she said coolly.

Adam turned to instruct the steward who hovered nearby and then enquired, 'How about some pastries?'

'Yes, that sounds good. I've quite an appetite.'

Adam grinned approvingly as he placed their order.

'You are also a good sailor then, Leonie.'

'Yes, must be one of the lucky ones,' she agreed. 'So, whereabouts is your home, Adam?' How refreshing it felt to enquire in this easy way.

'The family home's in the Midlands but I've lodgings in Streatham. It's where scribblers, stage actors, musicians and the like choose to live; all-night trams run out to Streatham – necessary when one works into the small hours.'

Did she detect an air of amusement, of being gently patronised? 'Much livelier than Devon then,' she offered. 'By the way, I caught sight of you writing in your notebook yesterday.'

'I was merely describing how this fine ship rides out a storm – no sordid tales.'

'Oh, really?' Leonie widened her eyes.

'Yes, I know it's a scurrilous rag.' He cocked a brow. 'Here on board, my job is to report the interesting ports the *Britannic* visits; in particular, translate the troops' experience on the voyage and their part in the celebrations in Australia, all for the general public back home.'

Leonie noted he did not denigrate the readership of this low-brow newspaper, one certainly not allowed over the threshold at Downshill. 'Civilians are kept in the dark, aren't they? So many hundreds of troops, I imagine they're awfully cramped on board.' She was finding it easy to talk with Adam, to express herself. It was on the tip of her tongue to refer to his horse skills when the steward's arrival interrupted and it slipped from her mind. They waited until he'd left.

'I'm lucky to have landed this job. I have the officer's permission to visit the troops' quarters down below decks. They've recently been fighting the war out in South Africa; a tough bunch of fellows.' Adam whistled. 'The Tommies – that's what the other ranks are called – make me welcome. They're well provided for – sometimes I have my meal with them in their canteen.'

'That must be interesting.' Leonie was hesitant to voice her opinions but ventured, 'Sketches in the press make the South African war look like school boy pranks – jolly cartoons, you know – our superior troops fighting ignorant farmers. It's wrong, don't you think? Have you been out there? Out to South Africa?'

Adam gazed at her thoughtfully. 'No, I wish that I had been there. But I've studied original reports – which are edited for public consumption.' He nodded. 'Your sentiments reflect my own. I've come to believe those Boer farmers are amongst the bravest civilians you could combat. After all, they are only trying to protect their homeland; what's rightfully theirs.'

For several moments they were both silent, each sipping their hot drink and taking bites of the pastries. It was hard to realise she was having this conversation with a man she'd just met, and she found herself intrigued to know more about him.

As if he had been thinking along the same lines, Adam suddenly spoke. 'And you, Leonie? What was your life like back home?'

'It probably sounds dull but I enjoyed living in Devon even while I longed to take up employment. First step is to become a skilled photographer, so I took lessons. That's what I plan for the future; to become professional.' She'd given more information than intended and was annoyed to see Adam merely nod.

'I wish you luck; my view is that determination will help fulfil one's aim.'

She couldn't read his expression.

They'd finished their snack and, grasping the edge of the table, Leonie got to her feet. 'Thank you for the snack but I must go and see to my aunt. She's been awfully seasick. Will you please excuse me?'

***

Leonie opened their cabin door and peeped inside. She saw her aunt was propped up against the stiff bolster and her cheeks looked pink again. Her eyelids fluttered open and a fond expression softened her features as she gave Leonie a weak smile.

'I'm so pleased to see you looking better.' Leonie leaned over and pecked her aunt on her cheek.

'Yes, thank you, dear. I do find myself improved at last. But I shan't be too hasty. Will you pull the bell, please? I'll ask Lottie to bring me a light meal. Have you managed to amuse yourself? You've been gone quite a while.'

Her words held a question and, pleased to find her aunt in good spirits, Leonie was still buoyed up by her meeting with Adam Mallory and couldn't prevent her mouth widening in a smile. 'I had a hot chocolate with one of the passengers.'

'Oh? Who was that? Have I met the person?'

Leonie avoided her aunt's scrutiny and decided to hedge. 'Perhaps you do…' She hesitated, keen to be truthful yet not upset her aunt. 'I do find Selina Rogers good company,' she said by way of compromise. She turned away and busied herself with straightening the bed cover. The only publications delivered to Downshill House had been Church magazines apart from *The Lady*, *Woman's World*, or others of a similar nature. Leonie gained her wider knowledge of the world in the Reading Room at the Public Library in Exeter.

Ruth closed her eyes. 'I'm not sure I approve of that odd person Miss Gibson, nor her secretary.'

Leonie frequently sensed shadows of something else, some undisclosed trouble lurking behind her aunt's disapproval, and she determined not to rise to the bait. She spoke evasively, 'Oh the crew arrange plenty of activity to keep everyone occupied.' She prayed the voyage would have a beneficial effect and restore her aunt's good will.

'Well then, you must go and join in.' Ruth's head sank back. 'I shall be content to rest.'

Making sure her aunt's various items were to hand; her perfumed handkerchiefs, spectacles and copies of *The Lady* magazine, Leonie pecked Ruth's cheek and left. She was seized with an appetite for everything; her new companions and for all the excitement of life on board this splendid ship.

***

Leonie spotted Selina wandering along the deck. As she drew near, Selina grabbed her arm. 'Let's find some amusement; see if we can waylay some handsome officers?'

Leonie found herself dragged along, although her mind filled with thoughts of the pleasure she'd found in Adam Mallory's company. 'I was going to join the others in the saloon,' she said.

'Oh? Well just spare a few minutes with me, all right? Anyway, I should be doing some typewriting.'

'Yes, of course.' Leonie had no wish to spoil their new friendship. She saw many officers standing alone at the rail, some smoking a cigarette or cheroot, and to her relief Selina made no attempt to invade their privacy. Soon though, Selina found the chance she'd been seeking.

'Good day officers,' Selina greeted a party of officers strolling past. It was enough to stay the men's steps. 'And good day to you, young ladies,' came the cheerful response.

Leonie smiled her greeting but stood a little apart, observing Selina.

'Have we not met?'

As Leonie stood a little way off, one of the officers moved towards her.

'Please allow me to introduce myself,' he said. 'Clyde Ferguson, Highland Light Infantry.' Then without giving her time to introduce himself he declared, 'I regret there was an unfortunate incident… some while ago, in Devon?' They were out of earshot of the others.

Astonishment suddenly gripped Leonie. However could it be? It had occurred over two years before, yet she recalled the scene in a flash. Back then he'd been in country clothes; but this smart officer was definitely the same man. She'd been wandering the fields taking photographs when a strong hand had shoved her down in the ditch. She'd wrenched her ankle and he'd begged her forgiveness, claiming he'd awoken from slumber beneath a tree and believed some ruffian crept up on him. It was an unlikely tale, she'd thought. Later, she'd heard him introduce himself to her aunt as an army officer, back on leave from the South African war and staying in a nearby Devon village to deal with his deceased guardian's estate.

Shocked to see him again, she became aware of appearing rude.

Captain Ferguson hesitated. 'I'm still mortified. I beg you once again to accept my regret and apology for my disgraceful act.'

'Of course.' Leonie rallied, although still unconvinced about his behaviour all those months ago. 'What an odd coincidence,' she said coolly as she extended her hand to him. 'I'm Leonie Grant.'

'My pleasure, Miss Grant.' He stood erect and briskly shook her hand. Then clearly seeking a diversion he asked, 'May I introduce my companions? We're all from various regiments, you see. Edward's is the Gloucester's, Henry's the Seaworth's. Mine's one of the Scottish regiments – Highland Light Infantry. We're thrown together on this voyage.'

'That must be interesting.' Leonie noted how well groomed Captain Ferguson was; his moustache clipped in strict military fashion and just as in Devon, his dark brown hair parted straight as a ruler down the middle, and was forced to admit she found him agreeable. 'I'm very pleased to find us aboard this ship,' she said.

'Delightful for us to meet officers from the South African campaign,' Selina remarked as she and

Leonie took their leave. She turned to Leonie. 'You seemed to be hitting it off with that stiff looking officer. Come on; tell me what he's like.'

Leonie shook her head, still bewildered by the coincidence, and she revealed no more as they parted.

***

At dinner one evening a few weeks later, Colonel Waring mentioned the enormity of provisions needed for the troops, since as catering officer it was his responsibility to organize rations.

'How interesting,' Leonie remarked. 'Such a large number of men – no doubt with huge appetites. I wonder how it can be managed?'

'Very messy and with much noise, I expect,' Selina interjected with a laugh. 'Is that not so, Colonel? Mind you,' she added quickly, 'I'd be perfectly happy to have the troops up here to dinner instead of them stuck down in the ship's bowels – would liven up our saloon no end!'

Later Colonel Waring spoke to Leonie. 'If you really would care to see the galley, I should be honoured to escort you. That's if you don't mind noise and terrific heat.'

She was pleased he'd perceived her genuine interest and not thought she sought a means of gossip. 'I'd like that very much, thank you.' A chance to see people at real work, she thought, and maybe understand why Adam found pleasure in their company.

The following morning Colonel Waring led the way down steep stairs. Leonie lifted her skirts clear of the treads and slid her free hand down the safety rope. In the hope of being inconspicuous she wore her plainest skirt of dark brown Holland with a high-necked grey blouse, her thick chestnut hair pinned back into a tight bun and covered by a light grey shawl.

More narrow steps zig-zagged steeply down.

'Do please hold onto my shoulder if you feel dizzy, Miss Grant.'

'Thank you, I can manage perfectly. I've found my sea legs.'

'You may find the Tommies rather uncouth. I trust you won't be offended?'

'I'm not concerned. I lived in a village where the yokels often swore oaths.'

For an older man and one fairly corpulent, the Colonel was nimble on his feet. They had to raise their voices over the noise which increased the lower they descended; judders and creaks as if the ship would split apart. Shouting above the din, the Colonel explained, 'Those sounds are from the giant crank shaft lying in a wooden gulley beneath our feet. Stretches the whole length of the ship and drives it along.'

How ignorant I am. Leonie shook her head with irritation at herself. 'I've never considered how the *Britannic* actually moved through the seas.' Her lungs filled with the strong odour of burning oil, smoke and gas. Then came a strong whiff of rotting vegetation; but none of this deterred her.

Hollering above the din, the Colonel pointed out the ice room inside which whole animal carcasses were refrigerated. Standing on a metal grid at the foot of the steps Leonie jumped as a loud hiss of steam escaped a vent and dampened her cheeks.

'Imagine what it must be like for the horses down in the hold,' he said as they stood side by side. 'The mounted officers give them endless care, but they never get used to the ship's motion.'

The Colonel laid a hand on her arm. 'Be ready for the heat,' he warned, heaving open a heavy steel door. The heat rushed at them like a blast furnace and threatened to knock her off her feet. She waited as he exchanged a few words with the Sergeant Cook in charge and she inhaled the fungal smell of yeast and the strong odour of boiled meat as she dabbed her damp face with the edge of her shawl.

She shook her head. 'We passengers up above have it so easy.' A growing concern for the men down there sobered her thoughts. As her sight grew accustomed to the artificial lighting, she marvelled at the mechanics of food preparation; the massive iron contraptions; implements for chopping, mixing and grinding; the long metal rods inserted into baking trays which moved on squeaky rollers into the gaping ovens. Some of the cooks had a sweat rag tied about their forehead. Their work seemed dreadfully dangerous and she hoped there were no accidents.

Leonie averted her eyes as the pastry cooks nearby exchanged ribald jests with each other as they moulded the dough. It mystified her how Adam could enjoy the company of men such as these.

Colonel Waring was having a few words with the Quartermaster and before long they left and returned to the upper deck. The Colonel remarked, 'Rather cramped down in their quarters you see, so they come up here at dawn for exercise. Fresh air is most invigorating for the men.' He smiled at Leonie, his face round and genial.

'I've seen field officers capering about the decks very early in the morning,' Leonie had to hide a smile, 'wearing strange short trousers cut off at the knee.'

'Indeed so,' the Colonel nodded.

It occurred to Leonie that Captain Ferguson appeared not to take part in activities. She then felt bold enough to suggest, 'Perhaps the stuffy War Office should consider employing female domestics to do the cooking – voluntarily, of course. After all, it does seem unfair that men have to go to war and also work in those conditions.' She fancied the Colonel's moustache twitched.

Her lungs filled with wonderful fresh sea air. 'Thank you for taking me to see the galley for myself. It's a salutary lesson to see how the soldiers work.'

Later, returning to the cabin Leonie was pleased to find her aunt absent as she dragged off her soiled clothes. She poured cold water into the china wash bowl and splashed her face to cool her cheeks. Changed into a simple cotton frock, she pulled on light canvas boots and became aware of a total absence of sound. The constant thrum of engines had ceased; the ship must have anchored. Snatching up a straw hat, her parasol and camera, she left the cabin and was soon climbing the companionway and out into the afternoon sunshine. She gave a start as Selina attracted her attention.

'Do hurry, Leonie!' Selina called out. She waved frantically. 'Everyone's going ashore here! The ship's anchored at Port Said for coaling.'

A huge barge loaded with coal lay alongside the ship and black smuts were already flying about. 'Go ahead, I must find Aunt Ruth. I'll try to catch you up.'

She almost collided with her aunt who, recovered from her sickness, stood soberly attired in maroon shantung, her wide-brimmed hat secured by ribbons under her chin. Aunt Ruth tapped her parasol on the deck.

'There you are, Leonie. Wherever have you been? I'm ready to go ashore and these kind ladies suggested I join them,' Ruth spoke crossly. 'Whatever are you wearing? You look like a housemaid!'

Leonie halted in her tracks, furious with her aunt.

Ruth plucked Leonie's arm. 'I looked about the saloon for you at luncheon, where were you?'

'With Colonel Waring, Aunt,' she retorted. 'He was kind enough to take me down to the galley to see how food is prepared for the ranks.'

'Well!' Ruth Fox exclaimed. 'I hope this sort of behaviour doesn't become a habit – attracting attention of the lower ranks, indeed.' She was looking Leonie over, her face wrinkled with displeasure. 'It'll take more than a few missed luncheons to trim your height. Now you'd better hurry. If we don't get off the ship we'll all be black as chimney sweeps. I can't guarantee you a place on the ferry.'

Leonie frowned as her aunt swept towards the dispersal area, but couldn't remain angry for long. Her mouth twitched in a smile, glad that Aunt Ruth had no idea of what went on in the galley. She'd be very offended if she knew Leonie had been ogled by the troops down there.

With no wish to put her aunt in worse humour, Leonie changed into a grey silk gown and, bunching her skirts, she gripped her parasol under an arm, slung her camera strap over her shoulder and with the help of waiting seamen, made it down the rope ladder slung from the side of the ship and stepped into the last ferry before it cast away.

Looking back Leonie saw the *Britannic* was now besieged by barges of coal and lighters filled with coolies whose task was to 'coal' the ship. Shielding her eyes from the fierce sun she watched skinny men swarming like crabs up the pristine white hull. What terrible lives they must lead, she brooded.

The passengers' small craft eased between dozens of Egyptian ships in the harbour. The air was filled with the clapping and chanting of half-naked little boys who did a jig, standing in a frail homemade craft at risk of capsizing. '*Throw silver dollar, throw shiny guinea,*' they implored. Leonie clutched her camera as the ferry rocked and took some snaps, resolved to add them to her collection for an exhibition. There seemed to be injustices everywhere one travelled.

Chapter Three

Once ashore on their wobbly sea legs the civilian passengers found themselves thrust full tilt amongst a heathen throng. Port Said greeted them with dusty heat and raucous screeches, maimed beggars and a plague of filthy, ragged infants who held out beseeching hands. Impudent small boys hauled scraggy beasts towards the passengers. '*Good donkey ride, Lady, Sir, Highness – see big city*!' they demanded, using scraps of Pidgin English.

Leonie caught sight of her aunt staring wildly about in distress, searching for her. She'd become separated from the other passengers and was clearly relieved as Leonie manoeuvred her way past squabbling natives towards her.

'Oh my goodness, dear! I'm so glad to see you,' Ruth exclaimed.

Leonie took her arm in an affectionate gesture. 'We'll be quite all right if we stay close together,' she reassured.

Ruth wasn't at all sure. 'Disease must be rife!' she exclaimed. 'The sanitary arrangements must be far from adequate; oh dear, the stench is indescribable!' She stared aghast as barefoot ragamuffins hopped over the open sewers that carried a sluggish trickle of filth down to the harbour, and used her closed parasol as a weapon to fend off the grubby hands which plucked at her sleeve. She gripped Leonie's arm. 'We'll need a dose of Syrup of Figs to cleanse us after this!'

There was no relief from the sun. It beat down mercilessly and forced them to make frequent stops to regain their breath.

Leonie furled her parasol and handed it to her aunt. 'Will you please hold it for a moment? It's all a marvel; I must take some snaps.'

Ruth frowned and waved her parasol about. 'Whatever do you find good in this dreadful place? Ugh! beggars everywhere.' She brushed a gloved hand down her sleeve to dislodge a mosquito and plied her fan with vigour. Her attitude was easy to read, it was clear to Leonie that she must wonder what had got into her niece, whose behaviour was utterly wayward.

'I'm quite taken with the strangeness of it all,' Leonie said as she retrieved her parasol.

'Mercy upon us, we should have stayed on board.'

'I can't agree. Surely you find this fascinating? It reminds me of Ali Baba and the Forty Thieves.' Leonie's rejoinder didn't relieve her aunt's anxiety.

Ruth's alarm stiffened her features. 'Come!' She tried to pull Leonie away and raising her voice above the din she declared, 'We'll find our purchases and get back to the ship and a good tub to scrub ourselves clean!' The sight of a bundle of rags asleep in a doorway was enough to quicken her steps. Both of them were jostled by insolent youths, which did nothing to calm Ruth's mind. 'It seems once a place becomes frequented by foreign tourists, the manners of its inhabitants deteriorate!' she exclaimed. 'It's quite useless,' she choked, 'however shall we purchase silk shawls?'

Leonie encouraged her as the crowds thinned and her aunt clutched Leonie's arm protectively. 'Even if we discover the shop,' Ruth shook her head, 'we'll never be able to communicate our needs.' She cried out with relief as they came upon a group of passengers from the *Britannic*.

'We'll be inside this coffee house,' they indicated. 'Do both join us when you've finished your shopping.'

Her morale boosted, Ruth let out a sigh. 'Ten minutes,' she declared, turning to Leonie. 'Then we'll join these passengers.' Her attention was suddenly arrested by a young gentleman who leaned over a stall haggling for some object, and she gave a start as he turned around and waved. His face looked bright with recognition as he spotted Leonie and indicated they should wait till he'd completed his transaction. 'That young man appears to be bargaining with confidence,' Ruth stated. 'I don't recall seeing him aboard. Are you acquainted?'

'Only in passing; now I think we should go on, Aunt.' Leonie tugged Ruth's arm but she held her ground. She lowered her parasol and scrutinised Adam.

'Well, he does seem to be a personable young gentleman. My! That's what we need, a gentleman to escort us who can translate our requirements to these foreigners.'

'Do let's go, Aunt.'

'Whatever's got into you? You're quite content to mix on board with the rabble below decks but unwilling to meet a civilised gentleman?'

His transaction had come to an amicable conclusion and a bulky object was passed into the young man's arms. Ruth seemed heartened as he freed a hand to tip his panama hat. 'Good day to you ladies. Adam Mallory,' he introduced himself.

'Mrs Ruth Fox and my niece, Leonie Grant,' she exclaimed, her smile including Leonie, who guessed what would be going through her aunt's mind – *what a delightful young gentleman*, with thoughts forming that she must cultivate his acquaintance for Leonie's sake.

'How do you do, Mrs Fox. May I be of assistance?'

Leonie noted the distinctive cut of his light linen suit and silk cravat.

'Mr Mallory,' Ruth extended a doeskin gloved hand, 'I couldn't help but notice your flair with the market traders. It appears you are *au fait* with the local language?'

'It was more a case of forceful persuasion, ma'am.' Adam demonstrated a fierce scowl which lent an appealing cheeky look to his features and Leonie had to swallow bubbles of laughter.

'I am certain there was more to it than your terrifying stare, Mr Mallory.' Ruth's rejoinder was encouraging.

'Maybe a smattering of colloquial French aided by a few Arab oaths did the trick,' he said with a grin.

Ruth straightened her back. 'Mr Mallory,' she ventured, 'I wonder if we might prevail upon your good nature. We are having some difficulty in discovering certain items and making purchases.'

Adam Mallory's response came quickly. 'I've finished my errand, so it will be an honour to assist you, Mrs Fox,' he replied with a ready smile.

Did she imagine the slight wink he gave her behind Ruth's back?

It was clear to Leonie her aunt would be horrified if she knew Adam's occupation.

Dodging the outstretched hands and loaded pushcarts, Adam led them confidently through the narrow streets.

'Don't tarry, Leonie!' Ruth was annoyed when Leonie stopped to take a snap of an old man sitting on the ground, working at his Singer sewing machine.

Adam led them inside a warehouse and it took a few moments for their sight to adjust in the gloom, for dark blinds covered high windows to shield bales of cloth from the bleaching force of the sun.

A noxious odour filled their lungs; cloying smells which seemed to issue from the person of the fat shopkeeper. A guttering oil lamp illuminated a small circle around him and his face and bulging body had the guise of a wax dummy, and if Aunt Ruth hadn't been escorted by a charming gentleman Leonie was sure she'd have fled outside.

'I shall do my best for you.' Adam clutched his hat and strode forward, clicking his heels to rouse the fellow from his trance.

'*As-salaam alaykum*,' Adam bowed his head.

The shopkeeper shrugged off his lethargy, scrutinised what he saw as likely customers, and he rose to his feet ready to do business. Arabic salutations preceded a dialogue between the two mismatched men before the shopkeeper picked up a little brass bell from his desk and rang it vigorously.

Ruth clutched Leonie's arm as its jangle fetched a stooped crone out from the shadows, carrying a tray with tiny coffee cups and a pewter pot. Her face pinched, she declined the cup with a shake of her head and Leonie knew there was no way that her aunt would press her lips to it, for heaven knows the state of the washing water. She jabbed Leonie in the ribs. 'Don't drink,' she ordered, her annoyance a heavy frown as Leonie, like Mr Mallory, drained the coffee.

'Oh dear! I do feel palpitations coming on.' Ruth's mouth dropped, her eyes widened as she turned to Leonie.

'Be patient just for a little while. I'm sure we'll be all right,' Leonie smiled her reassurance.

At the ring of the shopkeeper's bell a tall Egyptian entered, bowed and was given instructions. He returned a short while later bearing armfuls of silken shawls.

'Ah,' Ruth gasped as each delicate shawl was cast before their eyes, fine as cobwebs and glistening with silver, gold and metallic thread. Her voice strengthened. 'I suggest these would suit us,' she indicated various shawls to Leonie, 'and we'll take gifts for our hostesses; these pretty ones. But first we shall have to see what price is set,' she declared in a business-like manner, having no intention of being cheated by this native person. She nodded to Adam as he advised,

'Try not to appear too keen, Mrs Fox. Look as though you find them not entirely to your taste.'

Leonie stared in fascination as the shopkeeper busied himself with an abacus, shifting and sliding the beads on the wires. He sighed, shook his head and looked at Adam before quoting a price. But Adam also shook his head and made his own offer. The shopkeeper spread his arms and raised his eyes as though asking Allah to save him from these infidels.

'He's pretending he'll be ruined; just wait,' Adam advised.

Ruth eased her back on the hard seat and smiled. Mr Mallory's charm, his confidence in dealing, had obviously made an impression.

Leonie could read her aunt's mind and guessed it followed the line of: *this young gentleman might make a fine choice for Leonie*.

Leonie fixed her sight on the strange scene and held her breath as the pace of bargaining grew faster until finally the purveyor gave in, his hands spread in an expansive gesture.

Ruth opened her reticule and handed Adam a wad of notes she'd exchanged on board. Counting out the requisite number of Egyptian pounds, Adam passed the rest back to her before handing the purchase money over to the shopkeeper. During this time, the shawls had been wrapped in tissue paper, then made a neat brown paper parcel tied with string.

'*Alhamdu lillahi*,' was repeated several times by Adam and the purveyor of shawls with deep bows.

'He's saying, thanks and praise to Allah,' Adam translated and the two ladies inclined their heads.

'Thank you, Mr Mallory. However can we begin to express our gratitude?' Ruth exclaimed happily as they regained the street. She snapped open her parasol. 'We'd absolutely not have been able to purchase a thing. I'm very much in your debt. However do you come to speak the language?' she rattled on. 'Perhaps you will consent to join in a game of cards one evening?' Dazzled by the bright sunlight and overcome with pleasure she stumbled and would have fallen to the ground had not Adam caught her arm.

'Aunt!' Leonie exclaimed as her aunt's features paled. 'It's all been too much. Here, let me find your salts.' She reached inside Ruth's reticule.

'Oh dear, that noxious air in there made me feel faint.'

'I'll hail a conveyance,' Adam said purposefully. 'You must return to the ship and rest. That fetid air was abominable.'

At that moment a horse-drawn gharry drew alongside and a compelling voice hailed them.

'Halloo there,' a large lady in the gharry called out. Jet bugle beads danced on her veiled hat as this person leaned forward and bade the driver to halt, oblivious to the honking horns as traffic built up behind. 'My dear lady, you are from the *Britannic*, I presume? Then you must permit me to return you to the ship. Amelia, Lady Wilson,' she shouted down. 'I have room for one passenger.'

Ruth hesitated in a dilemma, uncertain and unwilling to leave Leonie unchaperoned even though this young man was a gentleman. She was feeling too queasy to protest when Leonie spoke.

'I shall be perfectly all right in Mr Mallory's care.'

'Well do come then, madam,' the lady demanded imperiously.

'Thank you, how very kind. May I introduce myself?' Ruth murmured weakly. 'Ruth Fox, with my niece Leonie.' Her heart thumped with concern as she was hoisted up and settled onto the seat, the parcel placed on her lap.

'I shall escort your niece to the ship as swiftly as possible, Mrs Fox,' she heard Mr Mallory declare.

'Well that's a satisfactory arrangement then,' Lady Amelia boomed, allowing no dissent. 'Be sure not to forget the time though,' she wagged a finger.

Just then the driver gave up all hope of restraining his horse and the gharry jerked away at a clatter. Ruth looked overwhelmed with alarm that she'd allowed Leonie to remain in the company of a young man. She turned her head and her backward glance could have done nothing to solve her anxiety, for Mr Mallory had taken hold of Leonie's arm!

***

'Those pungent smells with the heat must have overcome your aunt.' Adam turned a serious face to Leonie. 'Sea air will probably see her right as rain.'

'I'm sure it will. That was awkward, wasn't it? I suppose I should have admitted we had already met but...'

Adam grinned. 'If you had, then do you suppose your aunt would have allowed me to us escort you both? May I take your arm? We'll go quicker like that.'

They walked as fast as was possible while avoiding obstructions and Leonie nodded, conscious of the feel of her arm tucked in his. She found it hard to breathe, but managed, 'You're right. And we'd never have been able to buy those shawls.'

'So it was all for the best,' Adam said confidently. 'I know we should hurry to the ship but all right if we stop for a moment? I'd just like to scribble a few notes.' Carefully resting his parcel against a wall, Adam took his notebook from an inside pocket.

Leonie watched his pencil fly over the page, intrigued by the squiggly shapes. 'May I see, please?'

He leaned towards her. 'It's a kind of code; shorthand – a means of writing fast.'

'Just like Egyptian hieroglyphics.' Leonie peered closely. Excitement surged in, overwhelmed by his flair, his confidence, his sense of humour – did it matter he wasn't a real gentleman? She couldn't deny flutters behind her ribs at being unchaperoned with this interesting young man in a strange country.

'You're very familiar with Arab customs and you speak the language. How is that?' They resumed their hurried walk, dodging stray dogs and chickens.

'Oh, in my line of work you absorb all sorts of facts,' he volunteered, still keeping up a stiff pace.

'Really?' She failed to keep the scepticism from her response.

Adam may not have heard. She felt her reserves weaken, conscious of the clean, male scent of him amongst the pervading stench all around. She caught her breath, aware her gown clung damp on her back. What if the perspiration pads under her arms were damp?

'Am I going too fast for you?'

'Not at all; I'm used to walking in the countryside. What's in your lumpy parcel by the way?'

'A hubble bubble – hookah pipe. It's for the Tommies – they've become real pals.' Seeing her mystified look, he went on, 'It's a fiendish devise which Arabs smoke. They all sit in a circle each inhaling through one of the pipes attached to coils leading from the hookah. Strange, eh?'

'Was that the funny sweet smell the shopkeeper reeked of, do you suppose?'

'No, that was hashish.' Adam gave her a sidelong glance. 'An opiate, sends them into a trance. I'm told even the native policemen use it.'

'You seem familiar with the substance. Have you tried it?' she joked.

'No, my father is a strict disciplinarian, not that I ever had the urge to take drugs.'

'Oh, and your mother? Is she strict too?'

'No, Mother is delightfully lax, and my three sisters give her quite a time; the girls love me escorting them to London on shopping trips.'

'What fun it sounds.' She was running out of breath but determinedly pressed on.

'Too many females ganging up can be a bit stifling, you know. One reason I'm glad to be away from home. My youngest sister, poor dear, hasn't escaped. Her desire to marry a certain person was firmly clamped down upon by my father.'

'Why ever was that?'

'Oh, you know; considered beyond the pale. The fellow was born out of wedlock. Even my mother has reserves about that sort of thing. How about your family, Leonie? Am I correct in supposing Mrs Fox is your only close relative?'

Leonie drew a deep breath. They'd passed through a dark passageway and briefly cool air refreshed her. 'Yes, that's right.' Despite her usual inhibition she found herself talking, her sentences broken as she related brief details of her past.

'My uncle died a year ago.'

'You have very fond memories of him?'

'Yes, I do. He encouraged my photography; gave me this good camera on my twenty first. Said it was important to record everyday life for posterity.' She stopped to snap an old man harrying a laden donkey.

'Your uncle was a fine person then and must be missed. I can see why you are taking snaps. How do you think your photographs might be used?'

She began to hurry along again to keep up with Adam. 'I intend to have an exhibition. If that goes down well, it will give me confidence to pursue my aim of a career.'

'Mmm, sounds a good project. But not one I'd recommend for an amateur, especially a female,' he said. 'You'd have to compete with experts. Hey! I wish we could go on talking, but we'd best get back to the ship.'

'Who are you to decide if my photographs aren't up to scratch?'

'Sorry, didn't mean to offend,' Adam cast her a conciliatory glance. 'Can't help being outspoken.'

'Perhaps you'll eat your words one day.'

'Happens all the time. Come on, let's get going, shall we?'

There was no alternative. Adam Mallory was leading her through more narrow alleyways as if he had a map in his head.

Scenes went by in a whirl; men crouched over potter's wheels; hammering pewter pots or brewing coffee on paraffin stoves. Leonie halted briefly to take photographs. Intrigued, she saw men hunched over a game of skill with small stones; frail old men pulling heavy carts, their bodies clothed in rags. 'It's so distressing, all such hard toil.'

'Maybe, but it's always been like this.'

'Don't you feel concerned at all?'

'What's the use? We can't change them overnight to our idea of how things should be, even if that's what they'd want.'

Leonie frowned and made no reply.

'Sorry,' Adam grinned at her, seeming to relish her frostiness. 'I'm afraid it's my habit to stir up reactions. Blame *News of the World*. Come on, let's be friends, eh?'

'Very well, but don't foist your presumptions on me.' Perhaps Selina was right – she should be wary of revealing too much of herself. Then as the fun of being alone in this young man's company overcame qualms she asked, 'Where do you think all the women are, Adam? The place seems full of men.'

'At home, preparing food, I believe; most women only venture out early to market. Even then they must remain covered from head to toe.'

'I suppose you men believe that's how it should be.'

Adam made a face. 'Mmm. Maybe…'

'Pest! You men need a lesson in what's fair.' As they neared the harbour Leonie's ears filled with the scrape of sharp knives on leather, the boom of beaten copper and the strident shouts of street vendors. How offended Ruth would be, Leonie thought, as they passed men chewing betel nuts and spitting in the street. She averted her eyes, aware of their stares.

Distracted, she was caught off guard as a hard shove in the small of her back sent her reeling. Her heart plummeted. A robed man snatched at her arm. It happened fast; the glint of steel; hands grappling for her camera; Adam yelling as his boot shot out; a yelp and scuffling feet. When she looked up the assailant had gone.

Adam helped her to her feet, his hair dishevelled and hat in his hand. 'Leonie! Are you all right? My fault; shouldn't have brought you down these back alleys.'

'I'm just fine.' Her heart pumped hard, warming her cheeks.

Bending down, Adam picked up her parasol whilst keeping hold of his parcel.

'Thank you for fighting him off.' She should have said more, but didn't. He was right; she'd been foolish to take risks with no knowledge of these people's culture.

'We should head for the ship as fast as we can,' he urged. 'There may be more scoundrels about but that one won't be back in a hurry.'

She smoothed her skirts and jammed her straw hat over hair sprung loose in the fracas. 'Don't worry. I wouldn't have missed any of this. It's my fault bringing a camera; temptation for that fellow. Adam, your hand's bleeding!'

Adam glanced down. 'That rascal was a bit too quick.'

'Wait. Hold the camera, will you? This will have to do,' she fished up her sleeve for a cambric handkerchief.

'Please don't ruin it on my account.'

'It's fit for the rag bag, really,' she said. 'Keep your hand steady.' She leaned close, acutely aware of him as she wound it around his hand and his warm breath fanned her cheek. Concentrating, she tore the end in two and tied a knot. 'There, that should help for now.'

'Thanks, Leonie. I wouldn't mind a few more wounds if you'll agree to dress them for me.'

She took a deep breath as he took her arm protectively and guided her hurriedly towards the harbour. Passing an alcove, she gave a start. Two army officers were having a heated exchange.

'*Damnation to you, Renton…*' Leonie recognised the voice – Captain Ferguson, the Highland officer from that incident in Devon.

Adam stopped, his head cocked to one side. They were out of sight but within earshot and Leonie felt embarrassment rush in. She tugged his arm, 'It's their business, not ours.'

Instantly she regretted her words. Adam turned and frowned. 'Thought I might help,' he said crisply. 'I've got to know Captain Ferguson as a friend.'

Leonie's cheeks burned. But was that the truth? Adam's attitude to his work was hard to pin down. Almost at once they were surrounded by a gang of scabby urchins who chanted, '*Baksheesh, baksheesh,*' thrusting out grubby hands. To her horror Leonie saw that one of the small boys had only a bare stump for an arm. 'Oh, it's too cruel.' To think she'd ever thought some of her Sunday school pupils deprived. Even the poorest labourers didn't throw their children onto the streets to beg. 'So there's really no one to care for them?'

'The sad fact is they have to fend for themselves. Families can't feed so many mouths.' He was urging her away.

'If only I could give them something – I've already given away my few coins.'

'No matter.' Reaching under his jacket Adam extracted a handful of coins and threw them on the ground. 'They only know hunger and squalor, poor little devils,' he murmured as they left the urchins scrabbling for them in the dust. 'A different world, is it not? The reality contradicts those pretty, mystical tales of the Orient we read in books as children.'

'That's true.' Heartened by Adam's caring tone she added, 'People's lives here are so different.' Clearly he had experience of the world way beyond her limited view of life. Yet he could only be a year or so older than she was, she guessed.

They'd reached the harbour at last. Together they hurried through the dock gates. They stepped into the ferry and soon the vast white hull of the *Britannic* loomed above the bobbing craft which plied between ship and shore. Up the accommodation ladder they quickly climbed. Leonie's head reeled with the scenes she'd witnessed in the company of her unusual escort. 'It's been an extraordinary experience.'

'Thank you, Leonie. I'm afraid I let you down back there.'

'Not a bit of it. What if my aunt and I had been alone?'

They quickly bade one another farewell. Her feelings about him were confused and she longed to sort them out; but right now she must devote time to her aunt's needs.

***

'Ah... you are back at last,' Ruth exclaimed peevishly. Then her face brightened as in a rush to tell her own story she put Leonie's to one side. 'What a time I've had. Delightful people; Lady Amelia made such a fuss of me. Can't wait to write and tell them back home.' She bubbled with pleasure. 'You should have seen, everyone we passed doffing their hats, her ladyship kindness itself, having the gharry sweep right through the dock gates to the launch.'

'I've been concerned, Aunt. Are you quite recovered?'

Her tale cut short, Ruth picked up her lamb's wool puff and dabbed clouds of white powder over her bare neck and shoulders. 'Yes, thank you, dear. That awful place, it did make me queer for a while but dashing along in the conveyance in a breeze, I was soon feeling better. Utterly charming,' she continued, arching her brows. 'I would have been invited back to their residence without a doubt, had the ship not been due to sail.'

Leonie hid a smile, suspecting that the passengers would be regaled with this story at dinner, yet pleased her aunt had enjoyed herself.

Replacing her powder puff in its bowl, Ruth leaned forward and peered at her reflection. Then, turning round, she said, 'Now I want to hear where you went with that young man. I trust he conducted himself well?' She looked away, fiddling with the toilet articles in front of her. 'Such a kind gentleman, coming to our aid like that and speaking the language too. I'm quite impressed.'

Leonie made no comment except, 'Without Mr Mallory's help we should never have been able to buy our shawls.'

'We'll undo the parcel after dinner,' Ruth suggested. 'Decide which shawls are for whom. I really must see Mr… and express my gratitude.'

'Mr Mallory.'

'Is he travelling alone? I don't recall seeing him amongst your new acquaintances.' She frowned, beginning to look uncertain. 'You're very quiet. Is anything wrong?'

'No, Aunt. It's all been fascinating. Mr Mallory made lots of notes…' Oh dear, she'd not meant to say that.

'Lots of notes? Whatever for, may I ask?'

'Well, he's a reporter, and I expect he was gathering information for his newspaper.'

'My word! A newspaper reporter? A common hack!' Ruth exploded. 'And I allowed you to be alone with him?'

This was too much. 'What's wrong with a newspaper reporter? Adam is a perfect gentleman.'

'So, it's Christian names already? And which newspaper is he scribbling for, may I ask?'

Leonie couldn't stop the words slipping out. *'News of the World.'*

'Dear God!' A dull red stain spread over Ruth's powdered neck. 'Are you a fool? Are you telling me this person is employed by a gutter rag? And you've been roaming that dreadful place in his company?' She let out a sharp cry. 'And knowing this you allowed him to escort us…'

She made it sound shameful and somehow this took the gloss from Leonie's pleasure. She burst out, 'You act as if you have a right over me. I've come of age, so I can be trusted to make my own friendships.' Unable to stop words boiling over, she cried, 'Besides, you're not my mother!'

'That may be.' Ruth's tone deflated. She snatched up her smelling salts and inhaled deeply. Leonie's unexpected rebellion must have worked, for she lowered her voice and it took on a pleading note. 'It's just my concern for you, dear. I'm afraid we've been rather isolated from the world in our village. However shall we tell who anyone is if they step out of their rightful class?'

Leonie heaved a deep breath as she tried to see her aunt's point of view. 'If that's meant to imply Adam Mallory is not a gentleman, you are wrong. People have a right to choose their own role in society.'

'It makes for a topsy turvy world I must say. However, I appreciate Mr Mallory's assistance – goodness knows how he learned to speak to those Arabs.'

Leonie curbed her resentment and decided that her aunt, though but fifteen years her senior, had lived in an outdated society. Shamed by her outburst, she determined to make amends.

She watched as her aunt poked her hair with fretful but practised fingers. A pronged, tortoiseshell comb was stabbed into the hair at the nape of her neck as she eyed Leonie thoughtfully in the mirror.

'As long as you are not harbouring silly notions about the first man you come across? You've lived a sheltered life, dear.' Her voice shook. 'I'd prefer you not to see Mr Mallory. Newspaper reporters are of an unfortunate…' she hesitated to use the word '…breed. There are fine officers on board you might befriend.'

Leonie had nothing to gain by furthering the row. 'I'm sorry I said harsh words. I'm always grateful for your care and promise to make myself agreeable to the officers on board.' She gave her aunt a peck on the cheek and was rewarded with a fond smile. 'I'll leave you to finish dressing first, shall I? Then I'll take a quick tub to wash the grime away and change my clothes.' She heaved a sigh of relief that this little spat had been resolved quite amicably.

***

After Leonie left the cabin, Ruth fumbled in her toilet case for her flask of brandy and took several gulps. She then completed dressing automatically. Her heart beat fast. Waves of fear pricked her spine. A newspaper reporter? That odious *News of the World* – the very devil at ferreting out secrets. *Oh, Leonie*! Her fingers locked together in fright, an unconscious habit when disturbed. What dire characteristics had she inherited…? It took a huge battle of will to fight off the terrible secrets which threatened to overwhelm her and break down the careful scaffold of her life.

Chapter Four

The *Britannic* was once again spick and span after the coaling at Port Said, her decks scrubbed and sanded back to a blond smoothness by the seamen.

Adam didn't appear at dinner. Leonie hopefully scanned the passengers. Later, she strolled along the decks with Selina, still unsettled by the row with her aunt. Her heart gave little flutters as she cast about for Adam. Not a sign of him. The ship had resumed its passage southwards and Port Said slowly disappeared in the gloom behind them. The two young women stood by the rail. 'Look, isn't that lovely?' As often when she gazed at lovely sights, Leonie's spirits rose, entranced to see how the sandy tinge of the sound merged with various shades of green as the ship entered deeper water.

'Worth painting,' Selina nodded. 'Pity, I'm no artist, though. By the way, you were a quiet mouse at dinner. What did you get up to in Port Said? I didn't see you there.' She turned, eyebrows raised. 'Bobby and I had a whale of a time, buying trinkets. Did you get back to the ship early?'

'No, Aunt and I were there for ages, trying to find somewhere to buy silk shawls, and we got lost for a while.'

'But I heard your aunt tell everyone how she was brought back in style by some dignitaries – quite an adventure, it seems.' She turned a questioning face to her friend, brows furrowed. 'So, how did *you* get back?'

It was no use, she'd have to tell. Drawing a breath, Leonie began her story. 'We had no luck shopping. Then I spotted a passenger I recognised who looked as though he knew the ropes. Aunt was delighted and asked him to come to our assistance. He proved our saviour. After we'd bought the shawls – dreadful stuffy place, my aunt felt unwell. Luckily, that Lady drew up…'

'Hold on,' Selina cut in, 'let's hear it slowly, eh? This *he* person,' she insisted, 'tell me who "he" was. Hard to believe your aunt would turn you over to a stranger, passenger or not – elderly was he? A high up sort of person?'

Leonie had the grace to blush. 'No, to be honest it was that reporter, Adam Mallory. He offered to escort me back to the ship.'

Her friend's eyes widened. 'Our saucy reporter, eh?' Selina threw back her head and laughed. 'Oh Leonie, you are a dark horse. Did Mrs Fox know who he was?'

'No. She was quite shocked when I told her what he does and that newspaper he works for.' Leonie's mouth twitched. 'We had angry words before dinner.'

'Never mind, it couldn't have upset your aunt too much; she was in fine fettle at dinner, wasn't she? Now I want to hear all – come on, what's he like? Where did he take you, eh, up some back alley?'

Leonie grinned. 'Yes, he did. But just to take a short cut. Oh Selina, it was such an adventure seeing lives of the natives in the raw. He's quite knowledgeable, speaks the lingo too.' She just couldn't go along with her aunt's views about newspaper reporters. Whatever was it about them that raised her fears?

'Sounds like you've lost your heart to the fellow.' Selina leaned closer, 'Confess – try anything on, did he?'

'No, it wasn't like that. Anyway there was hardly enough time to take photographs. He raced me back to the ship.'

Selina sighed, 'I envy you. Haven't had a minute alone with a fellow myself unless you count a conversation with that surveyor, sober old Mr Kershaw. Mind you I do admit it was fascinating hearing him talk about his expeditions around the world.'

'We don't know half of it, do we?' Leonie quickly changed the subject but her thoughts remained with Adam. Whilst Selina continued chattering her mind drifted off as she went over and over every single minute she'd spent alone with him, hardly daring to guess if he'd felt the slightest attraction to her.

'Is Mrs Fox your only relative?' Selina asked.

'Well yes, apart from my Uncle Sebastian in Australia. Apparently when my parents died I was adopted by my aunt and her husband, my Uncle Bertram. He was the local vicar.'

'How did your parents die?'

'Oh I used to try and find out but Aunt always managed to put me off. She would enquire, "I trust you are happy with Unlce and me?" I've always understood that my mother died in childbirth producing me. As for my father, it stuck in my head that he'd died while my mother was still carrying me so he never saw me. My grandparents looked after me until my aunt and her husband were married.'

Selina regarded her friend doubtfully. 'I'm trying to see things through your eyes. Our minds are strange; make us believe things even when circumstances tell otherwise, as if we're subconsciously afraid of the truth.' Her face cleared. 'Does it really matter? I mean you are lucky to have been brought up in a happy home.'

'Mmm, I know that. Look, it's getting dark. I can't take any pictures.' She peered down into the camera's aperture, unable to capture an image in the dim light. Huge bow waves, propelled forward by the ship's bulk, ate into the banks and surged back alongside, sending ripples to shift the pelicans on their stilted legs. 'It's so beautiful, isn't it? I wish I could fix this. If only there was such a thing as coloured film.' She shook her head. 'Good to share it with you though.'

As a curtain of darkness slipped over them Leonie suggested, 'How about a typewriter lesson? It's not late and you said Bobby's gone to play cards. Can you bear to teach a donkey?'

'All right, let's give it a try.' Selina nudged her friend, 'I've made a pig's ear of a torn hem. I'm counting on you to sort it out.'

After the typewriting lesson, Selina asked, 'Like to try these on? I've brought several.' She held up a pair of what looked to Leonie like floppy cycling bloomers. 'They're all the rage amongst a group of rich ladies in London you know. They call themselves the Rationalists – cycle about to show they can wear sensible clothing like males. I don't think it fair, do you? Men aren't trussed up like us in tight stays and long skirts.'

'I think I'll look silly in them.' Leonie stood up and undid the dozen small buttons on her bodice, and then untied the sash on her gown and dropped it to the floor.

Selina handed her a pair of striped cotton pantaloons. 'Not at all, you've got the figure for them. Not like me, straight up and down like a bean pole. Here, put them on and let's see. I'll show you mine first.' Selina reached into her trunk and selected some purple silk bloomers and stooped to pull them on. 'How do I look?' She did a twirl.

Peals of laughter leapt from Leonie's throat.

'Do I look that daft?' Selina wrinkled her nose.

'No, you look delightful. It's just,' she giggled, 'the price ticket's on the back!'

'Snip it off then, will you?'

Still filled with mirth, Leonie detached the ticket and showed her friend. '*3 shillings and sixpence a pair*. It was stuck on your rear.'

An overwhelming sense of how things would change in the future set Leonie's pulse racing.

'Aren't we lucky to have found ourselves on the same ship?' Selina chortled, giving Leonie a friendly hug.

***

The *Britannic* anchored off Suez under a baking sun, hot enough to crack the brazen blue sky.

'It's real Red Sea weather,' Bobby Gibson proclaimed, as if that knowledge should make the heat easier to bear.

Leonie raised her parasol in agreement. Wandering away she scanned the passengers for Adam, but he was elusive. Whatever could he be doing? Was he closeted in his cabin writing scandalous accounts? Her heart gave a little twist as she recalled exploring Port Said. Maybe he found the company of the lower ranks more entertaining than being with the naïve likes of herself.

She decided to write to friends in Devon and made for her favourite spot near the forward bulkhead, which offered a slight breeze. Sometimes at night there she stumbled upon grimy stokers snatching a cat nap, lying prone with fatigue. A sudden flutter of air caught her off guard and whisked away the sheet she'd started to write. Leonie sprang forward as the paper dipped and rose beyond her reach. A shadow passed her eye as an arm shot out and a man's fist closed over the paper.

'Here,' he said, 'yours, I think, Miss Grant?' Clyde Ferguson handed it over.

'Thank you.' Leonie stood back. She saw he looked exhausted. Deep lines etched about his mouth, his cheeks hollow. Surprised how it affected her she said on a whim, 'Please join me and don't be formal, call me Leonie.'

'Then please call me Clyde, forget the "Captain". I'm glad to have the opportunity to meet you again Leonie.'

She saw him frown, his grey eyes seeming to focus far away. 'This is another world away from home,' she said.

'Another world, yes,' he replied slowly.

She waited till he'd seated himself on a wide ledge. 'Where are you from when you're not involved with the war?'

'Originally from Scotland,' he spoke reservedly. 'But since boyhood I was away at boarding school then straight into the army. My guardians in Devon have now passed on, so it's hard to say where home is.'

His reply saddened her and unwilling to delve deeper Leonie stated, 'You are free to choose then.'

Clyde smiled. 'Follow one's dreams? Yes, that is a privilege, I agree.'

The conversation was in danger of coming to an end. Leonie racked her brains for something to say and found herself babbling, 'I've lived all my life in Devon. My aunt came from Scotland to be married. Grandfather was the ghillie on a large estate.'

'I see.' It sounded non-committal.

Oh dear, this was going nowhere. She sensed a gentle nature beneath his reserve, a person not given to flippant repartee. He was older than Adam, perhaps in his thirties, and very different. He made no attempt to leave but the silence which grew between them seemed not uncomfortable.

'I am interrupting your correspondence,' he said suddenly.

'No, I was only passing time with it, nothing urgent.' She had dismissed a thought of touring the decks in the hopes of bumping into Adam.

'You are making a long visit to Australia?' Clyde asked.

'Yes, permanent. We're going to live north of Adelaide with my bachelor uncle, my aunt's brother. He emigrated almost a quarter of a century ago.'

Clyde smiled at her. 'That's a big step you're taking if you'll forgive the presumption. Yet a wonderful thing when families can be re-united.'

They continued to converse spasmodically but she gleaned nothing to suggest what Clyde's row had been with that fellow officer in Port Said. She changed the subject. 'I'm told there will be marvellous celebrations in Sydney for the new twentieth century.'

'Yes, there'll be marches, displays and naturally we see to the men's welfare. We officers arrange interesting outings in which the passengers will be included.' He hesitated. 'Would you perhaps allow me to send you an invitation?'

Leonie nodded and smiled her agreement.

'Ah, will you please excuse me?' Clyde leapt to his feet. 'I've so enjoyed talking with you but unfortunately I must return to my duties.' He nodded and indicated below decks, looking somehow years younger as his mouth relaxed in a smile.

Chapter Five

Clyde did not immediately go down below decks but tarried in his cabin. Here on this ship, without the pressure that fired one up in combat, he felt in limbo, made much worse by this wretched episode with Renton. He needed to draw every ounce of energy in order to function during the day. He reached into a drawer. It was hard to resist a quick shot of brandy to steady his nerves. *I won't make this a habit*, he told himself. Off duty was the hardest time, when gambling ruled the roost as men had little with which to occupy themselves. His mind firmed. He would call Renton's bluff.

Clyde rang the bell to summon his batman. Clark had been his batman throughout their service in the South African campaign; a trustworthy fellow, keen as mustard and a sound soldier.

'Yes sir?' Private Clark stood erect. Clyde noted the man's smart turnout and reaching into his webbing pouch he pressed a coin into Clark's palm.

'Thank you sir, much obliged.' If Clark was surprised, his features remained blank.

'Are they feeding you well, Clark? Getting plenty of exercise?'

Receiving affirmation, Clyde nodded. 'Will you kindly tell Lieutenant Renton I'll be going down to check on the horses in fifteen minutes?' The nagging thought at the back of his head refused to shift; what if word got out? What if that young puppy of a reporter got wind of...?

The horses still suffered in rough seas. For the last three days they'd sailed through the calm waters of the Red Sea. Now, late afternoon on the fourth, the *Britannic* plunged head on into the Indian Ocean and began to wallow.

Clyde gripped the rails as he descended the companionway. Reaching the lower deck, he was briefly disorientated by the pounding of the propeller shaft as the ship cut through the swell. Pungent smells filled his lungs as he clattered down the final narrow steps; the strong stench of ammonia, of sweating horses and chaff, mingled with the acrid smell of coal dust and oil. Poor beasts, he thought. Then his mission came to the fore. He must sort out Renton.

Clyde recalled how months ago back in South Africa the officers celebrated a particularly gruesome battle with a fine dinner and demolished several crates of champagne with no compunction for the starving Boers. A few officers drank to excess. Normally, he himself curbed his drinking, but that night he needed something to calm his nerves. With a few brandies under his belt he'd talked freely to Lieutenant Renton about his odious father, the laird of a huge estate in Scotland; his notoriety as a plunderer of young women; and the old man's deserved ghastly end. He'd also revealed the change of his own name from the family name MacLeod to that of his guardians'; Ferguson.

Renton's youthful, devil-may-care attitude had seemed appealing. But the wretched fellow now threatened to contaminate Clyde with his father's acts. He'd discovered things certainly not known by Clyde's superiors and began demanding cash to keep his mouth shut – cash to pay for his drinking excesses.

Clyde's brows met in a fierce scowl. A pulse throbbed in his neck. He must put an end to it before Renton sold his story to that young newspaper reporter, Adam Mallory.

He was greeted by the shuffling, stamping sounds of hooves muffled by straw strewn about the horses' stalls and the clang of heavy buckets as orderlies sluiced them out in the aft. 'Good day, Jones,' Clyde said, as the groom responsible for Jasper's care came alongside. 'Has his hoof healed properly?'

'Yes, sir.' The man stood and brushed straw off his long khaki overall. 'That ointment cleared it up a treat.'

'Good man. I'll stay here with him for a while,' Clyde said, watching as the groom went off to continue his duties. He strained his ears, listening for footsteps coming down the ladder.

Hearing Clyde's voice Jasper's ears twitched and his hoof pawed the straw. Webbing shackles secured the horses to rings in the wall but allowed room for movement. A fine Cleveland bay, Jasper was built for stamina and speed and stood over sixteen hands high. Clyde marvelled how stoic were these creatures, lifted from their normal safe lives on some distant farm. He smoothed the horse's head and breathed gently into his wide, black nostrils and this contact served to help ease his mind. Kneeling down to check Jasper's powerful legs, his thoughts raced back to riding this fine horse into battle.

Lieutenant Renton's sudden presence caught Clyde off guard. He rose quickly to his feet and rapped out, 'Your horse, Byron – in good shape is he, Renton?'

'Yes, in excellent fettle, thank you, sir; a calm beast even in rough seas.'

Beneath the man's humble courtesy Clyde detected insolence. Delaying his mission, he pointed to Jasper's hoof. 'Poor fellow picked up laminitis. Cured now, thank God.' He spotted Renton's growing nervousness, eyes skittering about and anxious bluster in his tone, clearly wondering what his superior would say.

'I think you know why I wanted this meeting.' Clyde squared up and gave the other the full force of his keen stare. 'Got to stop, d'you hear? No more funds to bail out your drinking and gambling. Do your worst; shout it to the whole brigade! Matters not a toss to me,' he bluffed. 'What my father did was his doing and his alone.'

Lieutenant Renton's puffy cheeks flamed. 'Yes, sir,' he muttered.

But could he be trusted when drunk? Clyde supposed not. He barked at the junior officer, 'You'll be discharged quicker than explosives if you demand cash from me again. No more! Understand?'

Renton nodded, a red stain rising from his neck. He managed a salute before turning to take his leave.

Although it was still afternoon Clyde retired to his cabin and lay down on his bed. That unpleasant encounter with Renton down in the stables had proved unsettling. Thank God it hadn't brought on one of his 'episodes'. That was what the army doctors called them; tortuous nightmares when he lost his sanity and relived the gruesome scenes of war. Had this scourge gone for good? Had his mind healed?

Something else niggled at the back of his mind. It was something that Leonie Grant had mentioned. Yes, she'd said her grandfather was ghillie of an estate in Scotland. It would be the very devil if by a dreadful coincidence it could be the same place where he was born!

***

Over glasses of iced tea and lemon, conversation flowed as Leonie sat with Adam over tea in the saloon.

Adam spoke thoughtfully. 'I've a mind to try something else. I can't abide the idea of being a hack for the rest of my life. You should see some of the old fellows who've been in the trade forever. Noses sharpened, gimlet eyes, potbellied and reeking of stale tobacco from long, boring sessions sniffing around for titbits of news.' He laughed, and Leonie laughed with him.

'So, anything special in mind?'

He took a sip of tea and was silent for a moment. 'I'd love to travel,' his lively face looked suddenly solemn. 'May sound vague; but make use of my journalism to broaden people's awareness.'

'I think that's a very worthwhile ambition.' She realized how much she was growing to like him as the days went by.

'Trouble is my father may not think the same way. He's always assumed I'd follow him into his business; take up the reins long before he retires. I do owe my parents a lot, so it'll be hard to justify breaking away.'

His views reflected her own. 'I sympathise,' she said. 'In a small way, if I get the employment I'm after it will mean leaving my aunt alone in a strange country, a widow without her friends. It doesn't seem fair for her to depend totally on her brother.'

'I believe it's always been the same for the younger generation, don't you? So let's make the most of this voyage, eh? Enjoy everything on offer.'

They agreed on a date to meet again and Leonie returned to the cabin, thankful to find it vacant. Aunt Ruth must still be playing bridge. A swell of joy filled Leonie as she threw off her clothes and flopped down on her bed. She closed her eyes and went over the conversation she'd shared with Adam word for word, before sinking into a lovely doze. A warm flush suffused her whole body. This was what it must feel like to be falling in love, she mused. There was no way she'd adhere to her aunt's strictures not to see Adam. Ruth's ideas were fixed so far as 'one's proper class'.

If only Aunt could find some means of contentment, Leonie brooded, instead of being constantly on edge and ready to find fault. She reasoned how hard it must be after sharing a happy, conventional life with her husband and once again resolved to make allowances.

***

On the evening when they'd arranged to meet next, Leonie was relieved that her aunt had another arrangement to play a game of bridge. A half moon cast its eerie slanting glow over the hurricane deck as, concentrating on keeping from slipping over on the sloping deck, Leonie gasped when the large figure of Lieutenant Renton blocked her way.

'Miss Leonie herself,' he drawled. He leered down at her and held onto her arm rather longer than was necessary. His breath stank of alcohol as she pushed him away. Could this fellow be in charge of men's lives? Quickly, she pressed a hand on her stomach. 'A touch of the collywobbles,' she groaned, screwing up her face and she pointed to the rail.

'My dear young lady, do not let me delay you.' Renton backed away and waved her on.

Leonie found the secluded niche where steamer chairs were stacked. She couldn't ignore the slow thuds of her heart nor her ears sharpened on the alert for him.

The ship's rail rose and fell on the swell, the gentle motion pleasant. A soft whistle floated towards her like breeze blown through a keyhole and her pulse instantly took off on a race.

'Leonie, Leonie. Are you there? It's me, Adam.'

'Yes, I'm over here.' Her voice sounded tinny in the cool air.

'Oh good; I was afraid you might have forgotten. Look,' he said, hurrying to her, 'I've found an accomplice who's good at stalking.'

Surprised, Leonie saw a tiny black kitten nestled against Adam's chest. 'What a dear little thing.' She placed a finger under the kitten's chin, delighted when it purred. She stole a glance at Adam, noting his gentle expression as he gazed at the tiny mite.

'Who does it belong to?'

Adam's eyes flashed as he looked up. 'Well, I did wonder if I might find a soft-hearted young lady who'd accept him as a gift?' A question hung unspoken, but to defray the subject she asked,

'May I hold it? You haven't said where it comes from.'

'Rescued the poor little waif,' he said as he lowered the warm bundle into Leonie's arms. 'The ship's cats down in the galley produce too many litters – more than enough to deal with the rats. So, they have to be…' he thrust out his lower lip, shook his head and pointed out to sea.

'That's so sad; I can't bear to think of it drowned.' The kitten snuggled against her and purred loudly as it kneaded her bodice. 'We must save it. I'd love to have it in our cabin but…' her voice trailed off. 'My aunt… it's difficult.'

'I've been thinking, just a crazy idea. Oh, do let's sit down. First, I want to hear more about *you*, Leonie. There was no chance to talk in Port Said, was there? Don't even know if this is your first trip abroad?'

'Yes, it is my longest journey. I begin to realize how much I've missed.'

'There's plenty of time to catch up; sounds like you've enjoyed a pleasant, settled life.'

'What about you? Travelled a lot? I mean, speaking Arabic isn't a universal skill. However did you come to learn it?' Pressed against her breast, the kitten's purr resonated like the sensual tingles fetched by Adam's nearness.

'My father's business is in steel. He took us all around the globe on his assignments. When we stayed in India I caught a bout of malaria and missed out on my schooling, so the parents hired tutors. It was easy to pick up foreign lingo and I've had a fascination for languages ever since.'

'What times you must have had.'

Adam made no effort to enlarge. Instead he remarked, 'But you'll be looking forward to a new life in Australia?'

She thought for a moment. 'Yes, as I mentioned before I intend to make a career in photography. I know it won't be easy,' she said firmly. 'I'm prepared to take on any work at first to earn my keep.'

'To be frank,' he interjected, 'I think you'd be better off sticking to "any work". I understand Australians aren't good at accepting females in their own professions.'

'Well I shall prove them wrong! What's the good of women having the franchise if they can't be treated equal?' she demanded.

'I don't disagree, just stating facts as they are.'

'You men are all alike.' Her warm feelings switched to anger. 'Expect us to swan about on your arm like pretty pets.'

Adam threw back his head and roared with laughter. 'I was teasing,' he insisted.

Leonie sprang to her feet.

He grabbed the kitten as it leapt from her arms and, calming it, passed it back. 'Here you are. Oh Leonie, I really was only teasing. Can't help winding you up. It's what I'm used to doing with my poor sisters.'

For a moment, Leonie was unsure whether or not to believe him. 'Just as I said, you men think you can treat us like silly nincompoops.'

'Will you show me your pictures? I'd really like to see them, Leonie.'

Mollified by his change of tone, Leonie hesitated. He sounded sincere but could she believe him? Then pride in her snaps overcame doubt. 'Yes, if you like,' she said slowly.

'Why not tomorrow after breakfast in the saloon?' he asked.

'Yes, I'll be there.' Something about him puzzled her. He seemed such a mixture of personalities. These thoughts vanished as the kitten began to wriggle and dig its claws into her bodice.

'Here, let me take it.'

A pleasant tingle shot through her as their fingers touched as he gathered the ball of fluff into his arms.

Adam seemed not to be aware. 'I've got an idea,' he exclaimed. 'Let's make a home for it in one of the lifeboats. Are you game, Leonie? It'll need some sort of bedding.'

'Sounds a giddy idea.' Leonie's emotions swayed. 'Yes, we can't risk it being caught.' She giggled. 'What can I do?'

'Will you wait here a moment?' He dropped the kitten into her arms. 'I'll see what I can find. The Tommies will slip me food so it won't starve.'

'It must have a name.' She nuzzled her face in the soft fur. 'I know, how about Mischief?'

He disappeared and she waited, the kitten clutched tight to her chest. Night fell suddenly like a shroud and the moon cast shreds of silver ribbons about the ship. Moments later she gave a start as Adam padded quietly back.

'Hello, you were quick.'

'Had to beg a used flour sack,' he said breathlessly. 'I told the Sergeant I need it to store some things. I'm sure he wasn't taken in when I begged scraps of food from the Tommies.' A faint meow had Adam leaning towards her to stroke the kitten. 'Right, Mischief. Let's get you settled.' He turned and began to remove steamer chairs from the stack.

'What are you doing? Can I help?'

'Stop Mischief scampering away and keep a sharp look out, will you?' he called over his shoulder as he piled up the chairs. 'Hope these hold my weight.'

She watched as he lifted his leg and climbed onto the top of the heap. His feet were on a level with her ears. 'You're doing well,' she called in a hoarse whisper as he hopped from the chairs onto the gunwales of a lifeboat.

'I'll check if it's possible to reach down inside…'

Leonie jumped as a tall figure loomed out of the darkness.

'What the bloody hell's going on?' Alerted by shuffling noises up above, a stern voice rapped out.

Quickly Leonie thrust the kitten under her shawl and slipped back into the shadows as a ship's officer swung the beam of his hurricane lamp up into Adam's face. She winced as Adam fell backwards onto the chairs, which collapsed beneath him with a loud crash.

'Move that bright light away will you please? I'll explain.' Adam kicked the empty sack out of sight.

Leonie smothered her giggles at the spectacle. Adam look daft as he tried to appear sensible with one leg caught in the tangle of chairs.

'You'd better come up with a good excuse! Those lifeboats are not to be tampered with; not for any reason,' the sailor growled.

'I do apologise. I'm Adam Mallory, newspaper reporter,' Adam announced firmly as he tugged his leg free. 'Just doing research to report to my news editor about how things operate on the ship.'

In the yellow lamp light Leonie saw the sailor's face screw up.

'I suggest you get authorisation next time. What if there'd been an emergency, the call to abandon ship while you were playing around up there?'

It was fortunate that clouds hid Adam's face for Leonie could picture his pretence at being serious. 'Yes, sir, I won't do further research without permission.'

'Clear this up then.'

The sailor continued on his inspection and they both chuckled as his lamplight grew faint as it weaved about the deck further off. It was as if it were the most natural thing when they fell into one another's arms, the kitten squashed between them.

'You looked so funny,' Leonie gasped. 'Just doing research; don't know how you kept a straight face.'

Adam's breath brushed her face and she felt the strength of him through his light jacket as he leaned into her. Then Mischief squirmed, scratched their arms and instantly forced them apart.

'Leonie,' Adam said hoarsely.

Leonie's voice wobbled. 'Thank goodness he didn't spot Mischief. Whatever shall we do with her?'

The look Adam gave her held a query, but whether it related to their embrace or considering her question, she couldn't tell. Then his mouth lifted in a gentle smile. 'I think kitty will have to bunk down with me.'

Chapter Six

The following day Leonie determined to put more effort into keeping her aunt company. Ruth was looking pale and drawn again, certainly not as robust as most other passengers, who'd gained weight from their extravagant meals.

'Do let's go up on deck, Aunt. We'll sit quietly together.' She worried that Ruth was ailing for a disease and couldn't bear the thought of her not being fit to meet her brother.

Up here on the promenade deck a soft breeze cooled the air. Large canvas awnings made sufficient shade above the recliners where passengers relaxed, talking or reading a book. The deck steward, ever attentive, manoeuvred her aunt's chair into the spot she selected and placed another beside her for Leonie.

'What a pleasant way to spend our morning. I can still hardly believe we're on a ship sailing to Australia,' Leonie remarked cheerfully.

'I am finding it pleasant,' Ruth agreed. 'If only my dear Bertram had lived to share this experience…'

Leonie leaned over and laid a comforting hand on her aunt's shoulder. 'I do sympathise, Aunt. I'm sure your brother will give you a little of Uncle's loving support.'

'Dear child, I know you have my interests at heart,' she smiled at Leonie. 'As I do yours,' she added.

Each sensing a new, closer relationship they sat silently gazing out to sea. Leonie reflected that Devon was already becoming a vague image. Aloud she asked, 'Shall I order a glass of sarsaparilla? Or perhaps you'd prefer a pot of tea?'

'Thank you dear. A pot of China tea would be very agreeable.'

Provided with their refreshing drinks they sat and looked on at the group which surrounded a certain small person. Miss Bobby Gibson seemed to be the centre of attention. She wore a strange outfit for a tiny person, as was her custom. Today, an orange striped skirt flopped about her deck chair. A blouse of shot silk in vibrant green with voluminous sleeves, and her head swathed in a turban, gave her the appearance of a ripe orange plucked from a tree.

'Mind you,' Bobby reminded her audience, 'back in 1889 the voyage from England to Australia took us seven weeks. Nowadays it can be done in forty days.'

Leonie watched Ruth smiling as she replaced her tea cup on the low table and raised her head to listen, and was pleased her aunt made no unkind remark.

'They may have been noisier and, oh my! How they rolled in heavy seas. But for comfort and elegance you couldn't beat the old P & O liners; travelled with them quite a few times.' Smiles crinkled Bobby Gibson's face as she reminisced.

Ruth lay down a copy of *The Windsor Magazine* she'd brought to read. 'Well,' she declared, turning a bright face to Leonie. 'Perhaps I was a little too hasty in my appraisal. I do find Miss Gibson quite entertaining,' she whispered.

I wonder, thought Leonie, if Aunt would be so accommodating if she knew about her meeting Adam Mallory?

***

The following morning, Leonie arrived in the saloon with a photograph album, one of a half dozen not stowed with the rest of their baggage in the hold. Adam arrived soon after.

'May I order you a coffee, Leonie?'

'Yes please. Oh do tell me – did you survive all night with Mischief?'

'Well, she's quite a wriggler so I got hardly a wink...' He grinned, and she guessed it was not true.

'I made a bed for her in my haversack. Played out, I think; didn't utter a peep. She's eaten like a horse this morning so I've locked her in my cabin.'

They sat near to one another while Leonie slowly turned the heavy pages. She focussed on the photographs and, turning the pages, began to reminisce about each one. 'There's Bert, scything the back paddock and men following the plough…' she trailed off, suddenly aware Adam made no comment.

'I see,' he said slowly. 'They're very competent photographs, Leonie.'

'But? Go on, what's in your mind?' Her cheeks flushed, for she was sharing a precious, private part of her life.

'It's only that you said an exhibition in Sydney?'

'That's my intention,' she retorted, 'in fact I've already written to the gallery and they've suggested I present my photographs for them to review.'

'Well, it's only my opinion, but I don't think factual images of workers will receive rave reviews,' he said slowly.

'Would you mind explaining?' Her tone was sharp.

Adam straightened up and leaned back in his seat. 'I think Australians will expect to see, how can I say, images of modern architecture and the latest in design.'

'Well that's just your opinion. I believe my photographs showing real toil should promote great interest.'

'Please don't be upset. I'm not denigrating your photographs – I think they are excellent.' Adam touched her arm, his voice full of sympathy. 'But most well-to-do Australians – those likely to visit exhibitions – have gained their own wealth by sheer hard toil; had to pull themselves up by their boot strings, you know. They've left all the hardship behind them; won't want to see it all reflected back at them.'

Mortified, Leonie sprang to her feet and snapped the album shut. 'I won't give up,' she declared, her cheeks fiery hot. 'I'm determined to go ahead. I've taken hundreds of factual images.' She strained a smile. 'Even bad reviews are good publicity; I bet you can't dispute that?' She snatched up the album and turned to leave.

Adam stood and laid a restraining hand on her arm. 'Please don't be angry. I honestly admire your work. Look, I'll be around in Sydney until I join the *Britannic* again on its trip to New Zealand. I'll be happy to assist with an exhibition. I'd really like to be proved wrong.'

Relenting, Leonie turned back. 'I've always believed I welcomed honest criticism. You see until now, everyone just said things like, "Oh, that's a good picture Leonie," or, "Haven't you captured that well". I suppose it's about time I faced reality.'

'Do please sit down again.' He gave her one of his cheeky grins, head on one side. 'D'you know how delightful you look with your hackles raised? I love your hair when it springs free.' He made a movement in the air with his hands. 'Ripples like dark, golden sand in the breeze.'

Taken by surprise, Leonie's eyes lowered as she blushed. She drew a deep breath then looked him straight in the eye. 'What a clever ploy. You males think flattery will soften us females up but we're not taken in any more, you know.' Nevertheless, her mouth tilted with a smile.

Ignoring her remark, Adam asked, 'Where do you stay in Sydney? You said your aunt's brother lives near Adelaide.'

'With friends of Uncle Sebastian in the Bellevue district; his friend is a newspaper proprietor.'

Adam leaned forward. 'You'll be at the heart of things then, right there in the hub of Sydney city.'

'Oh I don't know about that,' Leonie demurred, 'Aunt and I will enjoy trips to all the celebrations and outings – apparently the officers will include the passengers from the *Britannic*. Uncle Sebastian plans to join us for Christmas and then take us both to his farm north of Adelaide.' She paused before asking, 'Where will you be staying then?'

'Here and there,' Adam said vaguely. 'I've good contacts who've offered hospitality. There's also a relative. May I ask a favour, Leonie?' he added. 'Will you meet me in Sydney when you have a spare hour or so? I have a feeling we shall meet soon anyway, perhaps in unusual circumstances,' he added mysteriously.

Even as she consented she wondered, whatever was that last statement meant to mean?

***

The following Sunday after morning worship, Ruth arrived on the promenade deck on Leonie's arm. A deck steward arranged a steamer chair, placed strategically for her so as to glimpse any passers-by she might wish to acknowledge. Declining further assistance, she looked up and smiled at Leonie. 'I'll be quite content here on my own. You run along and find your friends, dear.'

'Are you quite sure, Aunt?' Leonie's brows puckered. 'I will then, but you must call the steward to fetch me if you need anything. I shan't be far away.'

Ruth settled herself down. How pleasant Leonie could be, she thought with a smile. She'd brought some mending and frowned seeing the frayed hem, knowing their clothes were a problem. The few outfits they'd brought would have to serve for many occasions.

She breathed in deeply. The Sunday service had triggered memories of all those church services conducted by dear Bertram and she sent him up a prayer, for he was never far from her thoughts. He alone shared her secrets. Could Leonie still be seeing that dreadful reporter against her wishes? Her heart did a little lurch as she imagined his nosy questions.

Holding her spectacles up to the sky to check their brilliance, Ruth's thoughts turned again to Leonie, for Leonie seemed to have developed a strong wilfulness and a habit of attracting the undesirable which had renewed her fears. Taking deep breaths of sea air she pleaded, *please God, give me strength to offload my burden to Sebastian.*

Gradually the effect of warm sunshine and the gentle breeze of fresh salty air settled her into a better frame of mind. Picking up her sewing, she applied the needle with small, even stitches until the mending was finished. A pile of magazines lay nearby, while her legs were wrapped in a rug against possible draught. Here on the sheltered lee side of the ship, the swish of the waves and distant sounds of conversation lulled her into a doze. Her eyes closed. The sewing slipped from her lap and she tumbled into a dream.

She was hurrying, her steps faster and faster, unable to escape hundreds of reporters chasing her. She raced on, slipping and sliding on shiny photos, all identical, depicting a big bloated face which leered up, and its blubbery mouth was trying to suck her in.

Ruth jerked awake, but the horrid dream clung like a leech. She felt herself observed. Squinting into the bright sun it took a few moments to settle her breathing and wind the spectacle wires around her ears. When her sight adjusted it lighted upon an officer, his hand raised in greeting. Odd, she puzzled, there was a vague familiarity about him she couldn't place. Suddenly, the memory jolted to the surface. However could it be him?

'How do you do, ma'am? My apologies for coming upon you without warning. Clyde Ferguson,' he reminded. 'You recall that unfortunate incident with your niece in Devon?' He moved towards her. 'May I?' he asked. He bent down, picked up her sewing and placed it beside her.

Was she still dreaming? How could this be that young man who'd stood in her hall at Downshill? There was a tremor behind her ribs as if a mouse scampered inside a wheel. Flustered she said, 'Oh dear, I fear that Leonie – my niece has an imaginative mind...' Whatever was she babbling about?

But being an officer and gentleman, Clyde Ferguson chose not to hear.

'I beg pardon for startling you, ma'am. Yes, we have met before. In Devon, and not in the most favourable circumstance I regret to say.' He raised his eyebrows and receiving no response went on diffidently, 'I trust this remarkable coincidence of Fate may allow me to rectify...?'

This fine officer was definitely the same man who'd brought Leonie home that day after that incident in the meadows. Oh dear, that disgraceful episode she'd hoped to erase – all because of Leonie's foolish behaviour. She came to with alacrity and sat bolt upright. 'Why, what an amazing thing!' At once her brain skipped through any obstacles that might arise. She saw he wore Mess kit, obligatory for Sunday service, and she counted three pips on his epaulette. 'How delightful, Captain,' she exclaimed and extended her hand in welcome.

He took her hand and then ventured, 'You are visiting Australia?' He remained standing, his fingers stroking his clipped moustache.

'Yes, yes, to live with my brother. Do join me, please. Draw up that chair beside me will you?' She snatched a handkerchief from a pocket and pretended a sneeze in an effort to control her thoughts. 'What a coincidence, Captain, sailing aboard the same ship.'

'Indeed yes, it's quite amazing.'

She quickly turned things over in her mind. Normally a private person, she felt an urge to grasp this chance to enlighten him regarding Leonie's waywardness – but without denigrating her of course – for would he not be an ideal suitor? He was an officer and so must be a person of some means. She'd recalled his mention of settling his guardian's estate in Devon all those months ago.

'Mrs Fox, may I speak plainly?' He clasped his hands, turned his gaze to the ocean and for a few moments was silent.

She saw the lines deepen either side of his mouth as he slowly turned towards her.

'What I am about to say has never before been mentioned. I am confident of your discretion and only ask that you keep this to yourself.'

As he drew a deep breath, Ruth waited. A strange request and she felt flutters around her heart. 'You may be certain I shall honour your request, Captain.'

He began his explanation of his 'episodes' which occasionally afflicted him and how this had been the cause for the incident with Leonie in Devon. When he'd finished speaking, Ruth sat in silence for several minutes and tried to come to terms with what he'd disclosed and how it might affect a relationship with a young lady.

She scrambled good manners together. 'We civilians are shielded from the real horrors of war,' she remarked. 'I respect you for revealing the circumstance which brought about your momentary loss of reality back in Devon that day. I assure you; none of what you've told me will ever be mentioned.' As Clyde Ferguson murmured his thanks, words popped out of her mouth. 'Perhaps when your duties allow you will join our table for dinner one evening?'

'Thank you, I shall look forward to that. I've had the pleasure of meeting your niece on board.'

Ruth felt a rush of satisfaction. So, he'd met Leonie on board? Why hadn't Leonie told her?

As she watched him depart Ruth could hardly contain herself as she waited impatiently for the deck steward to attend. A little shiver ran up her spine as her thoughts ran ahead. This would be the start. When the ship arrived in Australia, she would contrive a meeting between Leonie and Captain Ferguson at some suitable venue ashore. There would be many military displays, parades and outings to celebrate Australia's entry into the Commonwealth. A smile of contentment lifted the corners of her mouth, knowing there would be invitations to grand parties in private homes. Most importantly it would be a chance for Leonie to partner this particular officer.

She'd almost dismissed her concerns about that young reporter, Mr Mallory. Just a brief shadow crossed her mind; for the problem remained of keeping Leonie from seeing him.

***

After Sunday morning service, Leonie wandered about the ship feeling restless, her mind filled with thoughts of Adam. He seemed such an unusual person and it was hard sometimes to take him seriously. She found herself standing beneath that lifeboat, recalling their amusing escapade with the kitten, and was unaware of Lieutenant Renton sidling towards her. As he came close, he tripped unsteady on his feet and as he let out an oath Leonie saw him. He was drunk and dishevelled.

The area was deserted. She tried to dodge him but Renton, powered by drink, swayed and stumbled against her and the bulk of him, strong as an ox, forced her back against the ship's rail. His foul breath filled her lungs as she yelled, 'Get away!' and pummelled his chest to no avail.

It seemed a miracle as Adam ran towards them.

Renton mouthed curses but backed away.

'He's disgustingly drunk but he only stumbled against me,' Leonie declared once he had gone.

Adam shook his head. 'Weird, isn't it? The Tommies all vouch for his bravery in the South African campaign; seems he's definitely not a coward. Perhaps drink buries awful memories.'

'Yes, but all the troops on board are specially chosen for their bravery, aren't they? Each must be heroic.'

'It doesn't excuse his gross behaviour,' Adam declared.

She persisted. 'That argument at Port Said between Clyde and Renton sounded serious.'

***

'I've just had a surprising encounter,' Ruth exclaimed as Leonie entered the cabin. 'Captain Ferguson joined me on deck. He tells me he's already acquainted with you…?' her voice trailed off expectantly.

'We have exchanged pleasant conversation. I sense he's rather a solitary man, pleased to find a listening ear. I find him quite agreeable.'

'Good!' The exclamation burst from Ruth's lips. She patted Leonie's arm, oblivious to any hint of distraction in her niece's voice. 'I've invited him to sit with me at dinner. I'm certain he'll agree to make up a four at bridge or a hand of whist later this evening,' she declared brightly.

***

Not long after a special dinner was laid on one evening. The passengers were a lively gathering, all kitted out in finery for the occasion. This was an important occasion to mark the anniversary of the *Britannic*'s achievement in 1896 when it gained the coveted Blue Riband for the fastest mail ship across the Atlantic. Tonight, calm seas meant all twelve tables in the saloon were occupied.

Leonie ran her eyes along the length of each table, searching for Adam. She'd hoped he would be seated at their table. His penchant for the rank and file intrigued her.

Clyde sat beside her aunt, Lieutenant Oliver Snelgrove at Aunt's other side. Selina sat on Leonie's right, Mr Kershaw to her left. She gave a little start as Selina tapped her arm. 'How well your aunt looks this evening, absolutely blooming. I see she's invited Captain Ferguson to sit next to her. Perhaps she'll be able to draw him out. I think he's rather a lonely person, don't you?'

'He seems guarded,' Leonie replied. 'Altogether remote but kind and courteous,' she added quickly, thinking: quite different from Adam's relaxed charm. She wore her second best gown of turquoise silk which had faded in places but she'd paid for it with money from selling her framed photographs at the church sale and it remained a favourite. Her hair was prettily dressed and fastened with mother-of-pearl clips. She gazed about and took in the luxurious scene.

The saloon glittered beneath the crystal chandeliers which picked out the ladies' jewels, uniform buttons and sparkling silver and cut glass. What elevated company they were keeping, she marvelled. Leaning down beneath the table Leonie picked up her camera and focussed on the scene. It would form a contrast with the snaps of Sunday school picnics with farmers' families, she thought. A little pang caught her off guard as the memory whisked her back to hay-making time in Devon; and then animated conversation returned her to the present.

Glancing at her aunt Leonie noted how relaxed Ruth looked, her green silk gown lending a youthful look to her appearance. Thank goodness Aunt had discarded her widow's weeds. To ease her dry throat she drank a whole glass of chilled water, which cleared her head. Leonie turned to question Mr Kershaw.

'Do you have business in Sydney, Mr Kershaw?'

'I do have a project,' he replied. The keen eyes seemed to absorb tiny details. 'Not in Sydney city; I'm a land surveyor,' he revealed. 'I shall soon be travelling up north. It's boom time in Australia; towns are expanding.'

Before long they got onto the subject of avoiding nasty diseases abroad. Leonie drank more water, pleased to find it steadied her mind.

'Diseases are a hazard,' he stated, 'especially if you are out in no man's land and the nearest civilisation is a two day journey away. One runs the risk of malaria, typhoid and many serious conditions.'

'It sounds dangerous.' She was finding him diverting company.

'Indeed.' His eyes narrowed in thought. 'Thousands of our brave troops fighting the Boers have been cut down by disease – more than lost in battle.'

As Leonie expressed her surprise he asked,

'And what of your interests, Miss Grant? Do you sometimes yearn for adventure?'

'Yes, I'd love to travel and photograph places not even on the map. I'm certain I could put up with primitive conditions.'

'Ah, is that so? You're a keen photographer, eh?' Mr Kershaw smoothed his mutton chop whiskers and eyed her keenly. 'It happens I may be in need of a competent photographer on one of my trips later on.'

Was it said in jest? To think she'd once imagined him a dull old fellow. Leonie's pulse raced. What if a chance did arise? But for a woman? So, making a joke of it, she said, 'I warn you, I might be first in the queue for the job!' And then without bothering to formulate her words she faced Mr Kershaw and asked him straight: 'If my skills as a photographer proved up to your requirements would you take me along on one of your trips?' She waited as he stroked his short beard.

Mr Kershaw neither patronised her with a smile nor exploded with a rebuff. 'It's a possibility,' he responded slowly. 'Many ladies in the early years of our Queen's reign have proved intrepid travellers; put up with more hazards than some men folk could manage. How would your aunt feel about it? I'd hire a female cook and there'd be a native boy to carry your equipment.'

Stirred by his serious answer Leonie kept her tone even. 'I've come of age and I believe my aunt has already resigned herself to my eagerness to travel. I intend to gain more experience as a photographer of course; must learn more about using a professional camera.'

Realising she was not dividing her attention among the others, Leonie saw they were all happily engaged in conversation with one another, so turned her attention back to Mr Kershaw.

Mr Kershaw seemed to come to a decision. 'Right Miss Grant, if you're determined then I'm willing to give you a chance on a shorter trip. You'd be under canvas, mind – I'd supply your tent and the basic things of course.'

Flabbergasted by his quick invitation she managed, 'Thank you Mr Kershaw, I really meant it; I'm prepared to rough it, as you say.' Excitement raced through Leonie's veins.

The subject was dropped and they got onto the subject of psycho-neurosis; which was all the rage. People held differing opinions as to its veracity. 'I'm very interested in these conditions,' Leonie remarked. 'Have you studied them?'

'I have developed an interest in the phenomena,' Mr Kershaw informed her. 'One of the facts I've gleaned from medical journals is quite significant. The extreme shock sustained by troops in battle causes trauma – a condition which might recur for a long time, even when they're home and safe. Unfortunately both the army physicians and those at home think otherwise – put it down to weakness of character.'

'That's awfully hard for any soldier afflicted. Until recently, I had no idea of the terrible strain the troops are under. Back home there's an emphasis on heroics, cartoons that make battles look glamorous affairs.'

'Well Miss Grant, what good would be done by disturbing the men's families back home?' He now addressed her seriously. 'May I give you my forwarding address? I should be honoured if you would contact me when you are settled in Australia. Perhaps then we might make any plans.'

Leonie slipped the card he offered into her reticule. 'I'll look forward to that,' she affirmed. It seemed almost too strange to consider and yet, what a wonderful chance, she mused.

She gave a start at the sudden noise and commotion further down the saloon. A man was yelling. Cutlery crashed to the floor, glass shattered and chairs clunked as men rose to their feet.

'Shut your dirty mouth, Renton!' the words rapped out. Hearing his name, the hairs prickled at the back of Leonie's neck. There was a stampede of feet as several officers leapt up and grabbed Renton and dragged him towards the exit. But he had a drunkard's strength. She crouched back in her chair as they struggled past. Renton's tirade burst above the hullabaloo.

'Father's a rapist,' he slurred, pointing at Clyde Ferguson.

An audible gasp rose around their table. Clyde's eyes narrowed, his jaw rigid as he and Oliver jumped to their feet.

'Chuck him in irons!' Outraged voices followed Renton as he was shoved out through the saloon door. Several male voices exclaimed, 'He ought to be drummed out. Put under arrest. Drink is the devil!'

Leonie suddenly spotted that Ruth was slumped on the table, her head down amongst crockery. Her seat swung back as she dashed to her aunt's prone body. Clyde and Oliver were already easing Ruth upright in her chair. Leonie brushed a lock of hair off the pale forehead and murmured, 'It's just too warm in here.'

Clyde muttered, 'Renton's gone too far this time.' Then brusquely, 'I'll deal with him right away.' Quickly excusing himself he marched from the saloon.

'The devil take Renton,' Bobby Gibson spoke for everyone as she placed a hand on Ruth's shoulder.

Despite their kindness, Leonie worried about Renton's odd effect on her aunt. Why had she fainted? She reached for Ruth's bead purse and fumbled for the phial of smelling salts. 'Breathe in, Aunt dear,' she urged. Ruth's face was grey as a sheet of card. Passengers crowded about to assist. Someone handed a glass of water. 'Please try taking a sip.' She pressed the glass to her aunt's closed mouth. 'Would someone please tell our stewardess?'

'Selina's already doing that.'

'Careful now, we'll lift her gently,' Oliver instructed a fellow officer. 'Carry her to her cabin.'

Leonie led the way as the men carried Ruth between them.

'Dreadful, Leonie, Renton's beyond the pale.' Oliver shook his head. 'The fellow's blind drunk and will be confined to quarters now. Please don't hesitate to call us if needed. We'll be on hand,' he reassured.

After the officers had gone from the cabin, Lottie helped Leonie remove Ruth's outer finery and get her into bed. 'I'll see if she'll take some Sal-volatile,' Leonie murmured, fetching the glass bottle from Ruth's dressing case.

'This may help the lady.' Lottie placed a cold flannel on Ruth's forehead. 'Those tight stays are the culprit if you'll pardon me saying. That saloon does get awful fuggy. She'll soon recover. Lost count the times I've seen ladies taken like this.'

'You're such a great help Lottie,' Leonie smiled at the stewardess.

Chapter Seven

After Lottie had gone Leonie sat on the bed beside her aunt. That unforgiveable slur Renton cast on Clyde leapt about her mind. It was cruel. She must find Clyde and offer sympathy. Yet, she brooded, Renton sounded so sure about something...

She took Ruth's small hand in hers and tried to put the events in order. Had Aunt fainted before Renton's outburst? Or did that come after? Leonie strained to remember. Or was Aunt concealing some awful disease? A little chill caught about her heart knowing just how much Ruth meant to her. She stared at the pallid face and mopped up the Sal-volatile on her chin with a handkerchief.

Ruth began to twist and turn, mumbling to herself. Alarmed, Leonie bent down. 'There, Aunt dear, you'll soon feel better,' she said soothingly with more faith than certainty. Ruth must be fit when they reached Sydney. 'Oh Aunt dear, I couldn't bear it if you were ill.' With a rush of affection Leonie threw her arms about Ruth.

Leonie could not know that in the joy of the moment, Ruth grasped a hope she might still bury all her dark secrets. But it must not be. A huge sigh crept jaggedly up her throat.

Leonie gave a start. She saw her aunt's eyes were fixed like grey stones upon her.

'Oh Aunt, that odious man Renton. Did he cause you to faint?'

A frantic shake of the head, Ruth's eyes were wild as a scared cat and her mumbling incoherent. 'Forgive my wickedness!' Ruth moaned. 'Oh dear God, I beseech you. I have sinned…'

A shaft of fear streaked through Leonie. What in heaven's name…? Aloud, she urged, 'Please don't fret!' Aunt Ruth was delirious; she didn't know what she was saying. Leonie sprang to the bell, ready to call the stewardess to fetch the doctor.

The shriek from the bed sliced through her action. Leonie's heart bolted. She turned and took the shaking hand her aunt thrust out. 'Whatever is it? Tell me! What can I do?' Aunt was scaring her. She sank down on the bed and put an arm about the quivering frame. 'Please, please let me call Lottie. She'll get you some soothing powders.'

'No, too late.' The words fell from Ruth's pinched lips.

'I must get the doctor.' Her tone firm, Leonie made to move but found there was more strength than she could have guessed in the hand that gripped hers like a vice.

'Leonie, oh my dear Leonie. I can't keep silent any more. Be prepared for a shock, dearest child.'

Seconds, minutes ticked by in tune with Leonie's heavy heart beats. Ruth's head flopped on the pillow and a great shudder ran through her body. Leonie held her breath, frightened for Ruth. She had to lean close to hear what she was saying.

'That evil brute – God help us!' She looked up. Her face was ravaged. 'My dearest Leonie, he took advantage of innocent maids. That beast in Scotland made you illegitimate!'

At first, her aunt's softly spoken words floated in the air; bizarre, unbelievable. They slipped from Leonie's grasp while she pieced them together like a jigsaw. Then all at once, that phrase slotted into place. Her heart missed a beat. Horrified, she exclaimed, 'I don't understand… your sister's husband – not my father then?' She got to her feet and stared down at the figure in the bed as if seeing a stranger for the first time.

Ruth seemed to calm. Her head rolled from side to side on the pillow. 'No. Please forgive me.' A ragged sigh escaped her mouth. She clutched Leonie's arm. 'The beast showed no mercy.'

Her words crashed into Leonie's brain. 'No, oh no,' she moaned. All those past evasions slid into her head, swirling in a vortex and gathering up secret looks and hints from the past while she struggled with the ghastly truth. She saw Ruth's anguished face peering at her, tears on her drawn face.

'Forgive me! Oh Leonie dearest, so cruel to tell you like this. Please try to understand; I was frightened to death you might hear it from someone else!'

Leonie stood, arms pressed rigid to her sides. Deeply distressed, her words spat like chips of ice. 'Is it true? You say I'm a bastard then?' Blood suffused her face, her throat swollen with angry tears.

She saw her aunt flinch as she raged, 'You made me believe in my father's death – I was so sad, thinking of your sister dying giving birth to me with no husband to comfort her!' Harsh words fell from her mouth. 'Did Uncle Bertram know? Answer me. Did you *both* keep me ignorant?' Her breath was tight. 'Was I not supposed to find out your sister was raped? I'm a bastard from a foul…!' She shuddered as images swamped her mind. 'Who was he? Tell me who that rapist was – the man who raped my mother!'

Ruth's relief at shedding one of her secrets after a lifetime hiding the shame had the effect of renewing her strength. She sat up quickly. 'The man's dead, buried and gone to Hell!' she snapped. Then, mortified by the manner of her disclosure, her tone softened. 'Leonie, dearest Leonie, please try to see how it was,' she implored. 'Bertram and I thought only of your best interests. Your grandparents adored you. You were such a sweet wee babe when Bertram and I married and took you in.'

Leonie couldn't relent. 'So, I'm the result of a horrible rape. Do you know what that feels like? Do you? I feel dirty, disgustingly soiled.' Hot tears stung her eyes and she fought to stem them.

Ruth slid from her bed and stood shaking in front of Leonie. 'You've not inherited anything from him, I promise.' She clutched Leonie's arm. 'You've no worry on that score. You're my family's side, the Grants through and through. We named you for them; gentle character, same features, chestnut hair…' Her voice pitched higher as she babbled on. 'Your grandparents Grant cared for you in the beginning. Then Bertram and I adored you.' She'd regained her composure as she beseeched, 'Haven't you always enjoyed a happy childhood?'

Leonie refused to be placated. 'So, there's nothing to worry about? Oh yes there is, a mountain of it.' For she knew it meant the end of her friendship with Adam. She closed her eyes, recalling the reference he'd made to a sister's thwarted affair with a man born out of wedlock. No man of character would be interested in her now.

She was aware of her aunt's scrutiny; saw compassion deepening the lines about her mouth and couldn't deny her aunt's concern. Confused by conflicting emotions Leonie blurted out, 'Don't worry, Aunt. It's not the end of the world. It must be unbearable to have lost your sister in childbirth and in such a way.' As an afterthought she added, 'I see my way ahead. I must make a career for myself now.'

Leonie garnered her strength and made for the door; bitterness hardened her words. 'I need to get fresh air.' Yet despite the awful, sudden revelation her affection for her aunt rose to the fore.

She turned back. 'Let me help you Aunt,' she insisted, and helped Ruth back to bed. 'I see what made you faint,' she stated, realizing it must have been Renton's slur about a rapist that dredged up her aunt's horrid memories. 'Try to get some sleep please. We're both overwrought. No, I'm all right. Of course I appreciate the wonderful care and love you and Uncle have given me.' She straightened her back. 'I just need to have a quiet think.' Then with a hollow feeling in her chest Leonie picked up her outdoor cape, turned and left the cabin.

Any thought for sleep had been banished as Ruth crept out of bed and reached for her little silver flask. Her heart hammered. Pouring a good measure of brandy into a glass she tossed it back down her throat and winced. *Poor, dear Leonie, please forgive me*, she prayed. She'd never intended to tell Leonie in such a horrible way but the fright of hearing that word 'rape' had triggered her act. If only she'd softened the blow, she fretted. How could she right such a terrible wrong to Leonie? Images flickered inside her head as the years rolled back to scenes she found too painful to relive. His name – what was the name of that odious laird? Osgood? Oswald? No, Osmond MacLeod, the terror of housemaids across the county; a monster... She poured more brandy into her glass and took a big sip, and cried aloud, 'Dear Bertram, help me! What have I done?'

She must not weaken. Sebastian must find them well and in good spirits. Soon they'd be off the ship and her fear that the young reporter might delve into her past and drag it up again in the newspaper would be gone.

What had she been talking about with Captain Ferguson? It was something she couldn't recall now... she'd gone all dizzy. Her head was filled with the terrible disclosure she'd made to Leonie. Not everything, no; she wasn't ready for that. Would she ever be forgiven?

What if that odious Renton really knew something? It had been written up large in the press at the time, all those years ago. She tottered to the looking glass, screwed up her eyes and peered closely at herself. Did she look a bad woman? A little nip of brandy could be depended upon to come to her aid. Taking another sip she took heart, deciding Mr Mallory seemed an honest young man, even if not a gentleman. Yet could she really trust a reporter who earned his keep from that scurrilous newspaper?

Strengthened by the alcohol, Ruth took herself to task. At least, thank the Lord, Leonie knew nothing more. As soon as the time was right she would unburden herself to her brother Sebastian.

***

Clyde fumed. Renton's foul insinuations made in public cut him to the core. As for Renton's behaviour to Leonie… Thank God she was a sensible young woman. A lesser female would have made a hysterical scene. He ran a hand over his head. He'd seen to it that the wretch was put under close guard for the rest of the voyage. Clyde released a deep breath, thankful his comrades assured him that no one would think any the less of him. But the stain stuck.

'Renton's drunken outbursts mean nothing,' they insisted.

Clyde's immediate concern was the disastrous effect he seemed to have on Mrs Fox. He recalled they had been conversing pleasantly just before she fainted. Could it possibly be because of something he said?

Grasping the ship's rail he stood alone high on the hurricane deck and stared over the slate grey sea, racking his brains as he tried to recall what they'd been saying. They'd been conversing about Scotland. But surely, reminiscences from years back had not made her collapse? Dimly, their conversation entered his mind.

'I see you are a member of a Scottish regiment,' he recalled Mrs Fox remarking, as she indicated the bugle set on its diagonal silver cross of the Highland Light Infantry. 'Ferguson is an old Scottish name. Where is your home in Scotland?'

'I have no home there now,' he'd replied. 'For my dear mother's sake, I returned to Scotland during vacations from boarding school. When my mother died, I was eight years of age. Her brother and his wife in Devon became my guardians. I was their heir and I took their name, Ferguson.'

Mrs Fox had lent a sympathetic ear, her interest genuine, and he'd found himself speaking of things he would not normally reveal.

'No relatives to draw you back to Britain, then?'

'My guardians have both passed on,' he explained.

'But your real father,' Mrs Fox pursued. 'Is he alive? He is not in communication?'

Clyde remembered delaying his response, fearful of dredging up buried memories. He'd taken a sip of claret as Mrs Fox turned expectant eyes upon him. 'My father met a gruesome end. Folk said it was his due punishment,' he'd replied flatly.

'Oh dear, I do apologise for probing.'

'Not at all.' He'd been anxious not to upset the lady. 'Years ago, it happened. In the Highlands, the

Blair Atholl...' All this came back with sudden clarity. That was when Mrs Fox collapsed – or was it after Renton's tirade and all the commotion? He couldn't be sure. Tomorrow morning he'd seek Leonie and try to find out. He turned from the rail, deciding to go to his cabin. As he flung himself down on his bunk there suddenly came the familiar dread noises swilling inside his head. Dark red blood blinded his sight; the whistle of explosives and crashes, screams of horses and the groans of wounded men deafened his ears. Clyde fought the horror of his fellow officer lying in deep mud, his leg torn off, pleading to be put out of his misery, as he sank at last into the all-enveloping darkness of sleep.

***

The ship lunged on through the Great Australian Bight.

Several days has passed since her aunt's dreadful disclosure. It sat heavy as a yoke and shadowed Leonie's anticipation for what lay ahead. Storm clouds scudded across the sky, tossed like massive grey whales. She took deep, even breaths and silently implored, 'Please God, let nothing more spoil our new life in Australia.'

'Plenty to look forward to on shore,' Selina declared. She seemed not to notice anything amiss with her friend. 'How is Mrs Fox? Has she said what made her faint at dinner the other night?' She held onto a ledge to prevent herself falling as the ship rolled.

Leonie hesitated. Burdened with the truth of her origin, she withheld the need to confide in Selina. 'Aunt's lost all zest,' she offered. 'She insists on taking her meals in the cabin and hardly pecks at them. I'd better go and sit with her.'

A little while later, a knock on the cabin door showed the stewardess outside.

'There's a gentleman waiting to see you in the saloon, miss.'

Leonie dabbed her nose with face powder, grabbed a crochet shawl and hurried to the saloon, expecting to see Mr Kershaw.

Instead she saw Adam.

'I'm afraid my aunt's a little under the weather. I can't stay.' She forced herself to make the excuse.

'Of course.' Adam's face lengthened, his eyes showing regret. 'Please convey my kind regards, won't you.'

There, she'd done it; she'd pushed him away. As his face lengthened in disappointment Leonie resisted a strong urge to throw her arms about him.

'We'll meet later?' His eyebrows were raised in a query.

Leonie turned away, about to rush off, but a spark of rebellion stayed her steps. After all, why not enjoy Adam's company before they arrived in

Australia? Her spirits lifted and she said, 'Yes, I'd love us to meet up later.'

She found her aunt reclining on her bed. There was no point in taking her distress out on Aunt Ruth. She still felt affection for her.

'Leonie, dear Leonie, will you try to forgive me?' Ruth's voice faltered. 'It was so cruel of me to tell you like that. My dear child, you are so dear to me.'

For her answer Leonie knelt down beside her and now the tears she'd held back flowed freely; for her aunt, for herself and her despair about Adam. 'Dear Aunt, it was a bad shock and I understand what a dreadful burden you've carried all these years. I couldn't have wished for kinder, more loving people than you and Uncle Bertram.' Then suddenly they were both crying and holding one another.

Ruth reached for her pocket handkerchief and mopped her eyes. She started to speak and her voice tailed off. 'You looked so despairing, dear.'

Leonie unbuttoned her tight boots. 'I just need a short nap.' Reaching for her slippers she suggested, 'I'll ring for Lottie. A mug of hot chocolate for us both, eh?'

Later on, after a rest, Leonie stood and pinned up her hair. She peered into the looking glass. 'I've promised to meet a crowd of friends. I'll be back soon.' She caught the anxiety in Ruth's face. 'Don't worry; I can deal with what you told me and won't throw myself overboard, I promise.'

Leonie made her way crab-like along the rolling passageway into the saloon to bury her problems amongst the company of friends.

***

The following day the air was fresh and clear. But Leonie's heart felt leaden as she looked about. She clutched her writing materials, undecided what to write to her friends, and stared into space. Out of the corner of her eye she grew conscious of a figure standing nearby.

'Leonie,' Clyde said quickly as she looked up. 'Am I interrupting? I seem to be making a habit of it. I've been hoping for a quiet word with you. Would you object if I light one of these?' he asked, taking a silver cigarette case from an inside pocket.

'Please do,' Leonie said.

Clyde spent a moment or two flicking a gas lighter before saying, 'I trust Mrs Fox has recovered?' He hesitated. 'I've been concerned I might have had something to do with her faint.'

'Oh no, how could you Clyde? Do please sit down here,' Leonie replied, quickly folding away her writing case. 'Yes – well, no, to your query about my aunt,' she added quickly. 'To tell the truth, not really well at all.' Scarcely waiting for breath, she rushed on, 'it's as if the stuffing's knocked out of her.'

'I'm sorry to hear that.' Clyde's mouth firmed. 'I'll stand if you don't mind. I've just come to apologise for the inexcusable behaviour of that junior officer, Lieutenant Renton. He's now under close guard.' He drew himself up and puffed on his cigarette.

What with her own troubles she'd almost forgotten the nasty incident with Renton.

His next comment must have been difficult for him. It fetched her sympathy.

'I've been concerned you won't wish to continue our friendship,' he ventured.

'Why ever not?' she asked, taken by surprise. 'Of course I'm your friend, Clyde.' She drew a breath. 'It was an unforgivable thing he said to you.'

'The fellow's a vile scoundrel when he takes to drink.'

She reached out a hand and touched his arm. 'Please, won't you sit down for a moment?'

'I appreciate your kindness, Leonie. Nothing like this will occur again.' His features relaxed, but he remained standing.

She caught his look of regret, his eyes shadowed. She sensed a tight hold on his emotions and could barely imagine the enormous responsibility he carried for his platoon in battle. Filled with the wish to put him at ease, she said, 'Clyde, I'm certain whatever happened, you are not responsible for Aunt's collapse. She's fatigued; the stress of leaving everything behind has caught up and taken its toll.'

He nodded. 'If I can be of any assistance, please let me know.' He was silent for a moment. Then, tossing the cigarette stub out to sea continued, 'We'd been conversing at dinner and on reflection, I wondered if my mention of a place in the Scottish Highlands could have affected Mrs Fox?'

Leonie frowned as she puzzled about a possible link. 'I know little about my aunt's life in Scotland before she married my uncle. She met Uncle Bertram when he'd travelled to Scotland on a fishing trip. My grandfather was ghillie on an estate and had made his acquaintance.'

'It's altogether a mystery, then.' Clyde spoke quietly, his brow creased. He added hesitantly, 'It would give me great pleasure to meet you on shore, Leonie.' His seriousness dissolved with a tentative smile. 'I'd be a poor escort, I warn you, totally unused to female company.'

'I shall look forward to that,' Leonie replied with a soft laugh. It was true, she enjoyed their platonic friendship. With this older officer there were no strings attached. She ripped a piece of paper from her pad and scribbled the Carters' Bellevue address. 'You'll be accompanying a female unused to being escorted by an officer, so we're quits! Here's where we'll stay in Sydney for the celebrations before we travel to my Uncle Sebastian's farm near Adelaide.'

They bid each other farewell and giving up the idea of writing Leonie made her way along the deck and reviewed the implications of Clyde's conversation with her aunt. His reference to Scotland could have dredged up things from the past. Scotland sounded like a vast place of crags, rivers and mountains so was it likely they knew places in common.

Thoughts of her aunt were never far away. Our human minds are unknown territory, Leonie pondered. She'd read and returned the medical journal Mr Kershaw had loaned her which gave details of neuroses that were too complex to throw any light on her aunt's behaviour. She found Ruth fast asleep and gently snoring when she returned to their cabin.

Spotting a drinking glass fallen over, Leonie took it to the wash stand. It smelled strongly of brandy. This was something new. Ruth was teetotal.

Disquieted, Leonie put down her writing case, collected her camera and returned slowly to the deck. Lost in thought, she gave a start as a familiar voice sounded at her elbow.

'I've been searching all over for you,' Adam said. He grinned and cradled Mischief against his chest.

Leonie's brain went swimmy. To cover up she leaned forward and tickled the kitten's ears. 'Mischief, haven't you grown.' Her heart failed to obey her head. With a huge surge of bravado, she made a sudden decision. Illegitimacy was no fault of hers. She would enjoy Adam's company for the rest of the voyage; there would be time to reconcile herself to life as a spinster once they reached Australia.

'Little monster, gobbles all the lovely food I get from the galley. I admit we sometimes share the same meal together.'

'Oh Adam, that's so funny, I must have a photograph of you with Mischief,' she laughed, quickly peering down to focus her camera.

'Now I'll take one of you holding her, shall I?' Adam passed Mischief over.

'Clyde Ferguson expressed an apology on behalf of that horrid Renton,' she volunteered.

'He's a real bastard, that fellow Renton, when he's drunk. Oh, forgive me, Leonie! I'm catching bad language from the Tommies.'

Leonie flinched. *A real bastard.* That's what *she* was. How could she ignore it? Mortified, she said, 'Can't stop, promised to take a message for my aunt.' She saw Adam's eyes widen in astonishment before she hurried away.

Chapter Eight

The voyage was nearly over. Leonie stood on the upper deck beside Bobby and Selina, each aware that they'd shared a momentous journey together. Everyone was keyed up, ready to disembark in Sydney harbour.

Ruth came over to Leonie and took hold of her arm. Determined more than ever to concentrate on making a career, Leonie had told herself that women had more chance in Australia. Yet dread of separation from Adam occupied her thoughts.

'Are you listening?' Selina suddenly nudged Leonie. 'Bobby and I will be staying right in Sydney city centre, at the Royal Victoria hotel,' she repeated. 'Promise to come and visit us very soon. Can't wait for all those outings with the military!'

The intense clarity of light and the salty tang of the swishing spray stirred Leonie's imagination. To take her mind off Adam she began to photograph her other friends. Turning to the shore she saw that houses dotted green slopes between the rugged headlands. In the broad sweep of a bay, the sails of small boats reminded her of winged insects skipping over the water.

'See, over there?' Mr Kershaw pointed out features clearly visible on land. 'You can just make out the Blue Mountains on the horizon.'

Leonie strained her eyes to the distance. 'That was kind of you to loan me that medical book. Does your offer – of employment – still hold, please?'

Mr Kershaw nodded. 'Provided you are serious?'

'I am, I assure you. Here's my contact address.'

Leonie shook his hand and they parted. For their arrival in Sydney she wore a fishtail skirt and floral silkette blouse with a pretty linen cape that set it off – a Shaw's mail order catalogue outfit bought for the princely sum of three shillings and nine pence three farthings. 'I don't mind wearing bankrupt stock,' she'd told her aunt.

She sensed Ruth's distracted mood, and placed a comforting arm about her shoulders. 'It's a huge wrench leaving our familiar life in Devon, but there'll be marvellous times to look forward to,' she insisted, though her cheerful words belied her sinking emotions.

'It's a blessing to have you with me, dear. You are still the same, lovely person you've always been.'

She caught sight of Adam on the deck. She spotted a look of concern tightening his features as he stared about, scanning the passengers; clearly seeking her.

'Look Aunt, we're rounding the headland,' she said. 'I'll be back in a moment; just going to bid a friend farewell.' Her legs moved of their own accord. Beyond sight of her aunt, she greeted Adam quietly. 'The end of the voyage,' she said. Her voice sounded unnaturally high.

'Maybe, but it's not the end of our friendship, Leonie?' He cocked his head and gave her a quizzical look. 'Or did you have that in mind?'

Emotion swelled her throat. She swallowed and shook her head. 'What's happening to Mischief? I shall miss her.'

'We've grown so attached she's got to come ashore with me. See?' He pointed to an outside pocket on his holdall. 'Snug as a bug in a rug.'

Leonie only wished she could be a ball of fluff so Adam could take her with him. Whether or not by accident she couldn't tell, but as the *Britannic* rolled over the bar at the harbour entrance, Adam's shoulder pressed against hers. She couldn't ignore the sensual rush which flamed her face. However could she forgo the chance of meeting him ashore? She looked towards land. Tall modern buildings towered above the pretty painted wooden houses which fringed the harbour. Reluctant to leave him, she prattled, 'What an adventure it's been.'

Adam sensed her mood. 'I wouldn't have missed it for worlds.' He looked her straight in the eye. 'We might never have met but for this voyage.'

Loud cheers sounded as the troops mustered below them on the lower deck ready to disembark and the noise of their cheering rose up, drowning his words. Adam raised his voice. 'They're a fine bunch of fellows.'

He was sensitive beneath the banter, Leonie thought. But would he really miss *her*? Or soon sail out of her life forever? She couldn't bear the idea.

The great ship ran along the shoreline. Strange trees burdened with bright red flowers caught her eye. Laughing a little too hard, she cried, 'They look like fat ladies in pantomime skirts.'

'Pohutakawas,' someone nearby explained. 'It's the Australian summer now. Always come into flower ready for Christmas.'

'There'll be miles and miles of gum trees. You'll see, they smell just like the ointment we put on sores,' she heard Mr Kershaw remark.

Her heart banged against her ribs as she forced her voice to sound calm. 'I'd love to capture all this on film. Too far away – black and white photographs won't do it justice.'

'I really do admire your photography,' Adam broke in. 'We shall have to organise an exhibition – perhaps at the Central Library?'

Surprised, she said slowly, 'I'll need to wait for the photographs I've taken on the voyage to be developed and enlarged.' Glad that her face was hidden beneath her parasol a sense of abandon swept through her as she added, 'That will be marvellous. I'll really look forward to your help.'

The excessive heat, tempered by cool offshore breezes, fanned their faces. Their light cotton skirts billowed. They watched as the long gangplank was fixed in place on the quay.

'I'd better join my aunt.' Her throat tightened. Adam clasped her hands in his. She felt her thighs grow strangely heavy. Glancing up she caught Adam's puzzled look.

'Are you all right, Leonie? Have I annoyed you somehow?'

'Oh no, Adam never, just nerves; wondering how things will be.'

He shook his head; smiled down at her. 'I'm going to miss our adventures, Leonie. You won't forget, will you?' He touched her hair and twisted a little curl around his finger. 'I have to go and make a report of our arrival.' From an inside pocket he took his notebook, picked up his baggage and started to back away. 'Don't forget, you promised to meet me again soon.' He gave her a cheeky wink. 'Who knows – maybe in unusual circumstances.' And at that moment, as if to make her presence known, the kitten's plaintive meow came from the holdall.

Leonie's smile faltered. Her hand lifted in a half wave. Then she turned with a heavy heart and went to find her aunt. Soon, holding onto hats, clutching hand luggage, skirts, and each other, they stepped purposefully down the gangplank onto Australian soil.

Leonie took deep calming breaths. The squeal of iron shattered her thoughts as giant cranes swung into action to disembowel the hold. Orders were barked at the thousand troops who trudged down the gangplank. She heard the neighing of bewildered horses as they emerged from the bowels of the ship, their hooves clattering like spilt marbles on the cobbles and everyone shouted to one another above the hubbub.

Bobby raised her voice above the hubbub. 'I've got a deadline to meet for an article. Means Selina and I will miss a few of the exciting events in Sydney.'

'If we get separated, we'll meet up soon, all right?' said Selina. 'Send a message to our hotel – the Victoria, eh?'

Ruth appeared at their side and at the sight of her expression, Leonie's face fell. 'What is it, Aunt?'

'It's Sebastian,' Ruth cried, as she displayed a telegram. 'One of the crew delivered this. Oh dear,' her face screwed up with anguish, 'I can't cope with it.'

Taking the wire from Ruth, Leonie read it out aloud.

'*DELAYED+TRACK DOWN+CARTERS MEET YOU OFF SHIP+HOPE BE WITH YOU SOON+SEBASTIAN.*'

'What if he's hurt?' Ruth cried. Her face screwed up. 'Adelaide is so far away. He might never get here at all.'

'Try not to worry, Aunt. Mr Carter will know more – Sebastian will have sent a wire to his office.'

Ruth's face sagged with shock and disappointment.

The news had spread. Passengers crowded around with murmurs of sympathy.

Leonie's heart did a plunge as Adam appeared holding a tumbler of water for Ruth.

'Do try a sip, Mrs Fox? It might help.'

Leonie stood watching, imprinting to memory this fresh sight of Adam.

Ruth seemed uncertain. Then with a weak smile she replied, 'How very thoughtful, Mr Mallory.' She raised the glass to her lips and took small sips.

'I'm certain you'll soon be united with your brother,' Adam said. 'I'd better take this back and go find my baggage.' Turning, he pressed something into Leonie's hand. A quick smile and in a moment he had disappeared into the crowd.

'Well, that was a kind thing to do,' Ruth smiled her pleasure. 'He's quite the gentleman after all.'

Leonie's pulse raced. She held a folded piece of paper in her closed hand and quickly transferred it to her canvas bag to save for later.

Mr Kershaw reassured, 'Your brother will be just fine, Mrs Fox. Flash floods happen all the time. The track gets washed out but no lack of navvies to shore it up. Mark my words, the train will be puffing along again before you can say "Jack Robinson".'

Ruth brightened a little. 'Thank you, Mr Kershaw,' she murmured, 'for setting my mind at rest.'

Leonie raised Ruth's parasol to shield her aunt's head from the burning sun, though the shade it cast barely gave any shelter. She felt oddly disoriented and sensed others felt the same way. The ship had been a tiny world, their days regulated and organised. Now they all huddled together in the shadow of a rust-coloured Customs House to escape the full force of the blazing sun, awaiting instructions. Ruth seemed to have recovered a little strength. 'I'm better now, dear,' she insisted with a tentative smile. She reclaimed her parasol. 'I'll hold it now, thank you.'

'Are you sure? I'll go and fetch some ice for your forehead, if you like.'

'No, thank you dear. I'd rather you stayed with me.' She shook her head. 'So upsetting when plans go awry; oh I do hope Sebastian gets here soon.'

Finally they stood outside and Leonie spotted a dapper man, waving a sign with their names. 'Come on Aunt,' she urged excitedly.

'Welcome, dear ladies!' their host Mr Carter boomed. His smile broadened as he gathered them both to his corpulent frame. 'My regrets that it is I and not your brother here to greet you. We have to blame Nature for his delay.' Released, they each received a kiss on the cheek from his wife.

Leonie saw a short buxom lady, her face wreathed in smiles. The silk bobbles attached to her straw hat danced about her plump cheeks. 'Dear Sebastian will be fretting most dreadfully.'

Leonie was instantly charmed by the free and easy way these Australians greeted new acquaintances, so different from the formality back in England.

Soon, Mr Carter had claimed all their baggage and settled them into a waiting buggy.

Mrs Carter chattered away as they clip clopped out of the dock area.

Dashing along through the leafy suburbs, Leonie marvelled at large clapboard houses surrounded by luxuriant gardens. Sub-tropical plants and trees reminded her of the pictures in a children's book. Arriving at the Carters' palatial home, she hardly had time to note the sweeping lawns, for suddenly a young girl dashed down the veranda steps

'Welcome to "Wahroonga",' she cried.

Aged seventeen, so four years her junior, Jane Carter had not lost her puppy fat nor her childish excitement. 'Leonie, I've been frantic waiting for you to come! See, my nails, bitten down to the quick.'

Spontaneously, they hugged one another. Leonie had imagined a younger child from her uncle's description and was delighted to find Jane almost a grown young woman.

'I'm thrilled to be here and meet you at last,' Leonie responded. She smiled, a little dazed; for it all felt so strange, as if part of her hadn't yet arrived.

At last she had a private moment. Leonie was desperate to know what Adam had pressed into her hand as she slowly unfolded the paper. She blinked. A tiny twist of chestnut hair wound through fair hair to make the shape of a heart! Blood rushed to her face. For a few mad moments she almost believed herself betrothed. But reality knifed in. She was an outcast!

Dinner that first night was a lively affair. Franklin Carter related tales of the early days. He refilled their glasses with smooth Australian port. 'Prices around here have escalated since the railways laid down more track.'

A glance around at the fine furnishings suggested his efforts provided a fair return. It could have been a stylish English drawing room, filled with antiques and fine Persian rugs.

The following day, Mr Carter received another wire at his office. Sebastian was due to arrive on Christmas Eve.

***

'Fate was cruel!' Sebastian exclaimed as at last he and Ruth were reunited with hugs, tears and laughter.

Happiness filled Leonie as she hugged the brother and sister, clearly so happily reunited.

Later, when Sebastian had scrubbed clean and dressed in city clothes, Leonie saw a handsome man, his face lined and darkened by years in the outdoors, his light ginger hair and moustache flecked with grey. A fun loving person, she believed, for he smiled frequently, though she suspected deeper emotion lay in his clear green eyes.

That night they all attended Midnight Mass at St. Mary's Cathedral. As she knelt to pray, Leonie felt a wonderful rush of peace, as if the burden of her birth had been whisked up to heaven. She listened with joy as her aunt's sweet soprano soared with Sebastian's deep baritone voice.

***

It was the most extraordinary Christmas she could have imagined. 'I must record all this,' she said excitedly, drawing them together in front of the Christmas tree for a photograph.

Franklin directed. 'I'll take some with this.' He indicated his large plate camera.

'What a beautiful camera,' Leonie exclaimed.

'Yes, these are used in the trade,' he explained.

'Leonie is a fine photographer,' Ruth declared.

Never before had Aunt praised her snaps. Leonie turned and kissed Ruth's cheek.

'Now if you'd like to give me all those rolls of film you've used, Leonie, I'll get them developed and some enlargements made.'

'Thank you, that's very kind. I'm keen to organise them.'

'So, is your photography a serious hobby?'

Leonie nodded. 'I'm very keen to make it a career.' She spoke boldly, having often suffered a patronising smile when she'd voiced her intention. But Mr Carter's eyes grew thoughtful as he responded,

'I shall be pleased to take a look at your work then, Leonie. We must have a talk later.' And then without giving her another glance he lowered his head under the black cloth and focussed his camera. 'Steady now everybody. Please stay still. Ready?'

Leonie blinked, dazzled by the light of the flash. Her pulse beat fast. So many things she'd need to know.

Fancy, cold fare for Christmas dinner; Leonie chuckled to herself as Mrs Carter's maids packed the picnic and carried it to the carriage.

Leonie scrambled aboard with Jane, whose ceaseless chatter enlivened the atmosphere. Soon they were cantering downhill towards Bondi Beach. Carriages raced one another, the occupants shouting festive greetings. It looked to Leonie like a highly coloured picture postcard; hot sun, blue skies, emerald sea and golden sand. At one point, she was certain she caught sight of Adam with another party of people. But she told herself her eyes were just dazzled by the sun.

It was a memorable day in good company, for Sebastian kept them all entertained with tales of the outback and Leonie felt healthily fatigued as they gathered themselves for the slow journey home, whilst the sun set in an orange, fiery blaze to the east.

Chapter Nine

The new twentieth century exploded about them as Sydney city welcomed 1901 with a cacophony of church bells and Leonie was instantly wide awake. Her fob watch showed it was 5 am.

A knock at her door preceded two maids bearing huge pitchers filled with scalding water. Leonie's tub was soon filled and the maids left her to bathe. Soon, soaped, rinsed and buffed dry, she dressed carefully in the outfit purchased at a good reduction during Marshalls & Snelgrove's sale. First she struggled with the tiny hooks and eyes of her fashionable S-shaped corset.

Thankful for the morning breeze through the windows, Leonie's thoughts were of Adam. Where was he now? A shadow slipped over her mind.

A tap at her door and Jane entered.

'Happy New Year. Wonderful New Century!'

Soon, powdered and perfumed, they left the room and hurried down the sweeping staircase. The others had also risen early but the ladies were so keyed up they could hardly swallow a mouthful. Sebastian and Franklin made up for them, tucking into eggs, ham, syrup pancakes and mountains of homemade bread.

Leonie felt she'd never met people as generous and outgoing as Australians. When breakfast was cleared away they all, the maids included, stood holding hands to say prayers together and sing a hymn.

Then they were all off to the city.

From an upper storey window in the offices of the *Sydney Herald*, Leonie stood amongst Franklin Carter's guests and stared down at the brilliant pageant below. Excitement was palpable as column after column of troops, resplendent in regimental uniforms, marched down Macquarrie Street. Each window in the buildings lining the route bulged with people waving flags, throwing confetti and cheering.

Chairs had been set for the ladies to command a good view. Ruth sat a little way off with Eleanor Carter. Leonie watched Sebastian holding the back of his sister's chair, leaning down to explain the various bands of marching troops. She felt enormous pride in her tall, healthy-looking uncle who wore an elegant dark tailcoat. Many other men were corpulent, their faces fleshy, waistcoat buttons strained over stomachs.

Who could remain sad on such an occasion? As she sipped her glass of bubbly wine, elation zipped through Leonie for all she saw and heard. 'Look at that glossy automobile! Whoever is that?'

'The Premier,' Sebastian explained. 'Nice jallopy, eh?'

'I reckon these troops are the very best.' Franklin's voice rang out across the room. 'Keeping up that fast pace over such a distance is no mean feat! Those uniforms aren't designed with our continent in mind; they must be sweltering, poor fellows.'

'Reckon they're fair dinkum, right enough,' another agreed. 'Been up all night spit and polishing their boots and shining up all that silver and brass.'

Leonie pictured Clyde Ferguson organising his troops under this blazing sun as she squeezed through tight packed bodies, seeking a moment's respite from the noise to think about Adam. She sat down on a swivel seat at one of the desks. This was the first time she'd seen inside a large commercial office. The typewriter was more modern than Bobby's. She noticed a speaking tube attached to a box and guessed it was one of the new-fangled recording devices. Running her hands silently over the typewriter keys she became aware of a quiet conversation taking place nearby.

With lowered voice, one of the men said, 'Seems things aren't going too well out there – y'know, in South Africa.'

Out of the corner of her eye she saw him tap the side of his nose. Pretending to be engrossed, Leonie fixed her sight on the typewriter and strained her ears to listen.

'I heard via the grapevine; all hush hush.' There was a pause and then he added, 'The Premier's holding back on orders to supply more Aussie troops. Significant, eh? And hear this – the requests for new uniforms have all but dried up. Someone's going to be bankrupt!'

'Keep this under your hat; but I can say this with confidence,' the other rejoined. 'There's many in government never been convinced our military should have been commandeered. Mark my words it's the gold mines they want – that's why Britain is fighting those Boers!'

The heavy flopping sound of overhead fans only allowed snatches of their exchange but she heard most of it. Instinct told her to store the information as they moved away.

She went to rejoin Jane and accepted another glass of champagne from a passing waiter.

'Here, I've saved you a bag of confetti,' Jane said, handing it over.

Casting the fragile scraps through the window, Leonie leaned right out over the sill and watched them fluttering down. She was reminded of springtime in Devon with clouds of apple blossom drifting in the orchard.

Without warning, her heart did a loop. She stared, transfixed by the sight of someone in the crowd.

Adam! He'd raised his panama to wave it at the marching troops. There was no mistaking his fair hair and features. Instinctively she called out, though there wasn't a chance of being heard above the racket. She stared; he wasn't alone. Gripped by disbelief, she saw a pretty young woman holding onto Adam's arm, laughing up at him. Their familiarity was glaringly evident.

Leonie hadn't known jealousy was a tangible thing. It leapt savagely about her breast, darted to her stomach. She recalled Adam's vagueness when she'd asked where he'd be staying in Sydney; his odd remark that they'd meet next in unusual circumstances. Adam Mallory was clearly attached. It felt as if her insides were scooped out leaving a hollow space. With an effort of will, determined not to spoil the day for the others, she dragged her sight away and turned to Sebastian. 'All this will just be an incredible memory one day, don't you think?' She spoke in a daze, as if someone else formed the words.

***

Early the following morning, unable to sleep, Leonie found a quiet place in the little sitting room to sort her photographs. She picked up the picture she'd taken of Adam holding the kitten and an ache settled behind her ribs. Don't be a fool. She tried to force away memories of the fun and adventures they'd enjoyed; but the pain wouldn't shift. She told herself life aboard ship was a fantasy, not a reflection of real life. To be far, Adam had never indicated anything beyond friendship. Besides, she'd made no bones about wishing to make a career. She scowled and slipped the keepsake photograph into her album, determined to find employment. It would give her a purpose.

***

A day or later when Leonie was off in the city with Sebastian, Ruth lay back in a wicker chair placed in a shady corner of the Carters' garden. Any suggestion of coolness was an illusion since the heat muffled and enveloped her. Anxiety tangled her thoughts; so many worries. Was this enormous step a mistake, uprooting them from all that was familiar in Devon? Could she find the courage to unburden her secrets to Sebastian or ever cope with this tiresome climate? And Leonie; she seemed far too strong willed. Oh dear, it was all becoming too much to bear. How long would she have to wait to gain her brother's company in privacy? She feared the rest of her secrets might tumble out if she didn't keep a tight rein on them.

A sky, bold as royal blue, dazzled her sight. Shielding her eyes she saw those nasty parrots strung along the telegraph wires, drooping like rosy daubs of paint. In the heat even they had ceased their screeching. She was reminded of a winter visit to the Tropical House at Kew Gardens where alien plants loomed through the hot swirls of steam and had scared her into an unseemly dash for fresh, cold air. She felt utterly disgruntled. Sebastian should be here, not off in the city. Once more she brooded; whenever would he be free so she could talk with him in private? And whatever was Leonie thinking? Going sightseeing in this appalling heat indeed.

Irritation pinched her lips. She glanced down and eyed her sewing box with disfavour. Nor could she be bothered to choose between the pile of magazines, or her writing materials placed near to hand on the garden table together with a little brass bell.

With an effort she eased the cushions behind her back and flopped back, tilting her head. Eyes half closed she became intrigued by the pattern of sky filtering through the silk fringe of her parasol clipped to her chair. Its shadow cast a dark pool that hid scurrying insects, she was sure. Giving in to languor, even the clink of ice in a glass and the heavy swish of a maid's departing skirts barely impinged on her mind. How very kind their hosts were, she affirmed; going to no end of trouble to make them welcome. Eleanor Carter had been concerned that Ruth would be content during her short absence to visit an ailing soul in the neighbourhood. In fact Eleanor's repeated, 'You'll be all right by yourself?' had been quite tedious.

Ruth gave a sigh of discontent and her brow furrowed. Franklin Carter had left early for his city office so this would have been a rare opportunity to talk alone with her brother.

'I've a little business in the city to attend to,' Sebastian had explained at breakfast. 'Perhaps you'd care to come for the ride, sister dear?'

Ruth tried not to notice how he slurped up his hot tea. Perhaps he wasn't used to genteel company on his farm. She thrust away the idea. 'Thank you Sebastian but I find this heat's just too much for a trip to the city,' she'd replied. 'I'll stay and rest in the garden. Do you expect to be long?'

'Not back till late this afternoon, I think.'

So another chance lost to speak in private with her brother. To her annoyance, he'd asked, 'How about you, Leonie? A chance to spend time in the city appeal to you? And perhaps a spot of sightseeing when I've done my business?'

'Oh yes! There are a few things I have in mind.'

Ruth sniffed, recalling how Leonie had jumped at the opportunity, always keen to roam about with her camera and new friends; God knows who these days. It could only lead to foreign notions. She took several deep breaths and gradually the warm air laden with the heady scent of bougainvillea and mimosa wrought a calming effect. Leaning forward she picked up the chilled glass of lemonade and took a welcome sip as a more charitable thought entered her head. Leonie must also miss Bertram, so she must not begrudge the girl an outing with her Uncle Sebastian. Besides, she reasoned, she could rest today knowing that in her brother's company, Leonie was unlikely to chance upon Captain Ferguson.

A bolt of fright caught her off guard. To think she'd considered Clyde Ferguson a fitting suitor for her niece! That was before she'd learned of his link to her past in Scotland. Fate was so fickle. Replacing the glass, she gazed around the large garden. Eucalyptus trees towered high above in the sky, their pungent odour drifting on the air and wide herbaceous borders in the English style flourished with all manner of exotic plants. She could hear the drone of a lawn mowing machine somewhere out of sight. Here she was, all alone with three maids and a gardener boy left with instructions to attend her needs. It was peaceful and quiet with no anxious faces hovering with bothersome enquiries such as, 'Did she feel stronger; was she comfortable? Did she need any medication? Did she think she'd be able to undertake the long train journey to Adelaide as planned, with Sebastian?' Why they all treated her like an invalid she couldn't imagine. Surely any lady approaching her fortieth year, travelling right around the world and set down in this blistering heat, would take a while to adjust? Small wonder she felt out of sorts, especially when the fright that

Leonie might chance to meet Clyde Ferguson never left her in peace. But of course, none of them knew about this.

Her pulse quickened as she mentally ticked off the days till the fourteenth of January. Not many days to go now. That was the date the *Britannic* would depart Sydney for New Zealand. Only then could she relax; for the ship would carry off her two big concerns. Both Captain Clyde Ferguson and that scurrilous reporter Mr Mallory would disappear from their lives. She smiled to herself. Her secrets would be safe. Once they were living in Sebastian's house near Adelaide, Leonie would be sure to meet one of those Australians who'd made his fortune and sought a cultured wife.

If only her dear Bertram were here, she thought wistfully. His staunch support, his wisdom and generosity of spirit had been so precious. He would have comforted Leonie when she learned the truth of her birth. Many times he'd urged to speak frankly to Leonie but she'd been too frightened. Then as the years passed, it seemed the necessity had receded.

What trick of fate had cast Captain Ferguson in their path; a person who must be familiar with where she'd lived in Scotland. Ruth bit her lip, determined to share her burden with Sebastian at the next opportunity. He was level headed and would be sure to offer sound advice. Mentally fatigued with worry, the excessive temperature gradually took its toll and she fell into a doze.

Something jerked her awake. Her eyes flew open and for a brief moment she believed Bertram stood there. Then as her vision cleared a tall maid dressed in black came into focus and she lurched back to the present.

'Sorry Mrs Fox to disturb you.' The maid spoke hesitantly. She was holding something out. 'Special messenger just come. It's for Miss Leonie; says he must wait for a reply.' Her face puckered with doubt.

'A note for my niece?' Ruth sat bolt upright. 'Quite so. I'll see she gets it immediately on her return.' She spoke with authority. 'I am aware what this conveys,' she said, waving the note in the air. 'Wait over there a moment.'

Ruth stared at the envelope. She noted '*For Miss Leonie Grant*' clearly written in black ink. Burrowing into her needlework box she reached for her scissors. She hesitated, turning the note over and over, trying to gain a picture of the sender. She decided that the flow of the pen strokes indicated an educated hand. But whose? Holding the envelope up to the sun she squinted against the glare but was unable to glean its contents. Hidden from the house she peered about, her sharp intake of breath loud in that quiet place. The maid was some way off. Heart thumping, she spotted how one tiny corner of the flap had weakened in the heat.

A burst of adrenalin coursed through her body, her face damp and flushed. The scissors fell from her lap. She could tell it would be a simple matter to raise the flap. She quelled misgivings as they surfaced. It was her right to protect Leonie and to establish the *bona fide* of the sender. Her next actions were slow and deliberate and soon the single, flimsy sheet lay wickedly hot in her hands. Spreading it out on her lap she lifted her eyeglass from the cord around her neck and fixed her sight on the signature. Shock sped her pulse as her eyes dived back and forth along the lines. Her body weakened and she sagged in the creaky wicker chair. With an effort she raised her head and as a child will, began to read the note in a slow chant.

'*Dear Leonie, I am hoping that you will be free to meet me on the 8th January at the Central Library in the city. Should you be otherwise engaged, perhaps you would propose another day? I shall be in the library all afternoon on the 8th, when you can hear the results of my enquiries. I look forward to your reply via this messenger. Please convey my kind regards to Mrs Fox.*

Your friend, Adam Mallory.'

Panic swirled in Ruth's belly. What had been going on behind her back? Leonie had given that reporter their address! His words rang in her ears –

'results of my enquiries with regard to…' Oh dear God, surely that must mean the reporter had discovered her secret!

She swallowed and sat upright as fear slithered around her insides. Her heart pounded dangerously fast. She'd been blind, all the while frightened Captain Ferguson and Leonie might be meeting alone only to discover Leonie had colluded with that reporter! To think she had thought him a gentleman, she anguished. Her troubled mind sought a focus.

For several moments everything went blank, till suddenly a glimmer of hope slid in. Why then – the matter was already dealt with! Picking up the little brass bell at her side Ruth shook it violently and didn't stop ringing until the maid came racing back. Out of breath, the girl stood gasping before her.

'Tell the messenger there's no reply, now or ever,' Ruth ordered the girl. 'Nothing more, you understand? Tell him to go.'

As the maid disappeared to the house, a hysterical cry left Ruth's throat which put to flight the startled birds. With shaky fingers she pushed the missive back in the envelope and grabbing her work basket, poked it right to the bottom beneath spools of thread, mending squares, tape measure and bodkins, taking no heed of the prick of a needle. The lid snapped shut, the catch was fastened. It was finally secure.

Her face burned, skin taut and itchy. Fatigued, Ruth flopped back on the chair. Slowly her sight fixed on a blob of blood swelling on her finger, and passing her tongue over it she was ill prepared as bile filled her mouth. The ground began to sway, her brain giddy as she retched as if to purge her past, her present and future. The world went dark.

How many minutes or hours had passed, she couldn't tell. Uncontrollably trembling she became aware of several faces, each with a startled expression, hovering anxiously above her.

Chapter Ten

'That was so kind of Colonel Waring; to invite us on this Hawkesbury River trip,' Leonie addressed her aunt, hoping to pump enthusiasm into her demeanour. It was a day or so after her aunt's collapse and she seemed to have only partially recovered. Lately she'd snapped at Leonie without provocation. Even her brother failed to restore his sister's humour. However could they all share a future together?

She was seated in an open buggy between Ruth and Sebastian as they rode through the hushed, leafy suburbs towards Redfern railway station. Even at this early hour, wide-brimmed straw hats and parasols were necessary to give relief from the heat. She gave a start as Ruth suddenly spoke.

'You've not felt the inclination to take a wife, brother?'

Sebastian turned his sister's query into a joke. 'I've had so many females offering me their fortunes,' he said, chuckling, 'would've set me up for life if I'd been so inclined.' That was all he was prepared to say and Ruth lapsed once more into her own world as they jogged along.

'Folk back home wouldn't believe any of this,' Leonie remarked. 'They'd be agog at the luxury

Australians enjoy. "Be prepared for rough conditions," they told me gloomily. "Australia's a wilderness with no refinement or decent sanitation.""

Sebastian threw back his head and laughed at her remark.

Previously, on her visit to the city with Sebastian they had visited a cool, lofty hall where a public exhibition depicted the future plans for the city's development.

'Sydney's so modern,' Leonie had declared.

'Boom time!' Sebastian had explained. 'Pennies scarcely rest in the palms of those developers. Cash flows in from lumber and mines and they can't wait to spend it. Mind you, I've admiration for the entrepreneurs. It's their canny brains and shrewd investing provides us all with new luxuries.' He shook his head. 'You won't shift opinions back home. Mind you, they'll get an eye-opener when they read in *The Times* about celebrations for our Inauguration into the Commonwealth.'

'I've just sent back cuttings from the *Sydney Herald* and some snaps I took of ladies wearing the latest Paris gowns. That should cut the ground from under their feet.'

'It promises to be dreadfully hot today,' Ruth murmured without opening her eyes. 'Thank heavens for this little breeze.' She lay back against the plush upholstery, her face protected by the delicate lilac veil which swathed her hat.

Leonie glanced up at the sky where the yellow globe of sun began to bore its way through the morning mist. Maybe Aunt was just tired. They'd had an early start, Leonie allowed.

The buggy juddered over cobbles when they arrived at Redfern station to join the party of civilians from the trip on the river.

Ruth asked, covering her nose, 'Ugh, whatever's that rank smell?'

'Boot factory back there. Tanning the leather hides,' Sebastian explained, 'employs hundreds of workers to fashion boots and saddles; there's big orders to supply the military.' Taking his watch from a pocket he remarked, 'Well timed, I believe. It's seven minutes before eight o'clock.'

Taking each in turn, Sebastian helped Leonie and Ruth down from the buggy and led them to a shady spot by the wall. 'Wait till I brag to my mates down South about the elevated company we're keeping today,' he chaffed, broadening his accent. 'Guess those fellows'll mark me a right dinkum swaggie telling tall yarns. I'll be forced to buy the booze!'

Ruth's mouth twitched, her features closing with unease until her brother took her hand and blew a playful kiss. 'Don't you worry, Ruthie. I'll chase the ruffians off my land!'

Leonie caught his wink and welcomed his efforts to tip his sister out of the doldrums. If anyone could revive her spirits, Sebastian would be the one.

Leonie was pleased for her aunt when she accepted an invitation to join the ladies in a superior train compartment towards the front. Ruth's departure left her with Uncle Sebastian in a compartment to themselves. Sebastian grinned as he spread out his pocket handkerchief on the seat opposite, stretched out his long legs and rested his gleaming boots upon it. 'No point in missing the chance to make ourselves comfortable.' Folding his arms on his chest, he turned to gaze out at the slowly passing scene.

Leonie whipped off her straw hat and leaned back. Desperate to find out more about the past she asked, 'Do you know of a laird, back in Scotland, who preyed on young women?'

Sebastian sat up straight, his eyes narrowed. 'Ay, there was a lot of gossip. But I was a boy, only seventeen when I emigrated and knew little of it.' He looked her in the eye. 'Why do you ask?'

'Oh, just something, nothing important.' She had no wish to spoil this time by asking if he knew anything about her origins. That would have to wait. Yet she still wondered how to bring the conversation around to her concern for Ruth.

The train rumbled on through stations with strange names. Leonie saw Pymble, Warrawee,

Berowra, which added to her delight at all the foreignness.

'I consider myself fortunate,' Sebastian said wryly, 'having you both cross the world to come here; gets a bit lonely living on one's own.' He slid suddenly upright and reaching for Leonie's hand, and drew her up so they could stand side by side at the carriage window.

In silence they surveyed the changing views as the train puffed its way energetically along a high ridge. Dense forests of eucalyptus sloped steeply down one side of the track, soon to be blotted out by billows of engine smoke. She gave a start as Sebastian spoke abruptly, raising his voice above the clatter of iron wheels and staccato chug of the engine.

'What do you suppose ails my sister, Leonie?'

Leonie gathered her thoughts. 'I've been waiting for an opportunity to speak freely but don't want you to think I'm complaining,' she replied.

'May I take it that Ruth is not as she normally might be? Am I correct that something is amiss?'

Leonie saw how his mouth firmed, his sandy eyebrows lifting to hint his seriousness. 'I've been concerned for ages,' she said quickly. 'Her moods are unpredictable lately. She seems angry with me but I can't think why.'

Their conversation was interrupted by a tapping on their compartment window.

'Five minutes to Hawkesbury.' A uniformed steward passed by their vision, knocking his way along the corridor.

'We'll talk again,' Sebastian assured her. 'I'll see if I can get Ruth to open up.' He squeezed Leonie's arm then opened the compartment door as Ruth joined them. Taking his sister's hand, he smiled down at her. 'Come; allow me to escort you from this noisy, iron monster.'

Leonie was happy to see her aunt's cheeks were pink, her mood animated.

'I've enjoyed such a pleasant chatter with those ladies,' she declared.

A great wave of relief swept through Leonie with the promise of a good day.

***

The party had reassembled on Hawkesbury's wooden wharf, ready to board a pretty paddle steamer which would take them to the picnic site. Waiting beside her aunt and uncle, Leonie gazed about at the company of fine officers; the dark blue jackets and trousers faced with the red of the Highland Brigades, green jackets of the Riflemen, the gold buttons; so many variations it was hard to take it all in, but she focussed her camera.

Tied up alongside the jetty, the steamer looked shady and inviting. Canvas canopies covered the three tiered decks which were linked by white latticework iron railings supported on balustrades.

Leonie spotted Selina and Bobby already on board, talking with Captain Waring. Finally they were all aboard; a bell clanged and the boat drifted slowly out into the main channel, its paddles thwacking with a steady beat, churning the brownish water to creamy foam.

'I'll take Ruth into the shade,' Sebastian said. 'Why don't you find your friends?'

Leonie turned to see Colonel Waring, his eyes twinkling.

'This is wonderful, Colonel. I really appreciate your invitation.'

'My pleasure, Leonie.'

'If you'll excuse me, I'll join you all later then.' Leonie wandered away. Melodies floated on the air as the band of the Highland Light Infantry played a selection of lively tunes. A welcome breeze tempered the noon heat, for the sun now powered down from a cobalt sky. She leaned over the rail and stared into the river. Why hadn't Adam said there was someone special waiting for him in Sydney? She jumped, thrown off kilter as her arm was yanked in a tight hold.

'Come with me!'

Her brain went blank, refusing to believe what she saw. It was Adam, but not the Adam treasured in her thoughts. 'Let me go! How dare you!' She struggled to free her arm but he held his grip and pulled her along with him. In a daze she stumbled towards the steps as he led her down. 'You're crazy!' she hissed.

The lower deck was deserted. 'What's this all about?' She faced him with a hot, furious stare.

He seemed to deflate and sadness lurked in his eyes, but she refused to unbend.

Adam murmured, 'I'd not thought you fickle.'

Taken aback she raised her voice. '*Me*, fickle?' The thwack and swish of the paddles and rumble of sound muffled her shout.

Adam's brow furrowed. 'You made yourself clear. My messenger reported back, word for word. No reply necessary, now or ever. That deserves an explanation.'

'Whatever are you talking about? What messenger?'

'Is this a game you're playing? You sent my messenger back with a flea in his ear.'

'The game's in your court. What note? Let's get this clear, what was it – your wedding invitation? I spotted you with that young lady!'

Adam laughed derisively. 'No wedding in the offing for me, so far as I'm aware.' He thrust his hands in the pockets of his linen jacket and doubt underlay his words. 'I can't believe you didn't receive my note.'

'And I don't believe you.' She tilted her head and gave him the kind of cold stare her school teachers had once done. 'Go on – try again! When did you send this supposed note?'

'Wednesday the 6th January; sent by messenger to your host's house – and it's a fact.'

Leonie's mind raced back to the previous week. There'd been so much going on; a note to the house could easily have been put aside. But he said the messenger had reported back... Quite suddenly, her legs sagged and she pressed her feet hard onto the deck to keep her balance. Oh, surely not? She hadn't been there on that particular day. Her face screwed up in thought and she recalled the 6th was Epiphany and the Christmas decorations were being dismantled. 'I spent that whole day in the city with my uncle, Sebastian,' she declared. All the while her brain was stunned; surely Aunt Ruth hadn't...?

There were a few seconds of silence. 'Maybe it was intercepted. I think we've been at cross-purposes, but that doesn't excuse your crass behaviour.'

Adam seemed to have grasped the situation and a humble note crept into his voice. 'I'll explain. In my note I asked you to meet me on the 8th January at the City Central Library. When the messenger returned to say, "No reply," I was devastated.' His face flushed. 'Oh Leonie, what an ass. It wasn't your fault; I see how it must have been.'

His behaviour just now had shocked her. What if it was just his dented pride? She scrutinized him, trying to discern the truth. But the need to believe him was overwhelming. 'Perhaps I now see it from your point of view. It would have seemed most rude,' Leonie acknowledged.

'I was frantic thinking you never wanted to see me again.'

The image of that fair-haired young woman failed to recede. 'So, I'll ignore this upset, but doubt we can still be friends.'

She saw Adam clench his fists. Several moments passed as he stared into the river before he turned and spoke. 'I was so upset. Please don't think badly of me. I really want to make amends. I wonder if the person who took the note thought it a kindness to break our friendship, since you'll soon be leaving for Adelaide to start a new life.'

'That's a generous thought. That person could only have been my aunt, who's been through a traumatic time leaving England behind. I'm sure there's good reason.'

Adam's eyes held the familiar eagerness as he asked, 'Would you please meet me in the city, Leonie? I've come up with an idea for your exhibition.'

'I'm not sure. I've been doing research myself.' He still hadn't mentioned the young lady she'd seen him with.

'Please give me another chance. Say you'll come to the Central Library tomorrow afternoon.'

'I don't know if that's a good idea.'

'Try to trust me. I beg you to be friends again.'

His crestfallen expression made him look terribly vulnerable. She felt a sudden flush of feminine power and couldn't prevent the words forming. 'All right, I need to return books to the library, so it happens I'll be there tomorrow afternoon.'

Adam heaved a sigh, 'Thank you, Leonie. I'll be waiting for you.'

'How come you're on the steamer?'

Adam's face crinkled with a grin. 'Oh, I managed to wangle myself on board claiming to make a report of the outing, so I'd best make myself busy.' He extracted his notebook.

She couldn't hold back her smile. He was the same Adam, up for a prank.

'Until tomorrow then, Leonie.'

She caught his tender look and gave him a tentative smile and half waved. Confused thoughts crowded in as she watched him disappear. He seemed to be two separate people; one the mischievous charmer and the other alarming and hard to assess. 'Damn Adam Mallory,' she muttered.

The noisy paddles had stopped, only the sound of excited voices floated over the water. Glancing to shore she saw the steamer was anchored in some shallows. She took several deep breaths before making her way back to the upper deck.

***

Leonie stood alone. Sebastian must have taken Ruth for a meander. Clyde Ferguson separated from his fellow officers and approached. 'Hello, Clyde,' she murmured.

'A fine way to spend a day, isn't it? How about joining me for a stroll ashore?'

The boat had inched towards a little island. There was a hive of activity as the crew got lines out and people crowded the rail waiting to disembark. She felt she could relax in Clyde's quiet company. 'Yes, I'd really like to stretch my legs, Clyde.'

'One hour, ladies and gentlemen,' a megaphone blared. 'The horn will sound for embarkation in fifty minutes. We must get away from Milsons Island on the tide.'

Spotting Sebastian guiding Ruth down the planks to the shore, Leonie drew back and waited till they'd disappeared. Then she took Clyde's arm and stepped ashore. Soon they were sinking up to their ankles in the soft white sand and it was impossible to walk with any grace. She grasped her parasol in one hand as Clyde took her arm and together they trudged forward. Crew members were directing people along a rough path to a clearing to one side. She heard the strains of harmonicas and banjos and a sing-song drifted back.

Reaching firmer sand, Clyde released her arm. 'Would you mind if we don't join them? I don't feel in the mood for all that jollity.'

'Me neither. Let's stroll about the island.'

They were both silent for a while. Gradually all human sounds faded as they wandered along the water's edge, their boots kicking up little sprays of damp sand. Only the squawk of ibex and cormorants, the buzz of cicadas and lap of water broke the silence. Ahead of their straying feet, she saw a wedge of rock covered in bright green moss beneath overhanging branches.

'Look, a bit of shade.' Clyde took a large pocket handkerchief from a pocket and spread it out. 'Do please sit down, Leonie.'

He sat beside her, one leg resting on his other knee. A serious man not given to easy talk, she knew, which suited her own mood. She placed her parasol against the rock and leaned forward, cupping a hand under her chin. How strange to be sitting here peaceably with the man who'd mistakenly assaulted her in Devon. A pair of river birds took flight, their wings flapping, and she stared until they disappeared.

She came back to earth as Clyde broke the silence. 'With regard to your aunt, I think there is a connection with the particular place I mentioned to her. Does Blair Atholl mean anything, Leonie? Is that where your aunt came from?'

'Why yes!' Leonie exclaimed. 'That's where my grandparents, the Grants, lived.' Leonie sat bolt upright. 'You lived there Clyde? That's incredible. Did you know my grandparents?'

'No, I never met your grandparents. As a child, I scarcely knew anyone other than our servants in the house. When my mother died, I was eight years of age and sent off to boarding school. Incidentally,' he said thoughtfully, 'my birth name was MacLeod.'

'MacLeod?' Leonie stared at Clyde. 'A MacLeod was my grandparents' landlord, I do know that. I once overheard my aunt telling Uncle Bertram that a MacLeod threatened to turn them off their land.'

Clyde stood up. He looked agitated and began to walk to and fro. 'Then that would be it. It must have stirred up hateful memories for your aunt.' He muttered to himself. 'When I was still a boy my guardians gave me their name – my mother's maiden name, Ferguson.' He sat down abruptly and beat his thighs. 'From boarding school I went straight into the army; never had the inclination to return to Scotland.'

Impulsively, Leonie reached and touched his arm. 'Makes me realize just how fortunate I've been. But it's an amazing coincidence, isn't it? Fancy us being on the same ship *and* having roots in the same place!'

'Almost too strange.' Clyde shook his head. 'What more do you know of Scotland from that time?'

'I believe my grandparents died when I was an infant. Aunt Ruth married the Reverend Fox and they brought me south with them to Devon.'

'This really is quite extraordinary. But why should it affect your aunt so deeply?'

'It's a mystery.' Leonie's mind raced, trying to grasp what she'd learned. Now and again, lively music drifted towards them from the other side of the island. What Clyde had revealed seemed unreal. Yet somehow, this particular disclosure seemed terribly important.

'Your grandparents were tenant farmers then?'

'I believe so. I wish I knew more,' she said thoughtfully.

'It's making sense. I wonder if...' He said no more.

'Your father... passed away when you were small?'

'He met his end in a nasty accident.' Clyde's mouth tightened. 'It was reported he fell foul of an iron trap set for a wildcat or badger.'

'Ugh, what a dreadful end.'

'I had no good feelings for him. He was a brutal husband to my mother.'

'I do see how the discovery would have dredged up unpleasant memories for my aunt. But it's all so long ago. Aunt shared a wonderful, happy life with my uncle. I can't understand why she should take against you when you were just an innocent child.'

'I agree. But if there is a connection, family feuds run deep, sometimes for generations,' Clyde reflected.

Leonie's mind raced back down the years to Downshill. She'd been looking for a pen in the bureau drawer and came across a newspaper cutting tucked beneath lining paper. Carefully unfolding it, the headline had leapt out; 'Notable Scottish land owner expires in horrific accident'. Despite the heat, hairs prickled at the back of Leonie's neck.

'I do hope Mrs Fox might be reconciled to me soon, before I sail on with the *Britannic* to New Zealand.'

Leonie dragged her thoughts back to the present. 'I'll tell Sebastian all about this if you agree. He's such a sound person; he'll be astounded too I'm sure. Fancy us all coming from the same small place on the other side of the world. I still can't take it in.'

'Neither can I. The coincidence takes some beating. Will you please introduce me to your uncle then?'

At that moment the fog horn vented a long mournful blast down the river.

'They're honking for us to board,' Clyde said, standing up and straightening his jacket. He shook his handkerchief and pocketed it.

Leonie willingly took his outstretched hand, overwhelmed by an odd affinity with this self-contained officer. 'I'm relieved to have had this talk.'

'We should do nothing to upset Mrs Fox. I really value your friendship, Leonie.'

'As I do yours.'

The sound of the boat horn came in short, urgent blasts.

'We'd best take a short cut over the dunes. They'll have our guts for garters if we delay the boat and miss the tide!'

How it happened, she couldn't recall. It must have been relief that barriers had been broken down, for she'd never believed Clyde could joke. They stumbled against one another clambering over the dunes and must have cut the most undignified pair.

Neither was prepared for the loud wail which greeted them, halting them in their tracks.

A dozen yards away Leonie saw her aunt gaping in their direction. She'd emerged with Sebastian from a track. Leonie clicked a mental picture; Ruth stark white against a dark background, a frightened look blanching her features.

Clyde reacted fast. Before Leonie could assemble her wits he'd reached them and introduced himself to Sebastian. 'Miss Grant was in danger of a snake,' Leonie heard him improvise. 'But all's well.' Then swiftly he turned, bid them all good day, and marched off to the boat.

It was fortunate the rest of the passengers had already boarded. Leonie shook her skirts and set her hat straight as embarrassed fury burst out. 'How rude of you, Aunt!'

Sebastian frowned and gave her a warning look as he took Ruth's arm firmly in his.

'Just look at you,' Ruth snapped; 'clothes dishevelled, your hair sticking out of your hat! What have you been up to?'

Leonie held her tongue. Aunt Ruth wasn't herself. As if to confirm Leonie's fears, Ruth struggled free of Sebastian and launched herself at Leonie. Then just as quickly, she wailed and sank down on the ground.

Horror-struck, Leonie stood stock still.

'The heat has touched her brain.' Sebastian's normal composure slipped as he demanded, 'Get up Ruth, hurry, else the boat will leave without us.' He reached down to lift her up. 'We're last ashore.'

Ruth stared from one to the other.

Sebastian's tone softened. 'Come, sister. We'll give you a hand.'

They each took an arm and slowly propelled Ruth toward the boat; for, eyes closed, she seemed unaware of what had happened.

'Heat too much,' Sebastian muttered over Ruth's head. 'Best get her inside in the shade, keep her calm.'

Thank heavens for Sebastian. Leonie expelled her breath. She tried to see things through her aunt's eyes. Surely a little untidiness didn't warrant that outburst? Any rational person would know she was safe in that officer's company. As they reached the boat she was relieved how Sebastian adroitly fended off people who pressed forward with clucks of sympathy, assuring them his sister just had a touch too much of the sun.

Once settled below decks in a stuffy empty crew cabin, Ruth soon dropped off to sleep.

'Don't take it to heart,' Sebastian took Leonie's shoulders in a hug. 'There's something odd going on,' he murmured. 'I'm going to sort it out. All right if I leave you for a while? Ruth seems out of it for the time being.'

'Yes, do please. Oh Sebastian, it's so good to have you here.'

Unsettled, she stood to relieve her cramped legs and, leaning against the door frame in the confined space, quietly removed her canvas boots. Shaking the sand into the waste basket, she slipped her boots on again. A warm wave of affection for Clyde lifted her mood. *I won't allow Aunt to unsettle this friendship*, she vowed.

Chapter Eleven

Sebastian went off in search of Clyde.

He climbed the two flights of narrow steps to the upper deck then stopped and took out his tobacco pouch. Striking a match, he lit up his pipe. Standing by the rail he watched the paddles churning water as the boat drifted out into the main channel and headed back down river. He puffed on his pipe, not wishing to join the rest of the passengers who were listening to the band playing below on the middle deck. Whatever ailed his sister? he brooded. Why had Ruth reacted in that unseemly manner so out of keeping with her usual demeanour? Why was she scared to see Leonie with that officer? The scene was indelibly cast on his mind. The two of them looked normal to him. He could well understand if a combination of champagne and hot sun had gone to his charming niece's head – but surely Ruth shouldn't find anything amiss in a mild flirtation. He must seek out that officer and sound him out. Drawing deeply on his pipe Sebastian hoped the man could throw some light on the situation.

Knocking out his pipe on the deck he replaced it in his pouch and with agile steps, bounded down towards the lower deck. His toes, jammed inside fashionable light boots, were pinched and he hankered for his familiar stout leather ones. He sat down on the steps to loosen the buckles as the band struck up a noisy rendering of *Where Did You Get That Hat* and soon had passengers clapping in time. Those bandsmen were giving their best in the heat, all trussed up in thick uniforms whereas civilians could wear cool linen and Shantung cotton.

He remained on the steps, brooding that his desire to bring Ruth half way round the world lay far deeper than a need to create a family to fill his middle aged bachelorhood. That, he accepted, brought solace; but there was also the desire to gain respectability that his sister and niece would provide that would ensure his smooth entry into Adelaide society.

Politics were his aim, a keenness to change things for the down trodden Aboriginal people who were mostly treated like dirt. Sebastian eased his shoulders as he ruminated. He fancied that the course of life was pre-ordained, that there were reasons for everything and, on balance, compensations.

He spotted the officer who'd been with Leonie approaching the bottom stair and it seemed the fellow was looking for him. Sebastian nodded and indicated they should retreat up above for privacy.

Throughout the rough and tumble of his early life in Australia, Sebastian had come across every kind of black sheep and scoundrel. As a consequence, he had fined tuned his judgement of character. Now, standing side by side with this officer, he took his measure and judged him to be honourable and certainly no philanderer seeking to get his way with his niece. 'I think we should introduce ourselves properly,' Sebastian stated.

The formalities over, Clyde said, 'I can't think why I frightened Mrs Fox. I seem to have an unfortunate effect on your sister I'm afraid. Leonie and I enjoyed a quiet stroll around the island, that's all.'

'I am certain you are not responsible for my sister's behaviour. Unfortunately she has been ailing for some while and, I think, is severely affected by the heat.'

'Leonie and I have made a strange discovery about the past. She plans to tell you about it.'

'I shall look forward to hearing, then.'

Clyde's face was set as he faced Sebastian. 'May I ask you to convey my deep regards to Mrs Fox? I should like your permission to keep in contact with your niece, once the *Britannic* sails on to New Zealand.'

Sebastian smiled. 'You have my assent on both counts. As for the latter, Leonie has a strong mind of her own.'

'Time runs against me,' Clyde seemed to voice his inner thoughts. 'Just eight days before we sail. I shall put my trust in providence.' Bending down, he brushed off sand clinging to his trouser legs.

Sebastian thought rapidly. 'Would you care to meet me tomorrow night, in Sydney city? Perhaps we can glean more understanding of this matter.'

'Indeed I would,' Clyde responded. 'Just name the place and time.'

Sebastian disappeared to join the rest of the passengers and Clyde's worries returned. There'd been another of those nasty episodes to shake his well being; ghastly memories of battles in the South African war. During his brief meeting with Sebastian, he'd felt a kindred spirit and wished nothing to spoil their friendship. Clyde cursed, wishing he had his brandy flask to hand. With an effort he made his leisurely way towards the bar. 'I'd like a long glass of iced cordial, please. Yes, laced with rum will do nicely.'

***

Sebastian had settled upon the Chinese quarter in Sydney, where they'd be unlikely to meet anyone who recognised them. From previous visits he had a rudimentary knowledge of the place.

Clyde had exchanged his army uniform for a civilian suit of brown linen, purchased off the rail that afternoon from a gentleman's outfitters. His steps lightened as he approached their meeting place, hoping Sebastian Grant might throw light on Mrs Fox's odd reaction to him.

The two men dodged hand carts and bicycles as they negotiated the narrow streets. For the moment, conversation was impossible. The air filled with the high pitched voices of Orientals. Tall tenement buildings hemmed them in, the leaning walls looking flimsy as a pack of cards. Their progress was hindered by vendors who stepped in front of them and plagued them with all manner of goods; satin embroidered slippers, ivory chopsticks and long bone pipes. They grimaced as a noxious waft from open sewers choked the back of their throats. Raising his voice over the babble, Sebastian yelled,

'I'm wondering if my suggestion is a good idea.'

'It's well with me; chance to see foreign life in the raw.' Clyde was finding it a relief to be away from the confines of the *Britannic*, in the company of this man.

The air hummed with twanging music. Above the clatter of wooden clogs on cobbles Sebastian said, 'Just getting my bearings. Ah, down this alley if I recall.' He led the way through groups of black-pigtailed coolies engrossed in a kind of game with dice.

At last, emerging onto a wider street, Sebastian nodded. 'Not far now.' A few minutes later, tantalizing smells tickled their nostrils and they arrived at Kim Wong's Chop House.

A broad faced Chinese man appeared on the threshold. Bowing and smiling he pulled aside a bead curtain and beckoned them into the dim interior. Then he swayed towards a door and summoned an underling.

As their sight adjusted, the men found themselves placed on a raised dais, screened all around with exotic plants. It suited their purpose well, for each welcomed the chance to speak of private things with no fear of being overheard. The Chinese at surrounding tables, intent on scooping up their food, took no notice of the white foreigners.

Clyde glanced about as several waiters entered their circle of light, bearing dozens of small dishes.

'No need to puzzle over menus. This dispenses with choosing what to eat,' Sebastian remarked.

Clyde grinned. 'Could have ended up eating God knows what,' he agreed. 'Heard tell they have a liking for dog and cat. But it all smells wonderfully toothsome.'

'Don't know about you Clyde, but I'm ravenous. Could eat a horse! I'll order some of the foreign poison to drink with it and then let's get stuck in.'

By the time they'd eaten their fill of Chow T'sai, Chow Mein dishes, noodle salads and fruit rice gruel and sunk a few cups of aromatic wine, they were satiated and ready to talk.

'This is splendid. What would the troops give for this as a change from their normal stodgy fare?'

'Warms the cockles of one's heart.' Sebastian wiped his mouth with a damask napkin. 'Bit of tucker like this'd go down well on the trail.'

Each seemed to be sizing the other up and liking what he found.

'Don't mind the smell of my weed?' Sebastian had taken out his tobacco pouch and, receiving Clyde's nod, proceeded to pack the bowl of his pipe. The familiar act settled his mind and readied him for the sharing of confidences. 'So,' he spoke, pipe between his teeth, 'Leonie told me where you originally hail from. Gave me quite a turn, I can tell you. Can hardly believe you could be Osmond MacLeod's offspring. No, it seems impossible.'

A cloud fell over Clyde's mind and it was several seconds before he responded. Then, casting off reserve, he disclosed how as a young boy he'd tried to protect his gentle mother from his brutal father's wrath. 'I was eight years of age when she died, and was fortunate to be adopted by my mother's brother and his wife. I jumped at the opportunity to change my name from my hateful father's and so took their name Ferguson. Incidentally, now they've passed on I've inherited quite a fortune.' He sighed. 'Unfortunately I have no use for any of it in the army.'

Studying the man opposite as he talked, Sebastian gleaned a complex personality, strengthened by severity; yet who'd retained sensitivity through the love of a gentle mother. His assessment was correct; Clyde was a man to be trusted – a man after his own heart.

'I'm honoured that you've told me all this. I hear from Leonie that Osmond MacLeod, your parent, met his end in a gruesome way. That would have been after I'd emigrated.' Sebastian shook his head. 'Can't understand why I never learned of it.' He took several drags on his pipe, surprised his sister Ruth had not written about such a dreadful thing.

After a moment or two, Sebastian continued, 'I'm familiar with animal traps. My father, ghillie on MacLeod's estate, demonstrated how they work when I was a growing lad. He warned me never to tamper with them,' he added thoughtfully. Staring straight at Clyde, his thoughts were unfathomable. 'Awful way to perish. Where were you at that time?'

'Away at boarding school.'

'I see.' Sebastian's heart began to hammer as again he brooded; why hadn't Ruth's letters mentioned how their landlord met his end? His pipe held mid air, he pitched his mind onto that terrible scene; a man caught in an animal trap. He shuddered. Surely their father hadn't been involved in a crime? He forced himself to fix the date of his father's death and let out his breath. Father had passed on before MacLeod met his gruesome end. The trap then could easily have been forgotten.

Something niggled at the back of his mind. No matter what, he must question Ruth. An idea came; he'd ask Franklin if he could obtain old Scottish newspapers. An account of the coroner's report at the time must have made sensational news. He fought to keep his voice calm as he muttered, 'None of us is responsible for our parentage, Clyde.'

'It's a terrible shock to discover your family was maltreated by my parent.' Clyde scowled into his drink.

'No fault can attach to you my friend,' Sebastian leaned over the table and patted Clyde's arm. He sat back in his chair and took a long pull of his pipe before continuing, 'I knew nothing of the laird's death till many years later when I met a bloke from the Highlands over in the Outback. I was picking up work wherever I could and not always privy to news from home.'

'I'm not ashamed to admit I had to contain a shout for joy when I was given the news by my Headmaster at school. With my mother no longer alive I wished never to set foot in Blair Atholl. After I'd finished school I went straight into the army.' Clyde straightened his back and shifted his legs. 'That's my life; always in the company of men. Never entirely at ease with the ladies... that is, until I met your niece. I'm happy for Leonie. She met a young man on the ship, Adam Mallory, a reporter. Has she mentioned him? But,' he added, rubbing his chin, 'where does this lead to your sister's rejection of me? When we first made acquaintance I was convinced of Mrs Fox's kindly feelings.'

'My sister's attitude must be connected to our mutual background,' Sebastian said. Only the soft shuffle of the waiters' slippers and the cadence of voices entered his consciousness as with a change of mood, he pointed his pipe at Clyde. 'You must be on your guard against all those shrewd matrons, seeking to marry you off to their daughters.'

Clyde's laughter lacked humour. 'Then it's a good thing I'm not in the marrying mood. As for my finances, I'd like nothing better than to find some good cause to redress the balance of my father's greed. I wish I'd had the chance to run the devil through with twelve inches of steel!'

Sebastian turned and clicked his fingers to summon a waiter to replenish their drinks. Then refilling his pipe, he looked up and asked, 'That righty-o with you Clyde?'

'Fine, our throats could do with slaking.'

'To our friendship, long may it continue,' Sebastian said, raising his cup.

'To our long friendship indeed.' The chink of porcelain sealed their pledge. Clyde gripped his throat and Sebastian guffawed.

'*Moutai*, Chinese special,' he said. 'Kick of a mule, eh? Give us fresh wind.'

Despite the younger man's revelations, certain aspects bothered Sebastian. Why should Ruth direct antagonism towards this pleasant officer? Did she lack the charity to absolve the son for the dreadful deeds of his father? He puffed out a cloud of smoke, reflecting how the shock of discovering Clyde's background must have revived her memories of their family's persecution. He brooded about the futility of making sense of a sister he'd not seen for a quarter century. Ruth had borne the sole care of their frail parents after he'd emigrated. Yet her present malaise seemed rooted in something deeper, he reasoned. In his estimation it would be normal perhaps for her to display aloofness, not to express fear at the sight of Clyde. Deciding it was too much to unravel now, Sebastian took a swig of liquor. Piquant aromas wafted through from the kitchens. Rubbing his nose he muttered, 'Females – they are the very devil to understand.'

'Life presents a puzzle at times. There are other things which plague me. May I confide in you? I feel a natural sympathy,' Clyde said.

'By all means. I shall respect your confidence.' Sebastian sat quietly listening as Clyde revealed his dreadful episodes which overcame him, caused by the trauma of war against the Boer farmers. 'Poor devils rode only rough-shod ponies – no defence against our mortars,' Clyde said with a frown. 'But the worst of it is…' he hesitated.

'Go on Clyde, best to speak of it.'

Clyde stared away unseeingly. 'You don't always have time in battle to assess all that's around you.' He spoke fast, clearly determined to get it off his chest. 'Shots came from an old farmhouse; I eased my horse back, took aim and fired in that direction; a terrible scream – female; I charged over, leapt from my horse and…' Clyde gulped.

Sebastian waited silently to give his new friend time to recover.

'I'd murdered her child!' Clyde slumped on the table, his head in his hands.

'You weren't to know,' Sebastian declared as he reached and placed a comforting hand on Clyde's shoulder. 'Could just as well have been one of those Boers; could have fired back and you'd then be the goner!'

Clyde raised his head. 'That's what I keep telling myself but it still causes these "episodes" to afflict my brain.'

'Terrible thing, wars,' Sebastian reflected. He sighed. 'These episodes you have are not unusual; they're the result of deep shock. Will it help to give you an example?'

Clyde inclined his head, straightened his shoulders and sat up.

'I've come across many a miner surviving a disaster underground, suffers delusions like you describe,' Sebastian explained. 'I've worked with men who've fought bush fires, seen their homes go up in smoke and livestock incinerated – all of them go through hell and get terrible repeats of it in their heads.' He nodded, his clear green eyes registering sympathy. 'They'll go one day, disappear of their own accord. I assure you. That's Nature's way.'

Clyde released his breath and tipped the rest of his drink down his throat. 'Thank you for listening. I know that makes sense. It's a relief to talk of it.'

Anxious to alleviate the doleful turn of their conversation Sebastian spoke cheerily. 'Would you care to hear my tale?' From the gleam in Clyde's eyes he could tell his story had a ready audience.

'I was almost eighteen years of age when the ship docked in Fremantle,' Sebastian declared, 'a real greenhorn, ripe for any rogue or swindler. I soon got wised up though. Tried my hand at anything going, till it was found out I was useless at it,' he grinned. 'Drags man to lumberjack, jack of all trades, learnin' along the way. Hoarded my earnings and kept my ear to the ground. One day, this brute of a fellow thought to get the better of me.' Sebastian scowled into his cup. 'A wager, to see who'd dare abseil down this cliff – a sheer drop, several hundred feet it was. We reckoned there was gold down there in the stream. We tossed a coin to see which of us would go down first. Fell to me. I swung out facing the rock, held my breath and felt for footholds. Then the rope went slack.'

Clyde tensed as he waited for the other to continue.

Taking a deep breath Sebastian went on slowly, 'Fate was on my side; threw myself onto a ledge. The fellow thought I was a goner of course, crushed on the rocks at the bottom of the gulley. So he comes swinging down.' Sebastian stopped talking for a moment, his thoughts far away. 'I kicked out hard and shoved him as he went past – instinctive like, as if my boot had a will of its own. The fellow lost his grip.' He paused. 'I hear his hideous scream of a night sometimes. I was lucky to escape with bruises. Felt my way up testing a hold in the sandstone till I gained hold of scrub, reached the top and got on my horse.' Sebastian thumped the table. 'So,' he directed his words across the table, 'I'd say we both get repeats of nasty scenes, wouldn't you?'

Clyde nodded. 'Thanks friend, you've put things in perspective. Best put it behind us, I agree.'

'No use harkin' on it. Get on with the present,' Sebastian concurred.

'Your tale is a salutary lesson. It's either him or you, the truth of the matter.' Clyde raised his eyebrows as he enquired, 'And now you've made it, achieved success – all the goals you set for yourself as a lad?'

'Well, still takes hard toil to make a decent living but I reckon you could say I'm lucky; paid off those artful bankers, own my farm and a few thousand acres. Wheat did well till '98, then the rust pest finished it off all over South Australia, so forced to sell off my fine team of Clydesdales to the knackers – almost broke my heart, I don't mind saying.' For a moment he was silent. 'Now I'm on to something new – grape vines.' Animated, he leaned forward and sketched parallel lines in the table cloth with his thumb nail. 'Rows and rows of 'em. Good north slopes y'see, facing the sun. Conditions right-on, 'cept when the weather's fickle.' He shook his head. 'Nothing comes easy on the land.'

'That's always been my dream,' Clyde muttered. 'Working a piece of land, watching things grow. Maybe when I'm finished with the military, I'll achieve it.'

A distant hoot sounded from a vessel in the harbour.

'It's getting late; best us be on our way.' Sebastian took out his pocket watch. 'A quarter of midnight. What say you to riding Shank's nag, eh?'

Clyde was on his feet. 'Good plan, nothing to beat a good pair of legs. Think we'll find our way back through all those alleys?'

Settling their bill, they left Kim Wong's. Each man tall and rangy, they strode along with their boots ringing on the cobbles. They passed homeless beggars in dark alcoves. There came squeaks and scurrying sounds as night creatures emerged to forage. A companionable silence settled upon them, each wrapped in his own thoughts.

They'd arrived at the harbour. 'I'll pay a man to row me out to the ship,' Clyde said.

'I'll take a tram. By the way, you said the *Britannic* will call back in at Adelaide after you've visited New Zealand? When will that be?'

'We're due back in Australia on 27th February. There'll be a week in Adelaide before the *Britannic* sails home to Britain.'

'Then we must meet again!' Sebastian declared. 'You'll accept the hospitality of my abode north of Adelaide, I hope?' he asked, his brows lifting. 'My sister and niece will be there.'

Clyde's response was swift. 'I'll certainly say yes to that!'

'Hang on a minute and I'll give you instructions to find Corrimony. Shan't be able to meet you in the docks, I'm afraid. The grapes won't wait; busy time and I'll be overseeing the harvesters.'

Cordially shaking one another's hand when they parted, Clyde felt warmth surge through him, expanding his chest. For the first time in his life, he'd been able to relax in the company of a good friend. Now he could look forward one day to meeting Sebastian on his home ground – and to renewing his friendship with Leonie.

Chapter Twelve

Sunlight forced its way through the wooden slats of her bedroom window and seduced Leonie from a light, dreamless sleep. For a few moments she lay totally relaxed in her bed, absorbing outside sounds as thoughts of Adam flew in. His parting shot had been tantalizing.

'We'll meet very soon, you'll see – in quite unusual circumstances.'

What could he mean by it? She racked her brains but no explanation came.

The previous day Sebastian had decided to take Ruth with him back to his home north of Adelaide. Clearly on edge to leave he'd declared, 'Must get back; the grapes must be harvested.'

Aunt Ruth had replied, 'Dear brother, I look forward to being at Corrimony with you.' She seemed animated by the prospect.

A sense of freedom washed over Leonie with the thought that her aunt had been content to leave her alone with the Carters. Eleanor Carter had insisted Sebastian take one of their maids with him to Corrimony. 'Just till Ruth is in a fit state to find her own maid,' she said kindly and refused Sebastian's offer to pay for the loss of her servant. 'You're a dear friend of my husband,' she insisted; 'my pleasure to be of help.'

The maid, Molly, was of Irish stock, large boned with feet like giant pasties but her plain face reflected a placid, caring nature and Leonie knew she'd make life easier for Aunt Ruth.

'You stay on, Leonie, and meet the ship when it docks in Adelaide. Come later,' Sebastian insisted. 'You don't want to miss the rest of the celebrations.'

To everyone's surprise, Leonie and Jane had received a personal invitation to a special ball to be given by Lady Olga Stratton, wife of a government minister known for his generous contributions to the South African war. The event was in honour of the Imperial Representative Corps in recognition of their elite position.

'Well, well!' Franklin had remarked. 'Someone important must have put forward your names. Who might this be, Leonie?'

Leonie shook her head. 'No, I can't think how her Ladyship… unless perhaps a certain elderly officer added us to the list. Yes, I expect that's it. I met a charming old Colonel on board ship.'

Sounds of activity reached Leonie and stepping into the garden she was aware that the air was perfectly still, the eucalyptus trees motionless under a gentian-blue sky. Perfect for the trip to the party tonight, she thought, as excitement darted in.

She spotted Mrs Carter and two Aboriginal girls gathering fruit for bottling and, keen to help, was soon fighting off wasps while checking the fruit for blemishes. Large blue butterflies descended to suck the bounty.

The morning wore on, the heat almost suffocating, and all were unprepared for the sudden fray. 'There's a storm coming!'

Huge pellets of rain streaked down and crashed on outbuildings' tin roofs like a salvo of military drums.

'Oh dear, I hope we'll be able to get to the ball tonight,' Leonie cried.

'Don't you fret my dear,' Eleanor patted Leonie's arm. 'Take more than this to stop those river steamers. Not going to miss out on the extra trade these fandangos bring them, are they?'

That night, returned from his office, Mr Carter fished in his black bag and produced a piece of paper. 'There's a wire from Sebastian, Leonie. It appears our dear Ruth is much improved.'

Leonie scanned the message and let out a sigh of relief.

Mrs Carter beamed a smile. 'You young ladies must enjoy a bit of life before settling down.'

***

In place of their usual parasols, one of Franklin Carter's huge black umbrellas was held over their heads by Bridget, Mrs Carter's maid. It sheltered the two young women as they stood pressed together with a crowd of young people on the quayside near Princes steps, waiting to board a steamer that would take them to the ball.

'I'm almost too excited!' Jane gasped.

Leonie gave her young friend's arm a squeeze. 'It's going to be such fun!' she said.

She knew all the officers from the *Britannic* would be there. Disappointment took the edge off her anticipation as she brooded; if only Adam were invited. A sigh escaped her mouth… it was hardly likely he'd wangle an invitation despite his resourcefulness.

The deluge continued unabated as if a million buckets of water tipped from the sky. Both of the young ladies' finery was protected by two of Eleanor Carter's huge waterproof capes. She'd insisted on them taking her maid Bridget lest she be censured for not chaperoning the young ladies.

The wind stiffened, sending more rain slashing down. 'What a way to go to a ball!' Leonie exclaimed. She stood and leaned over the rail as tree branches hurtled by on the rushing brown river. The sight of toads big as tubs floating helplessly by, their yellowish bellies pulsating with fear, had Leonie almost done for. 'Poor creatures,' she murmured.

Selina tucked her arm through her friend's. 'I'm longing to catch up with your news. I'm trying to guess how many men you've got tucked up your sleeve already!'

'Perhaps Clyde Ferguson and maybe Colonel Waring,' Leonie laughed.

'Mmm, so you say. What about that dashing young reporter then? Bet Adam Mallory wangles himself an invitation!'

'I'm sure he's got a sweetheart, a young Australian,' Leonie said offhandedly.

Selina turned wide eyes to Leonie. 'What a rat. I thought he was sweet on you – poor Leonie, don't tell me you're not upset?'

Arrived at their host's private jetty they were confronted by a staggering obstacle. The storm had done its worst; the end of the landing stage had vanished. Leonie gazed ashore, seeing that a wide expanse of muddy water separated them from the lower reaches of the lawns.

Young men were casting off boots and socks and rolling up trouser legs, capturing the spirit of adventure as they jumped into the river. The fellows stood unsteadily, urging young women to leap into their arms.

Leonie cast a mischievous look at Selina. 'How about it? Let's show we can manage without them, shall we?'

'I'm game for that.'

The rain had ceased and, hitching up their ballgowns under their waterproof capes, they tied them up with their sashes before slipping off the ferry. 'Ouch!' Leonie was unprepared for the cold water lapping about her boots. Hand in hand, stumbling on stones, they got a fit of giggles when they were pulled ashore by immaculate flunkeys.

'The silk will soon dry out,' Leonie said, shaking her skirts and stamping wet boots. Dripping with water they were directed to a dressing room. Clouds of steam rose from high racks spread with all manner of wet clothing above a row of paraffin heaters. A bevy of maids handed out huckaback towels, heated curling tongs over spirit lamps and attended to footwear. 'More like the Mad Hatter's tea party,' Leonie said, laughing.

Bridget handed to them their dancing slippers and soon they were ready for the ball. The young women clasped their fans and hurried up flights of stairs to an ante chamber. Here, the regal figure of Lady Olga Stratton stood waiting to greet her guests.

As Leonie introduced herself and made a curtsey she was startled when Lady Olga said,

'Ah, I believe you are acquainted with my nephew.' She gave a pleasant little laugh and waved her fan playfully. 'He's just inside the ballroom.'

Leonie presumed she'd been mistaken for someone else but let it pass.

'Enjoy your evening,' Lady Stratton's mouth twitched in mirth. 'Any friends of my nephew are particularly welcome.'

As her friends swept eagerly past in a rustle of silk Leonie paused on the threshold of the ballroom and absorbed the scene. She saw Clyde and Oliver waiting to whisk Selina and Jane onto the dance floor. The lilting tones of a Viennese waltz swelled about her as she hovered, partially concealed behind huge urns of palms.

And then without warning her heart lurched. A familiar person stood nearby. He was elegant and composed, greeting guests as they arrived as if it were his normal role. Her eyes widened; for it was Adam, every inch the fine gentleman. Jealousy streaked in as her mind scrambled; for Adam was accompanied by a ravishing beauty dressed in pale pink, the same young woman she'd seen with him from the upper window in Franklin's office.

Leonie's head went all swimmy. The urge to escape blanked out her senses. Quickly she turned about, unprepared as the heel of her dancing slipper caught on her hem and she stumbled, knocking into a plant pot which crashed to the floor. Frantic with embarrassment she stooped and tried to free the slipper.

Adam had been alerted by the sound and flurry of movement; she caught a glimpse of him striding towards her.

'Leonie! Thank God. I've been frantic you mightn't make it in the storm.'

Briefly it came to her he seemed genuinely pleased and, furious to be caught in an unladylike position, she was obliged to raise her hot face.

'No need to curtsey, Leonie,' Adam remarked mischievously.

He was down on his knees extracting her heel even before a retort formed. Furious with him and dismayed by his obvious deceit, she was forced to clamp her mouth shut as a manservant approached.

'May I assist, sir?'

'No thank you, Stevens. I'm just checking to see if Cinders here fits this slipper.'

Leonie drew a deep breath. 'Fraud!' she hissed and felt tears press the back of her eyes. 'I don't understand. Who are you?'

The slipper was now eased back on her foot and helping her to her feet, Adam brushed back his hair. 'There's good reason,' he stated. 'I can explain everything later if you'll allow me.'

Leonie shook out her skirts and rapidly fanned her cheeks as she strove to recover composure. 'Her Ladyship said…'

'Yes, that's my Auntie Olga, to tell the truth.' Adam relaxed and grinned. 'I got her to find your address through her social network. Please forgive me Leonie.' His lower lip jutted in penance as he faced her. 'I honestly couldn't reveal things earlier.'

He must have caught her hesitation as she frowned and glanced over his shoulder once more at the young lady who'd been at his side. 'Oh, you must meet my cousin Penelope. I've been keeping her amused with tales of our escapades.' Then, as if it were an afterthought, he added, 'Penelope's only recently engaged.'

Engaged? Leonie scraped together good manners. Everything had been upturned too fast to take in. So Adam's cousin was engaged to someone else? The sense of relief slid through her as with a playful flick of her fan she tapped Adam's arm. 'I always knew you weren't cut out for a common hack.'

'No?' he asked, giving her a wink. 'Just wait until you read my sordid offerings I wrote on the *Britannic* then!' He opened his arms and smiled. 'May I take your arm for this polka – unless, that is, your dance card is already filled?'

Leonie became aware of all the young ladies who hovered about attempting to attract Adam's notice and felt her heart expanding as he placed his hand on the small of her back and clasped her hand in his. Pressed close to Adam's chest her heart thumped in time to the beat as she dipped and swung to the music. There was no denying her feelings as she breathed in the subtle aura of his eau de Cologne and clean linen while they twirled beneath the chandeliers.

All around them silks and satins, shiny buttons and medals flashed in the sparkling light. Leonie gathered her breath. 'I'm bewildered Adam. Please explain why you are…'

'I shall.' He smiled down into her upturned face. 'Let's enjoy the dance for the moment, eh?'

Suddenly Adam's mysterious comments made sense. *We might meet in unusual circumstances.*

'Tell me, what's happened to Mischief? Did you keep our kitten?'

'Mischief's lording it below stairs; given no end of special titbits. Cook says she's never had a better mouser. If you like we'll slip down there later.'

As the music wrought its magic she moved in unison until a flourish of fast bars brought the dance to an end. Briefly a picture flew in of Adam guiding her through the slum alleys in Port Said, but now he led her towards massive French doors. Leonie found they were high up on an iron walkway at the upper level of a glass conservatory. She might have strayed into a tropical rainforest. Strange spiky plants, towering palms and thick coiled stems bearing vivid flowers enclosed them.

'I've missed our adventures, Leonie. Come, let's sit here.' He'd brought them each a glass of champagne and indicated an iron bench tucked beneath the large leathery leaves of banana trees. 'Dancing's hardly begun so I don't suppose we'll be disturbed.'

Leonie's lungs filled with fragrant aromas. Only the faint sounds of dance music ruffled the silence. She could hold back questions no longer. 'Why, Adam?' she asked. A pulse throbbed at her temple. 'Was it all a pretence then; working as a reporter?'

Adam took his time to reply. Taking a sip of champagne he turned towards her. 'I do make reports. Look Leonie, I know I can confide in you. I had to be able to fraternize with the Tommies on an equal footing,' he said wryly. 'Let them think I'd come from a similar background so they'd feel able to talk frankly.'

She waited, trying not to interrupt his train of thought, unable to see any connection.

'You are aware that Britain and her Colonies are at war in South Africa,' he went on. 'I've been employed, in a manner of speaking, to uncover the reality of it – whether there's any danger the troops might rebel against army discipline. A lot of our lads are farming stock. Fighting Boer farmers must go against the grain for many of them. So what better way to assess their feelings than allow me to fraternise? I've come to admire them all. Those thousand Tommies on board were fighting in the thick of it.'

'I'm really impressed.' Leonie looked straight into his eyes, intrigued by his story. Still puzzled, she asked, 'But can't the officers relay that kind of information?'

Adam screwed up his face. 'Officers are trained to portray the positive; don't want the British to lose face. Besides, blatant propaganda on our side plays a big part in bolstering a cause. It was my idea that I mixed with the ranks.' He paused, sipped his champagne then continued, 'I know I can trust your discretion when I tell you what I'm really about.'

Leonie's pulse raced as she managed to reply, 'Any confidence you share will be safe with me.' Bubbles of champagne fizzed through her brain. The fun-loving young Adam now seemed more mature, a serious young man.

'My other mission in Australia is to discover the attitudes of those on whom our country depends. Will the factories producing arms go on supplying them? Find out if the wealthy factory owners are still prepared to make contributions to the war effort. Also it's important to see what newspaper columnists are reporting – read between the lines.'

Heat flushed her face as she marvelled at Adam's role. She couldn't help breaking in. 'What an incredibly important task. I'm so impressed, Adam.' Perplexed, she frowned. 'Why were you chosen to do this?'

'You might say it's happened by default,' he replied. 'My father in the Midlands has made important connections with the arms trade by supplying materials. He was keen to play a part in the war effort so pulled strings. He somehow persuaded the men in power that no one would suspect that his young whipper-snapper of a son could ferret out vital information. You see, through my aunt's network and social gatherings I'm able to converse with politicians; glean their willingness to provide more Australian troops. They open up to me whereas they might not to a British businessman.' He looked away as though considering whether to proceed. Then, turning back to Leonie, he started to expand.

'The military are getting uneasy. The South African campaign is not going well; whatever folk are led to believe.'

'I'm so impressed with your task, Adam.' Her thoughts were muddled. 'Is it not dangerous – I mean, what if you were exposed as a kind of spy?'

'No, because the enemy are over in South Africa – the Boers.'

'I've never understood why we had to fight the Boer farmers,' she said with a frown. 'They are just defending their own land, aren't they?'

'Yes, they are doing so; but I won't bore you with politics tonight. That's enough for now. You're not holding it against me, I hope? Annoyed with my deception?'

'No, to the contrary; I do envy you engaged on such an important mission.' She vigorously fanned her face but failed to cool her warm cheeks. 'Didn't the troops wonder about you, I mean having a posh accent and speaking foreign languages?'

'I got away with that by changing my accent. Also I let them believe I'd risen to the job of reporter because laid up in hospital most of my childhood I'd received tuition from well-meaning visitors; naughty eh? In truth I did spend time in hospital when Father was working out East. Caught malaria and my parents did hire private tutors.'

Beneath his boyish candour there was strength of purpose. Leonie gave a start as he lifted her gloved hand to his lips and planted a brief kiss. Suddenly she recalled the conversation she'd overheard that momentous day in Franklin Carter's office. 'I may have mentioned that my host Mr Carter is editor of the *Sydney Herald*,' she ventured. 'I watched the March from his offices. You might be interested to know what I overheard.'

Mindful to get it straight, she slowly repeated the businessmen's conversation about the South African war.

'Why Leonie, that's just the kind of information I've hoped to gain. Well done! Think *you'll* make a fine spy.' He reached inside his tailed jacket for his notebook and jotted down what she'd said in shorthand. 'You're in just the right place, staying with the Carter family. Franklin Carter will have his finger on everything of importance in the city.'

As Leonie watched him making shorthand notes suspicion flew in. Adam must have known that Franklin Carter was their host.

Doubt fixed her to the seat as all at once Adam's attentiveness seemed to make sense. He'd gained her confidence by sharing his. Had he singled her out for a purpose? What a stroke of luck for him, that her host in Sydney was the proprietor of the *Sydney Herald*, privy to every political twist and turn. Her heart sank and darkness fell over her brain. She was nothing special to him except as... Something painful and solid seemed to wedge in her stomach. Carefully, she set down her glass and got to her feet.

Adam noticed nothing amiss as he put his notebook away. Closing her fan she looked down and spoke quietly, 'Please know I shall respect your confidence, Adam. It's absolutely safe with me. I must say goodbye and go now to rejoin my friends.'

Adam's face registered his surprise. 'Forgive me, Leonie. I've monopolized your company.' He scrambled to his feet. 'Let me help you find them, then I shall have to do my duty by my cousin and her fiancé.'

'No, no. I'll soon find them. I loved our adventures on board ship, Adam. Let us part thinking of all those happy memories.'

Adam's jaw slackened. Shaking his head he pleaded, 'Leonie, you're not serious? You can't mean you don't want to remain friends? You are not really saying goodbye?'

She took some measure of comfort from his distraught expression and forced herself to say, 'I'm still a friend. I wish you good luck with your mission.' And then she turned quickly away, lest he saw how nearly his reaction persuaded her to stay.

Selina and Jane pounced on her as soon as she re-entered the ballroom.

'Hello Leonie, whatever have you been up to? Jane spotted you dancing with Adam Mallory – seems our young reporter's turned out to be a proper toff! Gossip's flying about.' There was a gleam in Selina's eyes as she whispered, 'What a turn up! Fancy our Adam hobnobbing with the gentry. Jane and I hardly recognised him. Tell us the secret. How do you ensnare these devastating young men?'

The two of them pressed close, eager to hear Leonie's tale.

Leonie forced her reply. 'Easy,' she said, raising her eyebrows and giving the girls a glance through narrowed eyes. 'Whisper something indelicate into their ear – always does the trick.'

'Oh, Leonie!' Jane's shock fetched a squeaky response. 'Not true, surely?'

A wry smile twitched Leonie's face and she left Selina to put Jane straight, for at that moment the dinner gong boomed through the crowd. Her heart was heavy. However was she going to live without Adam's friendship?

***

Colonel Waring took Leonie's arm and led her in to supper. Jane was placed beside Oliver and Selina seated by Clyde. Leonie's place card showed she was to sit between Clyde and Colonel Waring.

A lump of sadness wedged inside her. *You idiot*, she scolded herself. Why had she behaved so stupidly? Why make stupid assumptions? Adam couldn't have known on board who her host in Sydney would be. Was it likely that Her Ladyship knew anything of Adam's role as a spy?

It was too late to put things right again and for courtesy's sake she must make pleasant conversation with the Colonel.

Colonel Waring leaned towards her and whispered, 'Came as a bit of a surprise I imagine, discovering our young reporter is Lady Stratton's nephew? I regret I was not permitted to divulge his mission, Leonie.' He cocked an eyebrow, waiting for her response.

Leonie flinched. 'I've assured him his mission will be safe with me.'

'Quite so my dear. I see he's acquainted you with…' The Colonel nodded approvingly. 'That young man has my admiration. A lot of fellows being well connected would take advantage and slip into a soft occupation.' He held his wine glass to the light and turned to Oliver, his voice raised. 'A fine bouquet, eh?'

Struggling with her deep regret Leonie asked, 'Do you have family back home, Colonel?' For a moment she feared she'd spoken out of turn, for a shadow slipped over his kindly features before he replied.

'My dearest wife passed away in childbirth, many years ago. Our little infant did not survive her. But,' his features brightened, 'I am fortunate to have three dear sisters who produce countless nieces and nephews for me to spoil. You see, I have the best of it, for after a romp and play with them, I can return to my rooms a short distance away to recover.'

'And where is this? Where do you live when you are not away with the army?'

'Cheltenham, The Lansdowne Hotel; comfortable place; suits me down to the ground.'

Warming to him Leonie asked on impulse, 'May I correspond with you there?'

The Colonel's beaming smile lit up his crinkly eyes. 'My dear Leonie, that would indeed give an old campaigner pleasure.' He raised a free hand and gave his moustache a twirl. 'May I return the compliment and write to you in Australia?'

'I should like that very much.' She picked up her dance card and pencil and tore off a piece, knowing it would be pleasant to correspond with this charming elderly officer. 'I'll give you my uncle's address near Adelaide.'

Despite this pleasant conversation her appetite had gone. Attentive waiters constantly refilled her wine glass so she drank far more than she could manage. At the top table she caught a glimpse of Adam talking with his lovely young cousin as if he hadn't a care in the world. With an effort she made conversation with her companions, thankful when they were taken up with lively company at their other sides.

It seemed an age before the toasts and responses were over and she could leave the table. Dancing began again. She watched Jane dancing with Oliver, pleased that these two had found happiness. Her eyes strayed to Adam as he danced but she avoided his puzzled stare while moving silently about the dance floor with Clyde, finding him not expecting small talk. He seemed far away. 'I understand Uncle Sebastian's invited you to stay when the *Britannic* returns from New Zealand,' she ventured. 'I'll really look forward to that Clyde.

'I keep thinking about the strangeness of our shared beginnings in Scotland and feel so fortunate we've met.'

Clyde's tone was serious. 'Indeed, as I am, Leonie. My friendship with you and Sebastian is very important to me. I don't intend to forgo the pleasure of a visit to Corrimony.'

***

Later, as the dancing drew to a close, Leonie found she was separated from her friends. The orchestra struck up a few dramatic bars and the boom of a big drum bade silence. Suddenly, hundreds of coloured balloons descended from netting high up on the ceiling, bounced amongst them as long crimson streamers rippled down and weaved amongst the throng. Excitement rose as everyone struggled to disentangle themselves from whirls of paper and string.

Leonie tugged at the red streamers binding her until they pooled like blood at her feet. Amidst the noise of the melee, balloons burst with the ear splitting crack of rifle shots. She caught sight of Clyde. Alarmed, she saw his features twist; saw him dodge the laughing crowd and dash outside into the night as if the devil clutched his heels.

An awesome sense of foreboding swept over Leonie as she kicked aside the streamers and rushed after him. Everyone was too preoccupied to notice as she hitched up her skirts and sped like the lamplighter after him through the garden door. A wall of black enveloped her as she left the brilliantly lit room.

'Clyde? Clyde, are you there?' She kept her voice low. No reply came out of the dark. The smell was the first thing she noticed; damp and earthy like mushrooms picked at dawn. Everything was moist.

She peered up through the canopy of tree ferns and glimpsed a new moon, a slice of pale yellow melon, before it shied behind puffy clouds. She'd often enjoyed walking in the countryside at night. Drawing a deep breath she began to follow a narrow path. Wet shrubs brushed her gown. She ignored her soaked dancing slippers and stopped to listen. She stood stock still and the musky aromas of alien plants came with each quick breath. A breeze got up. Trees rustled their leaves in accord with her anxiety. A few yards further and a cave of darkness enclosed her. Her heart beat loud in her ears as weird sounds reached her from the river. Surely if Clyde were here he'd make his presence known? Unwilling to lose track of the house she turned and started to hurry back, unable to shake off her deep concern.

She found everyone pressed to tall windows at the other end of the ballroom. Selina grabbed her arm. 'Wherever have you been this time? We're waiting for the Grand Finale of the display. Aren't they fantastic,' she cried as a burst released thousands of stars in the sky.

'Oh!' she exclaimed, shooting Leonie an odd look. 'Your gown's soaking wet! Don't say you've been spooning out there in the rain with another conquest?'

Chapter Thirteen

Clyde's sight clouded as the crackling noise of gunshot fetched one of his worst episodes and swept him back to the Transvaal. Violent scenes swamped his brain; soldiers letting off rounds of ammunition at anything that moved; even old men and women, infants in arms.

He rushed headlong into the garden in an attempt to throw off demons, hurtled through sodden vegetation, his nostrils filled with the vile stench of rotting flesh. In his mind's eye he saw the astonished look on a Tommie's face, crushed under wagon wheels till the thwack of a Boer sharp shooter's bullet put an end to him. The Boers had brought in their 75mm Cruesot, a devil of a monster, and trained it against the tin roofed town the army defended.

All these images inflicted their toll as he drew ragged breaths and yelled up at the night sky. 'Damn all wars!' His feet began to squelch in mud so that only his headlong speed stopped him sinking as he plunged into a shallow river.

The shock of cold water cleared his brain and snapped him alert. He stumbled, trying to gain a foothold, cursing himself for floundering in the swollen river. At that moment the moon emerged from clouds and transformed the wide stretches of mud into liquid gold. He saw how the storm had left carnage of tree roots. Branches floated sluggishly past, beyond his reach. There was nothing to hang on to.

Like a shutter, clouds swallowed the moon and imprisoned him in darkness. Too many brandies confused his orientation. He lifted a foot, uncertain which way to turn. Shale shifted under the soles of his light buckled shoes and water soaked his tartan trouser legs. He'd lost his bearings. The current didn't make it any easier. He swore and clenched his fists, as water crept higher up his legs. If his feet got trapped in twisted mango roots on a rising tide he'd be done for.

Discipline taught him to remain calm, his mind sharp, but he was finding it hard to form a strategy. He could match a human enemy but nature possessed a will of its own. A white mist rose off the river like a wraith to enclose him in its embrace.

How many minutes passed as he strove to make a plan, he couldn't tell. There came a faint chug, chugging sound which broke into his concentration. The volume increased. He turned towards the noise as faint lights broke through the mist. He made out the lines of a launch, moving steadily down a channel in the river. The low throb filled his ears. Standing with the chill penetrating his bones, he knew they'd never hear his yell above the engine noise.

Without warning, a thunderous blast rocked the air and lit up the sky as brilliant as day. Green flares streaked like Verey lights and exploded high above. It dawned on Clyde that these illuminations were different from those in battle. They fell gently to earth in silent, luminous showers, multicoloured, magical. A flaring rocket caught his gaze. He followed its arched flight as it curved towards him and shone on his white epaulettes and gold buttons before it hit the surface with a splutter and fizzled out. His shoulders relaxed, finally accepting these were innocent explosions – the grand finale of the ball, the firework display.

The boat's engine had cut to a low throb. Clyde could see men on deck, their forms lit up like players on a stage. Then the engine roared to life, its oily fumes heavy on the air. Puffs of smoke escaped its stubby funnel as the vessel slowly turned and hove to within a dozen yards of him.

Clyde saw they couldn't come closer for fear of getting trapped in tree roots.

'Catch ahold mate!' As a massive rainbow shower burst in the sky, Clyde grasped the thick rope someone threw. Two men encased in oilskins hauled him towards their craft, their voices echoing over the water. 'Take a good hold, mate.'

Clyde heaved himself up over the thwarts. His shoes slid from under him and he fell, slamming his head on the gunwale. He was conscious of being dragged like a sack of sand as he blacked out. How much time passed he couldn't tell, when gruff voices impinged on his mind.

'Take a swig, sir.'

Cold metal pressed his mouth. Liquor chased like molten fire to his belly and punched him back to reality. Rising up on an elbow he found himself lying on deck without shoes, his bare legs covered with rough sacking. Several men squatted about. Wary expressions puckered their brows. He stiffened. 'I am greatly in your debt. Might have been a goner,' he said firmly.

'Reckon you were lucky we was just in the right place – tricky over that stretch, sir.' An old fellow squinted at Clyde. 'Got yer togs drying by the boiler.'

The other men stood, not meeting his eyes, and made a show of being busy.

'Much appreciated,' Clyde muttered. They must wonder what an officer in Mess dress of a Scottish regiment was doing wading in a treacherous river. At the least, they would think him a drunken idiot. He scowled, aware he owed them an explanation. It would be simpler if he understood himself.

The steam launch ploughed steadily on downstream as he trumped up a plausible tale.

'Damn fool thing to do,' he volunteered, his voice thick. 'Dropped my silver hunter watch. Went in after it and waded too far in the dark. Sentimental value, you know.'

The men on deck merely nodded and carried on with their tasks. The rest of the crew were down below and soon their ribald songs joined the sound of the spray as the boat plunged into the wider channel. A stiff wind now whipped over the bow and lashed Clyde's head. It cleared his brain and finally scoured it of foul images. To hell with these episodes, he chastised himself.

He made a sudden decision to see the war to its end, then hand in his resignation and settle in Australia. Working the land would ease his troubled soul and God willing, he'd still be a young man and one of substantial means. Raising his head he stared across the expanse of water and saw the twinkling lights beckon them into Sydney harbour.

***

Three days had passed since the ball but Leonie's worries increased. There'd been that frightening incident with Clyde at the ball and no word from him since. Also, she couldn't stop mulling over her conversation with Adam and the pain of her stupidity wedged in her stomach. She realized Adam had not made use of her and would have far more useful sources of information. Anyway, why hadn't she shown some spirit and asked him outright? How silly she'd been. In just a few days he'd be sailing away on the *Britannic* to New Zealand and that would be that.

Jane had been despatched on an errand and she sat alone in the Carters' dining room, sorting snapshots ready for her first exhibition in the foyer of the *Sydney Herald*. Yet her heart wasn't in it. Her mind kept wandering and she puzzled about Clyde's disappearance at the ball. Something dreadful must have happened to cause him to act in that weird way. She'd grown fond of this serious officer and wished she could help him.

A tap on the door broke into her despondent thoughts.

'Visitor for you, Miss Leonie,' Bridget announced, flapping a visiting card.

Leonie got up quickly, supposing that Clyde had called. Thank goodness! Now it would all be resolved. She hesitated. With Jane out visiting and Mrs Carter at her Women's Fellowship, it would not be done to receive a gentleman, albeit an officer, on her own. Such a silly outdated custom, she mused.

The steady drone of the mowing machine reached her. 'Please tell the gentleman I'll be down in the flower garden,' she instructed, aware the presence of the gardener should prevent a breach of etiquette and reflect upon dear Mrs Carter.

With no time to either change out of her plain gown nor attend to her hair, which swung like a fox's brush on her neck, Leonie hurried down to the garden, her photo album tucked under an arm.

A young man strode down the path towards her. Her mouth must have gaped in an unseemly way. 'Adam!' she exclaimed, scarcely able to believe her eyes. Struggling to retain composure she said, 'What an unexpected surprise.' Happiness filled her being and the unpleasant scene she'd set up at the ball vanished in a trice.

'Good day, Leonie. I was unsure whether I'd be welcome.'

Flushed with delight, Leonie managed, 'You are very welcome Adam. I'm afraid I wasn't very gracious.' She could scarcely contain her joy.

'You vanished at the ball; I searched everywhere for you but then I had to escort Her Ladyship in to dinner and lost sight of you.' He raised his eyebrows expectantly.

Quickly Leonie gathered her thoughts. 'You seemed so different,' she explained, 'from the reporter on the ship. I felt I didn't know you anymore.'

'Well let's hope I can put that right, eh? You'll allow me to stay a moment?'

Leonie couldn't hide her relief. 'Oh Adam, of course! It's so good to see you again.'

'Maybe you were a little harsh,' Adam replied. He grinned and brought a hand from behind his back. 'But here's a tiny token of our friendship,' he said, offering her a packet. 'Thought it might remind of our adventures in Port Said.'

'Incense candles! Oh, thank you Adam. They'll whisk me back there – I shall always treasure that time.' Her heart sang as up on her toes she blew him a kiss as if it were the most natural thing to do.

'Now I have a keepsake,' Adam said lightly.

She noted how easily he wore his buff linen suit with its green silk cravat. 'Do please sit down.' She indicated the white wooden seat. 'Will you have tea?' Her words sounded jerky in her ears.

'I must decline, thank you. I've just dropped by – running some errands for my Aunt Olga.' But he threw himself down on the grass, falling into a relaxed shape like a friendly dog. 'So.' He looked up mischievously, but his tone was uncertain. 'Wicked girl, running off from the ball and not saying farewell.'

'I do hope her Ladyship didn't notice my departure without taking my leave of her?'

Adam's face puckered. 'Well, she did remark that you were the only young lady who showed her disrespect.'

Heat flooded Leonie's cheeks before it dawned he was teasing, for his mouth twitched as he tried to contain his mirth.

'Oh, you really had me there. Tell me though, did Lady Olga notice?'

'I'll leave you to wonder,' Adam replied cheekily. 'Now what have you been up to since the ball?'

'Oh dreadfully dull, no exciting adventures to report. I'm ready to tackle anything on offer – jackaroo to lumberjack.'

'I've come to ask if you'd like to view the city lights this evening,' Adam asked. 'Will your aunt be all right about it? Lady Olga will be there with a crowd of socialites, but perhaps we can break away on our own,' he added mischievously.

'I'll come, Adam! She'll have to lock me up before I forego the chance!'

***

Adam took Leonie's arm as jostling crowds seethed about them. It was as if she'd entered a fantasy world; delight in his company heightened by the spectacle on show. Against the black night sky hundreds of coloured lights that festooned the trees formed a sparkling roof over Queen's Square and transformed it into an enchanted garden. Rows of red and white electric lamps lined every street. With upturned heads they both gazed spellbound at civic buildings cunningly decorated by what appeared to be sparkling gems.

'It's absolute magic!' Leonie murmured. 'I'll never forget this, Adam.' It was true; just as if her camera had imprinted the scenes on her brain.

Turning to one another they laughed to see how artificial hues made weird shades of mauve, orange and green of their faces, their teeth white as bleached bones. Could he guess even a speck of the elation he sparked in her, she wondered? 'I envy you the trip all around New Zealand,' she remarked when they paused to take breath. 'All those strange phenomena you'll see; thermal springs, volcanic mountains and such like. I'd give a lot to be able to photograph them.' They'd reached a quieter place away from the main attractions.

'Let's sit down for a while,' Adam said and he indicated a low stone wall.

Glad to rest her feet, Leonie found the stone retained the warmth of the daytime sun. Adam spoke reflectively.

'You know, I'll find it hard to settle back in the Old Country; can't see me sitting at a desk in some fusty newspaper office.' As if the idea suddenly hit him, he declared, 'Maybe I'll return here to Australia.' He gave her a sidelong grin. 'So when you're settled with a handsome sheep farmer and a brood of infants, will you throw a crust to a rough swaggie if he comes wandering by?'

'Maybe, but only if you'll not spurn a dowdy woman trudging about with her camera on her bent back,' she rejoined and set them both off laughing again. 'Look,' she ferreted in her reticule, 'I'll give you the address of my uncle's farm near Adelaide.'

Adam flipped over a page in his notebook. 'I'll take great care of this,' he said, as she wrote '*Corrimony Estate*' and the direction to take from Adelaide city.

Later that night as Leonie stood on the Carters' veranda to wave him off, ripples of excitement darted in with the prospect of seeing him soon at the Public Library.

***

Arrived back on foot in Sydney city, Adam walked fast, neither looking to right nor left. At half past midnight the illuminations were switched off and utter darkness descended on the dingy streets around King's Cross. This area was not to be ventured into by the faint-hearted at night time. From previous visits to Sydney he remembered a short cut to the ferry. At this late hour, the last ferry might soon depart so he must take the narrow alleys.

His heart was light as he went over the wonderful time he'd spent with Leonie. With a flash of surprise he realized that for the first time in his life he had serious thoughts about a young woman. As well as her charm and attractiveness, Leonie Grant shared all those interests he himself enjoyed and also his outlook on life. He respected her determination to make a career of photography. Thinking these thoughts increased his anticipation of meeting her the next day with the chance to voice his true feelings.

The air was still hot and filled with dust while heat from the flagstones rose up and wrapped him. Aware that muggers would be about he used his wits. The stiff collar and cravat were soon removed and stuffed in his trouser pocket. Stripping off his evening jacket he turned it inside out so the lining might make him less conspicuous a target for villains on the prowl.

Vagrants lurked in shadows, cackling and stinking of booze, but they formed no threat. His best defence was to walk fast with purposeful steps, neither dashing nor slow and careful, to avoid eye contact. Thank goodness he'd seen Leonie safely back to the house. This was a side of the city not frequented by good society.

As his thoughts again turned to their shared enjoyment of one another's company, he was overcome by the realization of his love. He cursed his stupidity for his lack of action; for he now feared it might be too late to discover if she harboured such emotion for him. Why ever hadn't he expressed his true feelings earlier when he'd had the opportunity? Why had it become a habit to behave in a flippant manner with her? He prayed she hadn't changed her mind about him and would keep their appointment. He longed to express his deep admiration for her before the *Britannic* sailed on to New Zealand. What a fool he'd been, always acting the joker.

He scarcely noticed the quarrelsome voices shrilling from open windows, accompanied by the sound of broken glass, the noises fading as he hurried down a street of shuttered shops. Nearing the ferry jetty, Adam released a breath of relief and casting off caution he broke into a run.

Without warning his body buckled, felled like a tree, and he crashed face down in the dirt. Pain seared his brain as hob nailed boots began to kick his chest, his limbs, his head; so all his senses merged in one tortuous mass. Strong arms grabbed his limp body and dragged it along the cobbles.

How long had passed before consciousness filtered in, Adam couldn't tell. Panic jolted him awake to find his hands tightly bound. A sack encased his head and grain dust choked his lungs. Adam blinked rapidly in an attempt to see and gradually his sight fixed at short range on chinks in the fibres. He saw he was lying on rough ground. Agonising pain shot through him with every twist of his body, but his struggles failed to shift the sack. *Keep calm*, he urged himself as panic rose in his throat. As he sank into darkness once more his last thoughts were for Leonie, and the strength of his feeling shook him alert and renewed his efforts to escape. A draught of air and heavy footsteps warned him to stay still. Whoever had kidnapped him might not show mercy.

'Keep 'im till 'e coughs up the dibs,' a man grunted.

'Toff's worth a guinea or two,' his companion growled. He kicked the sack and grinned as Adam yelped. 'Where's your cash?' he demanded.

Adam thought fast. Clearly these ruffians had planned his hostage for ransom.

His heart quaked. He found it hard to breathe and a shaft of fear leapt in. No one knew where he was. He could be thrown in the river and drowned and nobody would know. *You've got to act! Try anything*, he thought frantically.

Instinct had him pitch his voice in a low growl as he copied their manner of speaking.

'Guttersnipes! What the – you up to? Get this sack orf me! I'll get my gang of lads on t'you,' he yelled, mimicking the worst lingo he could imagine from an outraged Tommy.

Adam's words caught them off guard.

''E's no gent. You picked a dud 'un,' one of them gulped.

His ploy seemed to have worked as his two assailants turned their anger against one another.

'You dolt. Block'ead! This was your plan.'

'You was in on it – what now?'

They must have moved away. Adam strained his ears, but could hear only distant muttering while a heavy door was banged shut. It flashed through his brain that he could be here for days. What if he'd missed the departure of the *Britannic*? He thought of his missed appointment with Leonie. *I must see her*! *Dear God, what can I do*? His heart gave a lurch. *She'll believe I've stood her up on purpose.* After all, he hadn't given her much cause to believe in him, had he?

In an attempt to relieve his cramped legs Adam leaned back and felt a sharp prick on his shoulder blade. A nail? It stuck out of the wall behind him. Such a small thing but it fetched a glimmer of hope and served to reinforce his efforts. The sacking scratched his face as he tried to gain purchase on the nail head and after many minutes he got the nail hooked onto the sack. He struggled and, ignoring the agonising pain in his legs, finally dragged the sack off himself.

Peering about in the dim light Adam made out stacks of wood, lengths of iron and half-made barrels; a place for making beer kegs. Sweating with exertion he now began to work the nail against the cords binding his hands, each severed fibre giving encouragement to quicken his efforts. At last the cords dropped away and he set to work on freeing his legs.

His jacket had gone and with it his silver timepiece. With no way of telling the time, he made for the heavy door, thrust it ajar and escaped. The keen smell of the river filled his lungs and a faint light to the west showed dawn was rising. His shirt was bloodied and torn. As for his light trousers, they were smeared with river slime; but he set off at a steady trot in the direction of the ferry. The worst of his pains speared his left knee and only force of will kept him on his feet. Dock workers passed by but, accustomed to the presence of dossers, took no notice of the dirty man who stumbled along.

Not knowing which day it was, Adam knew he must get to the *Britannic* and find out if it was about to depart. He prayed there was still at least one day, so that he could meet Leonie as planned.

A story began to form in Adam's fuddled mind to satisfy the duty guard on the *Britannic*. It would mean acting a bit of a fool, but no matter. He'd say he misjudged a leap off a tram in the dark and knocked himself unconscious in his haste to reach the docks.

Panic set in. Would there at least be time to send Leonie a note to explain what happened before the ship sailed?

He hailed a sailor on board, who lowered the rope ladder which Adam slowly climbed, each movement bringing pain and sweat. A voice echoed outside his head from a long way off and seemed to be demanding something – but Adam couldn't tell what it was, as the deck rose up to meet him with a crash and he slipped into a void. Several days would pass before Adam was aware of the date.

***

It felt as if giant hands pressed down on Leonie's shoulders as she tormented herself with the agony of waiting for Adam to turn up in the Public Library for her exhibition. She hardly cared that the Head Librarian had shown an agreeable response to her sample of photographs, admiring their competence and fixing a date for the exhibition. Leonie's sole thoughts were centred on Adam.

She'd started the day filled with the happy prospect of seeing him and couldn't rid herself of the anguish she suffered when casting frequent glances at the clock which ticked away the time while her heart thumped with apprehension. When an hour, then two had passed with no sign of Adam while she pretended to search the book shelves, anger had swelled inside her. Even if delayed on important business, surely he could have sent a message? At first she'd racked her brains, refusing to believe he'd stood her up. An accident; yes, that was it, she tried to think. Finally, she'd left the library and made her solitary way back to Bellevue.

She recalled Mr Kershaw's comment: 'I may need a photographer on one of my trips.' Within a few minutes she had his poste restante address in her hand and was dipping her pen in ink. Pen poised, she hesitated. Soon, she must travel to Corrimony,

Uncle Sebastian's farm. Aunt Ruth would need her company in that strange environment. Any chance of her working would have to be in the vicinity of Adelaide, not on a trek out into the wilderness.

Leonie sighed, deciding to write him anyway. She'd send a pleasant note to remind him of their friendship on board and send him samples of her work; ask if he might consider employing her as his photographer at some later date.

Just to compound the misery of Adam's apparent duplicity her exhibition had turned out a failure. The early visitors merely muttered and moved away, which left her unsure of their reaction. As more and more people thronged the library foyer, voices were raised. Aghast, she overheard derisive comments. A smart gentleman said to his lady companion, 'We must go to Blundell's; have our picture recorded sitting in our new Phaeton motor car. This is nothing like we want.' He named a city photographer. And the lady's response: 'Oh Gerald, how lovely. I'll wear my new Paris gown and pearl choker.'

Leonie's heart had begun to pound as one forthright gentleman demanded of the crowd, 'Whose time is wasted? Why are these ridiculous things foisted upon us? I'll have a word with the librarian!' Soon there was uproar, everyone adding their tuppence worth. Mortified, Leonie had crept away, her face fiery red as their comments thrummed in her ears. Even worse she had to accept that Adam's comment had been right – 'They won't want to see pictures of toil…' These wealthy Australians were certainly not interested in the poverty and hardship of rural scenes from England.

Closeted in the Carters' empty morning room and fuelled by frustration, Leonie knew she had to accept the truth and focus on reality. If she was serious about a career she must research the market. If displays of wealth were *de rigueur* she would follow the trend.

Chapter Fourteen

At precisely 2.30 pm on Monday the 14th January, 1901, the Representative Imperial Corps were drawn up on Sydney's Circular Quay. The SS *Britannic* lay alongside, ready for them to embark for six weeks' stay in New Zealand.

Clyde Ferguson's gaze followed the line of uniforms and gleaming boots, thankful the army tailors had done an excellent job of refurbishment and his tartan trousers betrayed no sign of their recent immersion in the river. His mind switched off from the oratory delivered through megaphones by dignitaries who stood on a podium down on the quay, reassured that Lieutenant Renton was detained in custody on board. The man had been charged with being in an inebriated condition whilst on duty and was likely to be disgraced by a drumhead Court Martial. Clyde felt no stir of satisfaction, aware his own bad episodes might easily have led to a display of weakness. He clenched his rifle tighter. That damned war was the very devil.

He kept going back to his disgraceful exit from Lady Olga's ball. His heart sank. If only he could have a second chance to speak to Leonie and explain what demons were driving these ghastly episodes. He felt sure she would have understood. He admired her greatly but felt no romantic love, but deep feelings of another kind; the same feelings his dearest mother had once provoked. He would write her a letter to Corrimony and attempt to explain why he'd left the ball without bidding her farewell.

He hoped for Leonie's sake that young Adam Mallory would respond to her, for he sensed that Leonie was attracted to the young man. *I wish them well*, he decided.

'All embarked, sir!'

Clyde drew himself up straight and nodded to his junior officer. So they were all embarked. The city band took up a prominent position on the quay to send them all off. An emotive tune, a rendering of *Home Sweet Home*, inevitably squeezed his heart. Steamboats added their hooters as the *Britannic* weighed anchor and ropes were cast free. A great cheer went up from all the troops who lined the rail on the lower deck, echoed by those on shore. Staring sadly towards land, Clyde saw a dense wave of flags. His eyes ranged about the throng, regretful at being unable to pick out a familiar face. Only the prospect of meeting Sebastian and Leonie again in Adelaide in six weeks' time seemed to give his life purpose.

His brain clicked into focus as a loud shot rang out. Homing pigeons had been released from a box on the bridge. With a rustle of feathers they sped off into the cloudless sky. Clyde watched as they wheeled higher and higher, gaining their bearings. He marvelled how instinct winged them on pre-ordained routes; a pattern not so at odds with his own condition. His freedom was also constrained; his function controlled by command.

Turning away from the rail he stepped briskly towards the companion steps.

***

With the departure of the *Britannic* Clyde and Colonel Waring had been transported from her daily life; not to mention Adam Mallory. It seemed to Leonie that a wave of communal emptiness, like a period of mourning, enveloped the citizens of Sydney and this condition matched her own despair. Now, with streets and squares devoid of decoration, festive archways dismantled, flags and bunting discarded, everyone's spirits were deflated.

Adam had disappeared without a word and she couldn't deny her heartache was constant.

Selina Rogers and Bobby Gibson, booked for a series of meetings and lectures, had left for destinations elsewhere in Australia. 'Make sure you don't forget,' Selina told Leonie. 'We're meeting you in Adelaide in February.'

So, all her friends had gone away.

***

Adam surfaced to find himself lying on a narrow bunk in a small cabin. The smell of disinfectant and certain unguents filled his lungs as he spotted a white coat and cap on a peg. He must be on board ship in Sick Bay. Looking down he saw that one of his legs was encased in bandages. Tentatively he ran a hand down the rest of his body and his heart missed a beat. His chest was tightly taped beneath a stiff gown. The sensation of swaying alerted him to the fact they were at sea. Memories seeped in of being in pain, of climbing back on board. Then everything rushed back.

His heart thundered as he remembered his broken appointment with Leonie. Whatever must she believe? He winced, attempting to sit up as needles of pain darted in. Drenched in cold sweat, it struck him that his aunt would be concerned too at not hearing from him. How many days had he been here? He cursed himself for taking that risk through the slums. Flopping back onto the pillow he strained to remember Leonie's features, but they clouded and blurred.

A white-coated medical orderly stood beside him. 'You've come round at last then; been rambling. Colonel Waring said to let him know when you're awake.'

As reality caught up, Adam burst out, 'What day is it? How long have I been here!'

'A few days,' was the non-committal response.

'I must send a wire – it's urgent!' His heart quaked as he thought once more of his planned meeting with Leonie. Whatever could she be thinking of him? No doubt she'd decided once and for all he was actually a fraud. He must do something; anything – but what? Would she ever believe him again?

'You are to attend Colonel Waring now.'

'I'm unshaven, not decent.'

'Never you mind, young man. Brush and soap all ready here. I'll prop you up on the bolster. A quick lather and you'll be ship shape and Bristol fashion in two shakes of a lamb's tail!'

***

Each long blast of the steam whistle as the huge engine lumbered over a level crossing clutched at Leonie's heart like a sad lament. The train hurtled on with an incessant *thrum, ti'thrum* and seemed to chant, 'all-over-and-done, all-over-and-done'. She'd still not heard from Adam. Jane lay back in the corner of the carriage, her eyes closed; which allowed Leonie time to think. *Oh Adam*, she brooded, *why did you treat me like this*!

Fixing her gaze through the carriage window she saw they'd left the straggling outskirts of Sydney behind. Now and then she saw cattle, their long shadows pointing to the east. She could picture those early pioneers struggling with meagre possessions over this vast, uninhabited land. The sight of different scenery soothed her restless mood. The train laboured up an incline and Jane awoke with a start.

'Where are we? Haven't we got to Adelaide yet?'

At that moment a guard shouted, 'All stop Bathurst!' They'd stopped to take on water and give the passengers a break.

'Come on, let's stretch our legs,' Leonie urged. 'Might not get another chance for hours till we arrive in Adelaide.' Wrenching open the door, the views of a wide horizon set her firmly on foreign soil. Brushing smuts off her travelling skirt, she took Jane's arm as they strolled.

At last the train pulled into Adelaide and, slightly the worse for wear, they were greeted by Jane's relations. She and Jane were to stay with the Andersons for two days before travelling to Sebastian's farm.

'My dears, you must be quite exhausted,' Mrs Anderson clucked. 'We'll get you home at all speed.'

The spacious modernity of Adelaide was different from Sydney. Looking around, she saw how buildings were set in wide streets, landscaped on a plateau between the ocean and the Mount Lofty Ranges. As they trotted along a tree lined avenue, the only sombre note was the black cloth draping shops, a mark of respect for the recent death of Queen Victoria. The sight of these sad symbols of mourning brought fresh grief to Leonie's heart. Filled with despair, Leonie felt she'd gone so far away from Adam she'd never see him again.

***

Ruth had already settled into her routine in Sebastian's house and retired to her room after dinner each night, pleading tiredness.

Leonie's concern deepened. 'Aunt eats barely enough to keep a sparrow alive. She's been here for days. I hoped she'd be improved by now.'

'Ruth's well enough,' Sebastian replied. 'I've been assured that's so by a doctor I trust. Physically, there's nothing untoward. Time will heal, I'm certain.'

'Poor Aunt. I'd do anything to bring back her interest in life.'

'Just to know we care will be a comfort.'

Leonie and Jane had arrived at Corrimony at dusk, so there'd been only a brief chance to be reunited with Aunt Ruth at dinner and little time for conversation.

The maid entered the dining room, bringing a smell of carbolic. 'Is it all right to clear the table?' she asked.

'Yes, thank you Molly.' Sebastian gave the girl a smile. 'Has Mrs Fox settled down for the night?'

'Quiet as a mouse,' the girl replied.

Sebastian wore a loose smoking jacket in heavy green silk which, in Leonie's eyes, gave him the theatrical look of a character in a Gilbert and Sullivan opera.

'Right now, girls,' Sebastian's eyes twinkled as he guided Jane and Leonie from the room. 'Let's go into the parlour and make ourselves comfortable.'

Oil lamps hung on brackets and cast shadowy luminosity over heavy dark furniture. The smell of beeswax polish and old leather books clung to the room. Black horse hair sofas bulged with the newness of some yesteryear, for it was clear that Sebastian's daily life took place elsewhere. It was like a monastic den, Leonie thought. Once again she pondered her uncle's bachelorhood as she glanced around.

'Never had time nor inclination to burden myself with knick knacks,' Sebastian remarked as if reading her thoughts.

She hadn't intended criticism by her appraisal of his room's plain style. But she needn't have been concerned.

'I've something to show you,' Sebastian exclaimed, pulling the two young women along to a small cabinet. He slid open a drawer, half turning to catch their expressions as he lifted the lid. Nestling neatly on velvet trays lay two round pearly stones, gleaming in the lamplight. 'Opals,' Sebastian declared, 'each one unique. All I have left of my precious nest eggs, but worth a guinea or two,' he said.

'Oh, aren't they pretty,' Jane exclaimed.

'Heavenly,' Leonie agreed, mesmerised by their fragile beauty.

'By my reckoning it's when things are fine and dandy, that's when disasters strike. Not that I'm a pessimist, mind,' he hastened to add, 'but last decade saw more than its share of tragedy.' He placed an arm around each of their shoulders and guided them to seats. 'Thank my lucky stars I'd been able to sell a few of the pretties when the land boom collapsed. Most farmers were wiped out when the rust weevil finished the wheat.'

He was silent for a while. Suddenly he snapped alert. 'Whatever am I thinking of? Two beautiful young ladies and here am I going off on stilts!' He sprang towards a corner cupboard and produced a decanter and three ruby stemmed glasses. 'Time for a glass of good old Barossa port,' he announced, pouring the dark red liquid. 'This'll warm the cockles!'

Jane giggled. 'Looks delicious.'

'Perfect,' Leonie declared, taking a sip. She recalled how he'd even got a titter out of Ruth at dinner by mimicking a sheep drover's lingo.

'Settle back down and I'll spin you a yarn,' he said in that free way Leonie was learning to understand was the Australian manner. 'First thing first, though.' He topped up their tall glasses with the vintage port before adjusting his lean frame in a wooden carver and starting to talk.

'Wow, strike me, that was a laugh,' he guffawed, recounting a tale about his job collecting bugs. 'Devils, they were. Big 'uns and little titches. All had to be sorted, counted and boxed up to be shipped back home for some clever dicks to study under their microscopes. Guess they were trying to find a means of finishing the little blighters off before they bred too fast... Oh, I do beg your pardon, girls. I forgot my manners there for a minute.'

'No, no, do go on. It's fascinating, please don't stop. What happened next?' Jane urged.

'Right – but mind I don't blather on too long. Not used to having such sweet company hanging on my words.'

Leonie hid a yawn as tiredness threatened to envelop her, but her uncle's tales went some way to alleviating her sad mood about Adam. She knew she'd never get over Adam, but how long could she bear this feeling? She didn't know she'd dozed off until she heard Jane exclaim, 'What a painful experience.'

'Chance meeting with an old mate speaking of good wages brought me to Port Pirie on the Spencer Gulf. That's near a hundred and fifty miles north of Adelaide. The Broken Hill Lead Smelters,' he explained. 'Stuck that for two whole years and saved every penny I earned. That's how I was able to buy this farm. I called it "Corrimony" after your grandparents' old estate in the Highlands.'

His thoughts seemed to drift again. 'Those blast furnace chimneys belch smoke twenty four hours around the clock. Devil's Cauldron, we called it. Black as soot you got, dirt everywhere, ingrained in your pores. But there's another tale can wait,' he chuckled. 'Time to turn in.' He flipped open the lid of his silver Hunter. 'After one o'clock in the morning.'

***

Although Ruth had retired early to her room, she had no hopes for sleep. Her burden was now a part of her, a solid, malevolent thing that no amount of resting eased. As each day passed without the courage to share her darkest secret with Sebastian, the heavy weight of it drove deeper. She'd managed to tell him about Leonie's parent, the laird, and his reaction had been typical.

'Leonie's a fine lass and sensible too,' he'd declared. 'If there's one thing good from that evil laird, then Leonie's the one! Besides, our sister was a Grant like us, so she has inherited all that side of the family. I'll find a quiet moment and reassure her.'

Yes, Ruth thought. But before long she must reveal the rest. Wearing her nightgown, she sat stiff as a ramrod on a hard wooden chair as her mind ranged over her brother's and Leonie's reaction if she unburdened the rest of her terrible secrets, for there were more, and it was almost too awesome to speak of. She feared condemnation, horror, and worse.

Then as now she would think; why not keep the secrets? What good could come of revealing something that happened long, long ago? Until her heart gave a painful lurch.

In that moment, she prayed that God might arrange a way out; a swift heart failure to resolve her problem. Then she'd be re-united in heaven with her dear Bertram.

Her mind drifted this way and that as she tried to focus. Clyde Ferguson was surely no longer a danger? He'd been spirited over the seas to England. But there was still that other thing. Her sight strayed to her journal on the little bureau and she struggled to her feet and reached for her writing case. She must tell someone before it was too late. Her journal must suffice – she'd confide everything to its secret pages. She took the little gold key kept hidden in her reticule and unlocked it.

Several hours passed, though Ruth had no sense of the time until she'd committed to paper events which had never before been told nor written. Not even Bertram was privy to her worst secret.

There was such a release; it was as if her aching body belonged to another. She seemed to float high above the room, higher than the farm house, before collapsing softly onto her bed and slipping into a deep, dreamless sleep.

***

In the meantime Leonie spent a restless night, her head buzzing with umpteen worries; would she and Aunt Ruth be too great an intrusion on Sebastian's life? How would Ruth occupy her days once Leonie found employment? There would be no female companions of her class near here. As foreign sounds beyond her open window ended any chance of sleep, she slid out of bed.

For a moment she watched the sun's tremulous rise over distant hills and, aware that crisp dawn air would soon give way to burning heat, she made a hasty toilet. Wearing soft slippers she padded the length of the wooden veranda and gazed about to discover her surroundings. Unlike Devon farms where flower borders prettied the house, only a few hibiscuses straggled in a vegetable patch by an outhouse. Cobblestones linked the farm to large outbuildings; low structures she presumed housed farm workers. Sebastian had mentioned taking on extra workers for the grape harvest. It seemed they were already hard at work, for she spotted straw hats in the distance, all that was visible of them as they hoed between long rows.

Early morning sunshine crept higher over the fields and reached her, the warm rays suffusing her with memories of Adam. Sliding her hands along the wooden rail, she forced her mind back to Sebastian. At dinner last night he'd made light of his struggles over the years. She frowned, resolved to be independent and seek work as soon as possible in a photographic studio.

Her heart gave a little twist as the sharp cry of a baby hung on the clear air. Abruptly it cut off. Wherever had it come from? She jumped as squawking cuckoo burros riffled their wings and took flight. Staring after them her photographer's eye noted how the spire of a white Lutheran church breached the curve of a distant hill. A swarm of large winged insects rose from herbage and flitted past, adding to her sense of things foreign. Leonie mulled over her aunt's situation, aware how hard Ruth must find it, uprooted from everything she'd known in Devon and deprived of her husband's support.

Leonie straightened her back as someone called out to her and she saw a sturdy man of middle height stride into the yard. His craggy features broke into a smile as he approached.

'Good day, Miss Grant. May I introduce myself? Ned Bullen, foreman here.' Two sheep dogs crouched at his feet, ears cocked alert.

She found her hand taken in a firm grasp. 'I'm pleased to meet you. Do call me Leonie. I believe you've already met my aunt.'

'Yes, indeed. May I enquire how Mrs Fox fares? I've been away up country for a few days.' Holding a wide-brimmed hat in one hand he ran the other over cropped brown hair.

'Aunt is settling well thank you,' she said quickly, her words more hopeful than she felt. Ned Bullen seemed easy to talk to. She took him to be about forty years of age and he had the look of someone who could deal sensibly with the world.

'That's very good to hear. Would you kindly pass on my respects?' Ramming his hat back on he gave a low whistle and the dogs leapt up at his heels. 'I'm pleased to have made your acquaintance, Leonie. I'll be off now.'

As he disappeared beyond view an idea slipped in. Something hinted his enquiry about her aunt was more than mere courtesy. Her mouth twitched. She would try to arrange for her aunt to meet Ned Bullen again.

Chapter Fifteen

Six weeks had passed by at Corrimony and Leonie and Jane were now packed, ready to return to the Andersons' in Adelaide. The plan was to greet the *Britannic* when it docked in port.

Leonie was filled with trepidation. However would she react if she bumped into Adam? She couldn't prevent her feeling of longing to see him again. For courtesy's sake if they met she must give him the chance to explain why he'd stood her up at Sydney Public Library.

As usual, she was up early. She wandered down a steep hill and came across some shacks tucked in a gulley she hadn't realized were there. A line of washing swung from a tree; a couple of women's shifts and some infant garments. She pulled back just as a man emerged, his head lowered under the doorway. He straightened up and, taking deep breaths, stood and began to button his shirt. She watched him glance about and, with a dart of surprise, saw that the man was Sebastian.

There was only a slight shift of his expression as he caught sight of her. A man of action, he was by her side in several strides. 'I wasn't spying,' she declared, 'just wandering about exploring the place before I leave.'

Sebastian shrugged. 'Leonie, I think I know you better than that.' He stood feet apart, arms folded, his expression lightened by something. 'Rita's an Aboriginal,' he said quietly. 'I'm fond of the girl.'

Leonie realized an attractive man in his prime might seek pleasure with a female, but it saddened her it had to be an Aboriginal. It was none of her business and she turned to leave, but Sebastian caught her arm.

He let go again, saying, 'I regret if this offends you, Leonie. I hope we shall remain on pleasant terms.'

'Of course it doesn't offend me, and I'm always happy in your company.' Her sight flew to the shack as the muffled cry of an infant sounded. She heard Sebastian's deep sigh.

'Rita won't have things any other way – I mean, I've offered her and my bairn a decent room near the cook house but she refuses.'

So it was his child. Was that all he could offer? Men! They could take whatever they willed. She'd come to see that men could be devious; the same as women. Even Uncle Bertram had failed to disclose to his dear wife that their home reverted to the next incumbent on his death.

With a stab of annoyance she pondered that this must be a half caste baby. If Ruth found out it would be the death of her! Apprehension slowed her words. 'Does anyone else know?'

'My foreman does, Ned Bullen. He's discreet.'

'I heard the cry. Is the baby well?'

'Teething, I understand. She's a sturdy little thing.' His expression tightened. 'The child will be well provided for,' he muttered. 'Aboriginals have been treated badly for too long. Things have to change and I'm determined to make it happen for them!'

His words struck a chord for they reflected her views for people unfairly oppressed. A picture flew into her mind of the tinker family she'd come across in Devon heaving their heavy, ramshackle cart up a track. They'd been ostracised by the village. The woman had bobbed a curtsey and Leonie had asked permission to take a snap of their pretty infants. She'd been humbled when the woman accepted her simple gift of an embroidered handkerchief with grace.

Sebastian's keen glance locked onto hers, his thoughts hard to read. Curiosity overwhelmed her and she found herself asking, 'May I see her please? I'm not just prying, I assure you.'

'Mmm,' he muttered, and nodded. 'Yes, by all means.'

She followed him back to the shack.

'Rita, Rita? I've brought you a visitor, my niece,' he called through the door.

They waited on the threshold. She heard scampering sounds as if someone had hastily tidied up, and hoped she wouldn't cause embarrassment for the woman.

'Do please enter.' Leonie gave a start; for the voice which rang out was melodious and refined.

Sebastian ushered her inside ahead of him. It took a few moments for her eyes to focus in the dim interior before she saw a young, dark skinned woman, her head raised proudly with her arms about an infant on her hip.

'Rita, this is my niece Leonie, I've spoken of,' he said in a gentle voice. 'Leonie, this is Rita and Kalimna.'

Leonie stepped forward. 'I'm so pleased to meet you and your baby,' she smiled her greeting.

Rita nodded and murmured something under her breath.

Leonie looked down at the baby, who gazed up at her with huge, green eyes; eyes which were set wide apart beneath a shower of pale ginger curls. Leonie curbed a gasp, for had it not been for her dusky skin, the infant might have doubled for the beautiful painting of 'Bubbles' in the Pear's Soap advertisement. 'Oh, what a lovely child,' she burst out as her index finger was grasped by the tiny hand. She looked straight at Rita. 'What does her name mean?'

Rita's expression softened. 'Kalimna means "beautiful" in our language, Miss Leonie.'

'May I please come to visit you again?' Leonie caught the look which passed between Rita and Sebastian and saw him incline his head before speaking.

'Rita's employed to help in the kitchen,' he explained. 'I don't believe you've seen her there. She always keeps out of sight if anyone enters the kitchen. Kalimna stays here; Rita's mother cares for her.'

Leaving the shack, Leonie remarked, 'I'll respect your privacy.'

'Thank you. I've been looking for a chance to have a quiet word, Leonie. I'm not one to beat about the bush, as you will discover. My sister told me recently that she's divulged the circumstance of your birth. I just want to assure you,' he said, and turned to rest his arm about her shoulders, 'that nothing of that person has tainted you. I've grown very fond of you, Leonie, and couldn't wish for a finer young woman for a niece.'

His words had the effect of raising her spirits. She smiled up at him, unable to find words to express her feelings for this kind, generous man. 'I love being here at Corrimony with you. I'd better go and check Jane's packed and ready to leave.'

As they walked back in comfortable silence, she prayed Sebastian's secret would not hasten her aunt's decline. Her regard for Sebastian remained strong. It was as if she'd prised open a locked box and the contents spilled constant surprises. Each engrossed with their own thoughts, they climbed the hill back to the farm.

***

Leonie was aware of appreciative glances cast in their direction as she and Jane hurried along city streets; quite elderly gentlemen gave their canes a jaunty twirl as they passed by.

'I can't wait to see him again!' Jane tugged Leonie's arm to drag her along faster in her eagerness to meet Captain Oliver Snelgrove in Victoria Park. Leonie grasped her portfolio of photographs and used her parasol to shield her eyes, which played tricks in the dazzling light.

They'd returned to stay at the Andersons' in order to enjoy the events laid on for the *Britannic*'s passengers. Now, late February, the ship had docked in Adelaide Bay ahead of its homeward run to Britain, and the troops had come ashore.

Leonie's appearance belied the dull ache in her belly. She had tried to believe that a brief meeting with Adam would suffice; just the chance to put things right between them before parting for good; but knew she longed for more. Tension set her pulse racing as images of his quirky smile flew in and her eyes darted about in the hope of spotting him.

The sun glared from an electric blue sky. Their parasols gave little relief and the two young women hugged the shade beneath overhanging porticos as they headed down King William Street. Damp with perspiration, Leonie remarked, 'It's like being in a Chinese laundry!'

Jane giggled. 'It's easier for us Australians; we're used to the climate. Oh! I can't wait to see him!'

These two had clearly formed a close friendship and a warm feeling chased away Leonie's mood. 'Soon be there,' she said brightly. They waited for a rumbling mail coach to pass and it left a stir of air that fluttered the ribbons on their wide-brimmed straw hats. 'Stop a minute, will you please?' Leonie took out her camera and looked down into the view finder to take several snaps of street vendors.

Before long they reached Victoria Park where Jane and Oliver had arranged to meet beneath the dense frond of a tree fern.

Oliver raised his hand in greeting and started in their direction.

'Do go, Jane,' Leonie urged. 'I'll need to spend some time with these at the photographer's studio. Please give my best regards to Oliver, won't you?'

'I don't think Mother would approve of me being alone with a young gentleman.' Ready to dash away, Jane hesitated, doubt furrowing her forehead.

'I'll see you later at the Andersons',' Leonie reassured her.

Jane's face brightened. 'I'll see you back there then,' she called back, already dancing away. 'You know where to catch the tram…'

Waiting briefly until Jane and Oliver met, Leonie slipped away to find a quieter spot, noting she had half an hour before her interview at Lawley's Photographic Studio. If she gained employment there it would be a start to her career.

Leonie found a shady bench amongst flowering shrubs with views of the Lofty Ranges. She leaned back and tipped her parasol so it formed a curved frame around the distant horizon. Squinting into the sun she suddenly spotted a peculiar mark in the sky. Blinking fast, she stared at a strange dark smudge like the imprint of a sooty thumb in the clear sky. Was it an omen? For no reason, she shivered. When she next tried to fix her sight on it the mark had vanished.

Groups of soldiers from the *Britannic* ambled by and people wearing their best clothes stopped to admire the flowers. Lifting her fob watch Leonie saw there were still fifteen minutes to go before her interview. She gave a start at the unexpected sight of Clyde Ferguson coming along the path with a group of fellow officers and she straightened her back.

Catching sight of her as he drew near, Clyde's pleasure showed in his ready smile. 'Leonie, what a pleasant surprise.' Taking leave of his companions, he asked, 'Am I intruding?' Then with a slight smile, 'Seem to make a habit of it.'

'Not at all, it's so good to see you Clyde, a lovely surprise!' Leonie exclaimed. 'Look, I've only got a moment.' She hesitated. 'I'm going after a job. Do please sit down beside me.' She was shocked to see how thin Clyde's features were. He brought to mind an old army officer of her acquaintance back in Devon, a diehard of countless campaigns. He too had this steely, whipcord look.

Clyde sat down. 'Well done, Leonie. I assume it's to do with photography? I've been hoping to see you… to explain what happened that night at Lady Stratton's ball.'

'Look, if you have no other plans why not accompany me to the studio?' she asked on impulse. 'If you don't mind waiting, I don't expect to be long.'

'Yes, I'll be very happy to,' Clyde replied. 'I'd prefer to walk and talk.' His brow furrowed as he asked, 'Can you bear with me? I behaved like an ass that night.'

Chapter Sixteen

Sebastian tipped the floppy brim of his felt wide-awake hat down over his brow to shield his eyes from the glare. It was a scorcher today, all right. The sun powered down on the rigid rows of vines which stretched away to vanishing point on the horizon.

Whistling a tune between his teeth he stooped to pluck some leaves then turned them over in his hand. He spent several moments like this, meticulously examining the under surface before crushing them between his strong tanned fingers. Along the rows as far as he could see, bunches of grapes sagged warm and dusky and reminded him of Rita's plump breasts. He pushed the thought away. Just another couple of days and the harvest would be perfect and promised the best yield yet; superb quality too, he judged. Good thing that vines survived droughts; for there hadn't been a downpour for months.

His lower lip protruded as he grew pensive. He rocked back on his heels and felt a prick of apprehension. Sooner or later Nature bared her teeth. The crop seemed too good for comfort and memories of those poor bastards over to the east set him on edge. All wiped out, they'd been. Those fine, old established vineyards decimated by that little louse. Its name stuck in his head, *Phylloxera vastatrix* – it certainly had a nasty trick. In Geelong back in '75 they believed the plague was isolated. Then every few years it crept back and wrought more destruction in a wider area. Not one of those clever agriculturists had come up yet with anything to destroy the little sinners.

He rifled his fingers through the powdery soil and a long sigh left his dry throat as he considered the odds. His luck held so far. Yet the chance the scourge might drift his way was an ever-present threat chipping at his brain. Casting off gloomy thoughts, he sprang to his feet and shook out each leg of his breeches, freeing the fabric which clung to his prickly skin. He'd come to a decision. He'd tell Ned they'd start picking the following day. Everything was ready; the equipment sterilized in the cool distillery sheds and their regular work hands only waited for the shout. They'd need every barrel he possessed and some extra ones from his neighbours. People were always ready to help one another out at harvest time.

He chuckled quietly as his mind turned to an article he'd read in the *London Gazette* which told of the most advanced vinery project in the world, being developed just a few dozen miles away in the Barossa Valley. The writer spoke lyrically of the huge investment needed and the wonderful returns.

If his luck held he might one day have accumulated enough cash to invest in that new technology. There was no envy in his head. Any fellow who'd slaved to build a business deserved to benefit, although the way some of those wealthy entrepreneurs chose to display their wealth tickled his sense of humour. One had erected a family mausoleum on his land, an incongruous replica of a Greek temple, perched above a long flight of steps. As for him, once his time came he'd be happy with a patch of heather beneath a stormy Scottish sky, although that seemed unlikely. Australia was his home. Yes, he ruminated, that was about the measure of it.

Something made his nostrils twitch, the faintest whiff, but his head was so full of the coming work schedule it scarcely registered. With long strides he covered the acres back to his homestead, hailing his workers by name with a friendly wave as he passed through domestic fields.

Reaching the buildings surrounding the farm house he caught sight of his sister resting on the shady veranda. He raised an arm, about to call out in greeting, but received no response. So much, he thought, for trying to jolly her out of the doldrums. From his physician he'd learned that a constant tendency to sleep marked depression. Thank God for Leonie's friendly reaction to discovering Rita and the babe. He couldn't expect his sister to be so pleased.

Turning, he pushed open a heavy wood door to a stable and stepped inside. Within the cool, dim interior his lungs filled with the familiar smells of straw and ammonia which rose from the stalls. His horse Dante cocked his ears at his approach. Patting his flanks as Dante nuzzled under his arm seeking a titbit, he reached inside his cotton jacket. 'Here ol' fellow, I didn't forget.' Eagerly, Dante took the fresh grass Sebastian had plucked near a stream and made short work of it. Sebastian looked on with pride. Half Arabian, his faithful friend served him well; an intelligent beast that responded to every whisper in his ear or the slightest pressure on his flanks.

His thoughts turned to Clyde Ferguson and he hoped the young officer would take up his invitation to visit. Sebastian was sure he'd fit in here and wouldn't shirk at lending a hand when needed. Sort of man he liked; spoke straight out. They'd go riding; he'd be a fine horseman. Sebastian frowned as his sympathies rose for those Boer farmers fighting for their own lands. Somehow he couldn't forget that their plight ran parallel to the Scottish folk who suffered the infamous Land Clearances. But Clyde was under orders to fight wherever duty called. It struck him, being Australian, that the glorification of the South African campaign fooled the British public, rather like spreading icing over a dung heap – when the objective was to line the pockets of some British arms manufacturers.

Sebastian smoothed the silky hair down Dante's nose. Later, when it was cooler, he'd saddle him up and take a last look at the vines before nightfall. He tarried a few moments longer, his mind relaxing as he welcomed the cooler air on his hot skin. Before his sister arrived he'd have stripped off in the yard and sluiced himself down under the pump. He'd best go inside, run a tub and sit and soak; smoke a pipe of baccy. There was much to be done before first light on the morrow.

***

At dawn the following day Sebastian stood in the yard and looked about him. The hush was uncanny. Even the squealing sounds of piglets down in the pens sounded muffled. Concern puckered his forehead and licking a finger, he held it up. Not a breath of air. Staring back at the farm he saw the corrugated roof shimmering, thrown out of focus in the heat haze. He looked to the sky and his eyes screwed up against the white hot glare. Kites wheeled slowly in the thermals. A sudden dart of fear rooted him to the spot as, wiping a hand over the sweat beading his lip, premonition gripped him.

His body gathered itself for action and he was on the move, his long legs reducing the distance to the stable. He must get high up over the crest of hills and find what the elements had in store. Oddly, it took brute force to combat Dante's resistance. Never before had his horse needed dragging out into the yard. Against his normal calm a sense of urgency caused Sebastian to drive a fist into Dante's flank as the effort of heaving the horse tested his muscles and fetched curses. He was fully aware of animals' instincts and knew they could be relied upon. Dante's eyes showed the whites and his ears strained back. Something nasty was causing him to act this way. Throwing the saddle over the horse's back and fastening the leathers, Sebastian's actions lacked their normal gentleness as he made ready to go. Itching to be off, he hesitated. Then swiftly slipping the reins over the veranda rail he strode into the house.

'Molly? Molly,' he called, his voice low.

The maid arrived quickly.

He quickly reeled off instructions, allowing no time for questions. 'A big storm's coming. Get help fixing sacking to doors and windows. If Mrs Fox asks, I'm sure you'll think of something to calm her nerves. I know I can depend on you Molly,' he finished with a flash of his usual good humour.

'Don't you worry, Mr Grant.' Molly's plain face showed common sense as she absorbed the odd requests. 'Come what may, Mrs Fox will be well cared for.'

'Much obliged, Molly. Don't waste time now. I'll be back as quick as I can – a couple of hours at most.'

Thank God for a dependable servant. He drew a deep breath and hurried out to his horse. With the ease of long practice he untethered him, leapt up in the saddle, shortened the reins and was off at a gallop over the cobbles before Dante had time to baulk. If only Ned hadn't gone off to neighbours to collect more barrels... he could do with Ned's help.

Spotting some workers he shouted, 'Get the animals into the sheds and stay inside with them,' as he charged by. To others, 'Drop that and get down to the farm with sacking for the windows.'

Startled faces caught his mood and when he looked back, he saw they'd quickly complied. Leaving his domestic fields he headed up a steep bank, forcing Dante at a fast pace so the beast's chest heaved as he blew out hot steaming breaths. Suddenly Sebastian flinched. He caught a whiff of that same smell as the night before, but stronger now. It triggered a memory you could never forget if you'd struggled like he had over desolate miles of burned vegetation as an angry sun boomed relentlessly down; it was an acrid, throat choking smell.

He didn't spare his mount as they cantered over a high plain and climbed up a steeper track. He'd lost that smell. Maybe he was over-anxious with the grapes ready for picking. God knows he couldn't afford to lose the harvest. Yet whatever the elements had in store there was nothing he could do if Nature acted.

He reined Dante to a halt to rest him before climbing up the crest of the hill, and took deep, even breaths, ready to assess the worst. Then, kicking the horse into action, he made the final hundred yards to the top. Sebastian's heart missed a beat; his fears were founded. A short way off the hills were invisible, hidden in a dense black cloud that reached from the sky to the ground. The sun vanished, blotting out all light. Desperate to descend, Sebastian turned the horse about as Dante reared, his gums bared in a frightened loud neigh. Sebastian clung on for all his worth, throwing his arms about the horse's neck. He dug in his heels to bring the horse down to earth. As Dante's hooves hit the ground he yanked the reins and drove the terrified beast down the hill while in the corner of his eye he caught a glimpse of hell. A massive wall of dust rolled relentlessly down towards them, a roaring wind heralding its approach.

The howling blast was propelled like cannon shot. It hit them both. As horse and man floundered, it smothered them in a vortex that sealed eyes, noses and mouths with grit.

Chapter Seventeen

There were six of them at dinner that night at the Andersons' house, for as well as their hosts, Jane and Oliver and Leonie and Clyde were all made welcome. Delighted to have the company of two British officers, Mrs Anderson bustled about organising the maid. She reminded Leonie of a sprightly hen as she checked her guests had everything to their liking.

Leonie remarked, 'How pretty the fish look. Were they caught in the river here?'

'Oh no, my dear,' their hostess beamed and shook her head. 'No, the local fish is fit for the cat. This smoked Scottish salmon is shipped all the way out from home.' Her reply held no pretensions but was said in that Australian manner, with no thought of a slight.

How refreshing this is, Leonie decided. Back home a remark like that would have earned a snub. She caught the affectionate gazes between Jane and Oliver and memories of escapades with Adam swirled inside her head. Scolding herself for self-pity she turned to Clyde and felt a rush of affection, recalling their talk that afternoon when he'd unburdened his dread episodes. Besides which, she'd secured the chance to work at the photographer's, starting next month in March.

'Time for a toast,' Mr Anderson declared as the meal was cleared. He stood and waited till each of their glasses was refilled. 'Here's to the present company. May we all meet again one day soon.'

'Here, here,' their voices echoed.

'And a toast to Leonie, wishing all success with her employment.' He beamed at her benevolently.

'Thank you, I'll try to do my best.' Touched, Leonie felt her cheeks grow pink.

Without warning the strident jangle of bells rang through the house. Mr Anderson put down his glass as sounds of a commotion reached them. Feet pounded down the hall; a door slammed. With one accord they pushed back their chairs and rushed outside.

Leonie found a group of men crammed onto the back veranda. A hush descended as they all stared towards the distant tree line. Just in time she saw the horizon, a thin streak lit by moonlight before a monstrous blackness rolled over it, so dense it blotted everything out as if God shut down the world. 'Whatever is it?' She shivered despite the heat, her skin clammy.

'Dust storm on its way.' Without shifting his observation, Mr Anderson added, 'there's news over the telegraph – real duster by all accounts. Hot winds are sweeping down from the north. They'll pick up everything along the way.'

Leonie heard another grim voice. 'Brick fielder takes everything in its path for miles. It'll be a burning wilderness out there in the interior. What with the drought and the land scarified, there's nothing to stop its progress.'

The hairs prickled the back of Leonie's neck with the memory of that dark smudge she'd seen in the sky that afternoon. 'Sebastian's farm. What if it's...?'

'We'll have to pray they'll be safe, that's all; might swing in any direction.'

'It's about due for a brick fielder. Remember the last one? Threw everything at us, turned the place red; filthy stink over the city; took weeks to clear up.'

'Be a while or so before we get sight of it. You can smell it, never forget the smell. Reckon you can't beat Nature,' a man whistled through his teeth, 'land's been flogged to death; selectors squeeze every inch of soil. It's put paid to the wine harvest, bet my words. Don't bode well for their chances, poor buggers. Oh, beg pardon, miss.'

'Fix telegraph and the railways – yeh; dirt'll make 'em useless.'

A faint acrid smell twitched Leonie's nose. Instantly she was back in Devon and recalled stubble burning in fields after the harvest and little creatures scampering to safety.

She stood close to Jane, holding hands. 'Dear God, keep Ruth and Sebastian safe,' she prayed. She felt Jane squeeze her hand.

'I'm certain they'll be all right; your uncle knows what he's about,' Mr Anderson reassured Leonie.

Clyde suddenly appeared. He spoke rapidly. 'I've been loaned a horse and gig. Are you ready to come with me Leonie? I feel it urgent we get to Corrimony as quickly as possible and lend a hand.'

Leonie needed no bidding. 'I'll just be a few minutes. Please wait, Clyde!' Releasing Jane's hand she gathered up her skirts and raced into the house. Soon she was back, changed into serviceable clothes and boots and dashing down the steps to the driveway. She knew this moment would be imprinted in her mind forever. Clyde waited by the gig tapping his foot, wearing borrowed clothes; his uniform jacket exchanged for a waxed bushman's coat and a slouch hat, no longer that smart officer. She watched Oliver clutch Clyde's arm.

'I'll go in place of Leonie. I'm used to carnage… awful things.' He turned as she arrived. 'Let me go, Leonie. Surely it's best you stay with Jane?'

'No, thank you all the same Oliver. I must go to my aunt and uncle.' She grabbed the side of the gig and pulled herself up.

'Wait dear, take this scarf and mantle. It'll keep the dust off.' Mrs Anderson panted towards them and pressed a flask and towels at Clyde. 'You'll find these useful. We shall say prayers for you all. Now go as fast as you can – oh do take care, my dears. Go, and Godspeed!'

Jane came at a run and thrust Leonie's bag into the gig. 'You'll need your things!'

Leonie leaned down and quickly hugged Jane's shoulders as Clyde leapt in and stood gripping the reins.

'Hold tight now, Leonie!'

In a flash they were off up the leafy avenue, the horses' hooves scarcely touching the road as they raced beneath the trees beyond the outskirts of Adelaide. She heard the ragged breath of the horse as Clyde urged a creature used only to suburban streets into a canter over rough ground and she tried to steady herself.

'The main road's blocked, telegraph poles down.' His shout floated back.

Dusk was deepening, hastened by the blackness rolling over their heads. She heard the lamp squeak as it swung to and fro on the shafts, its glimmer now and then catching a winged insect in flight. However would he find the way down a track by this faint light? She and Jane had travelled down to Adelaide on a sealed road with a driver familiar with the route. She stared at Clyde's back, impressed by his skill, seeing how he stood and balanced in the swaying gig. It seemed like a mad dream.

A rumbling sound impinged on her mind and grew steadily louder. Then towards them, out of the gloom, came a motley collection of wagons piled high with people's belongings. Clyde shortened the reins and pulled over to allow them to pass. She peered into the darkness at the drivers and realized they were either children or aged men. Women carrying babies trudged beside the wagons and dragged infants along. Leonie shivered, guessing the able-bodied men must have been left behind to deal with the chaos. A twist of fear coiled inwards. Her heart thumped; slow, regular beats. Crowds shuffled by like biblical refugees, all heading towards safety. Her throat choked on the thick grey dust thrown up by the cavalcade which dimmed their visibility. She heard Clyde shouting to them and their disjointed replies reached her.

'Which way have you all come?'

'Turn back, mate!'

'Are we all right this way for Corrimony?'

'No use goin' that way; they'll be finished!'

'Where have you all come from?'

'Back of…'

Oh no, please God we are not too late, Leonie prayed silently.

The rest of their exchange was lost in the hubbub.

Ignoring their warnings, Clyde flicked the horse's rump. It bucked and pitched Leonie to the back, her arm striking wood. 'Ouch!'

'Are you all right? Hold on, Leonie.'

'Yes, it's nothing.' Her reply bounced back at her in the momentum of their race.

Suddenly they lurched off the track to the right and were rocketing hell for leather down a rutted path, the gig swaying to and fro over pot holes. She pitied the horse as it snorted and strained in the shackles, but Clyde forced it on with a crack of the whip.

***

'Woa, woa, my fine fellow.' As Clyde brought the gig to a grinding halt Leonie wiped a hand over her brow and tightened the scarf around her head. She watched as Clyde leapt from the horse, his face pressing the horse's neck and smoothing the sweating flanks to calm it down. He looked up at her with a gentle smile.

'Well done, Leonie. You're a good soldier. I'm told these folk will help us.'

Startled, Leonie saw Clyde had halted in a clearing surrounded by rough huts, and was bewildered. She saw the twisted branch of an acacia sprouted through the roof of a tumble down shack and there was no division between the huts and the scrubby land around them. A group of bearded men appeared. She realized they must be impoverished selectors who scarified the land then moved on. Clyde was in conversation with them and seemed to have gained their support. She sat in the gig nursing her bruises and noted how at ease he seemed. A thought filtered in. Could she and Clyde ever be more than friends? Then a strong pull of longing for Adam swiftly squashed the idea.

'Could shift this way any time.'

'Stone the lizards, mate. Best we get fixing down the roofs I reckon.' They made no move but stood about shuffling, casting sidelong looks at Leonie.

A thin bearded man came out of a shed leading two horses. With no idea what was going on she stared as he handed the reins of one to Clyde.

'Right-o mate. Take this 'un. He's a good chaser. And for the lady,' he turned a sharp face and squinted up at Leonie, 'reckon this 'un.' He tapped a sorry-looking nag's head with his knuckles and she realized with a stab of surprise that she and Clyde were meant to ride these two beasts.

Clyde looked up at her and explained, 'We can't drive this gig any further. Those travellers back there told me about these kind folk who'd be sure to come to our assistance. They'll lash down the gig and pile straw bales around this skittery creature until we get back for it.'

A big woman in layers of dun coloured shawls emerged from a hut. She strode over to the group, her weather-beaten face stern. 'Don't you lot crowd the lady!' She flung her words at the men. Clearly she knew what was going on for she soon got the fellows moving. 'Get some rocks for the roofs; fetch water in anything you lay your hands on.' Her sharp orders had an effect and Leonie watched the men skulk sheepishly away as she jumped to the ground. 'Please tell me, is there news of things ahead? We must get to my family at the Corrimony Estate.'

The woman's features softened. 'Can't say for sure, but farming folk is used to dealing with calamities.'

Leonie turned and took stock of the nag she was going to ride. It had an unhealthy looking dip in its back but appeared docile. Determinedly she fitted her boot into the stirrup, swung herself up and leaned forward to gingerly pat its head. Her only experience before on a horse was pony trekking on Dartmoor as a child, but she kept this to herself.

The woman and Clyde both led the nervous horse still in the shafts and coaxed it into a barn.

Leonie saw them emerge and heard the woman instruct,

'Keep on back down the track. You'll hit another to the right in a mile and half.'

One of the men volunteered, 'The place you're after lies ten miles up north.'

'My grateful thanks to you all,' Clyde shook each by the hand. 'We'll take care of your horses and ride them back in a couple of days.'

'Good on you mate. Don't be feared for the horse and gig.'

'Keep an eye out; there's folk looking for mischief,' the woman warned.

Clyde came over and made adjustments to the nag's bridle. 'Take care, Leonie.' His tone, though firm, came with a reassuring smile. 'Grip with your knees and duck your head or you'll be knocked off. Will you manage all right?' His eyes expressed concern. He was soon mounted up on a lean, muscular horse and, with a dig of his heels, led them away.

They crashed through untamed bush and she had to twist her body to avoid overhanging branches and razor sharp leaves which threatened to rip her clothes. The air was heavy with buzzing insects trying to colonise her face. A picture of Mr Kershaw flashed into her mind as the oily smell of eucalyptus came with each gasping breath. She gripped the reins as the howls and yaps of unknown creatures rose all around and concentrated on keeping up with Clyde. Her ankles chafed in her outgrown boots but fear for Ruth and Sebastian overrode discomfort. Without warning the old nag reared, tossing its head, ears pricked and eyes rolled up, and refused to move.

There was a sudden utter silence. It lasted briefly. Then a loud hissing noise and a terrifying roar rushed from nowhere. In an instant the demonic force of wind tore through the trees, slashing branches and all in its path as it swelled into the low pressure void.

'Get down Leonie. Lie down on the ground!' Clyde had turned to check just as his horse gave a violent lurch. The loss of a second's concentration was all it took.

'Clyde!' Horror-struck, she watched as Clyde was thrown and his head rammed against a tree trunk. Shock momentarily glued her to the saddle. He sank to the ground as her white knuckles clutched the reins, before a spurt of fear got her clambering down, terrified he was dead.

Her old nag reared, its mouth drawn back in panic. Then it turned and bolted off with her, crashing through the trees.

Chapter Eighteen

Adam winced as excruciating pain shot up his leg. Warned by the medic to remain aboard, he'd waited until the troops had all disembarked from the *Britannic* and then he had hobbled down the gangway, testing each foot fall. Gritting his teeth, he urged himself, 'Go on, and keep going.' The damaged knee was firmly strapped but caused an awkward limp and with the length of time he'd spent in Sick Bay his body was out of kilter. That rusty nail had turned his shoulder wound septic and fetched a prolonged bout of fever.

He stopped to regain his breath and mopped his hot face. Sweat trickled from his arm pits and soaked his flannel vest. He sniffed an oily smell off the sea and saw several vessels were discharging their waste. Keen to breathe fresh air, he hobbled painfully on and with some relief spotted a passing gig for hire. 'Can you take me to livery stables? I need to hire a good horse.'

'Off a ship, are you? Haven't you heard? Devil of a brick fielder on its way – dust storm, picks up anything in its path. In your shoes, I'd sprint back to the ship – no chance when one of them throws its weight.'

Despite the stifling heat a chill flicked down Adam's spine. 'What, it's blowing this way?' He limped slowly forward and clutched the side of the wooden gig.

'No means of telling; might blow itself out over the Lofties. Then again, it might twist down here. Still want me to take you?' At his assent the driver lowered himself off his seat and got down to assist Adam and thrust him into the conveyance.

'Much obliged.' Adam eased himself into a sitting position just in time before the driver flicked his whip and the horse trotted on. Above the clatter of large hooped wheels Adam heard the driver remark,

'Reckon there'll be chaos soon enough.'

A jolt of fear jerked his heart. What about Leonie? Was Corrimony in the path of the dust storm? He clamped his teeth as the gig jolted over cobbles and prayed he'd be able to find the farm and that Leonie would be safe. They'd arrived at the stables recommended by the driver. This time Adam declined help and eased himself down onto the path.

'G'day. Good luck young fella. Take care now.' The driver was clearly satisfied with the payment for his fare.

'Thank you, I will.' Adam limped into the yard and watched a group of mean-looking fellows in hob nail boots shift apart. Their type fetched his gall, reminding him of the attackers who'd caused his injuries. A muscular man in leathers emerged from the stables, shirt sleeves rolled to the elbow. He squinted at Adam.

'Looking for something?'

'I am.' Adam strengthened his voice. 'I need the hire of a good horse.' He looked the man in the eye as the ostler looked him up and down.

'Not jumping ship, eh? What would a young fella like you know about horses then?'

'I own horses back in England.' It was a civil response. 'Do you have one for hire?' 'Horses in England, eh?' the man stroked his rough hairy chin. 'Without putting too fine a point on it – I understand it's just wealthy folk back home owns horses, 'cept in trade as carters and the like. So where do you think of riding one of my fine mounts then?'

'Out to the Barossa Valley; not within walking distance, I imagine?'

The man chuckled rudely and blew out his ruddy cheeks. 'You might manage it in a day's quick march. Not on that,' he shook his head, indicating Adam's injured leg. 'It'd be a perilous journey anyways – dust storm heading there by all accounts. Telegraph poles and trees will block the roads. You still reckon to ride out on that crook leg?'

'I've got to get there; important business.' Charged with stubbornness, Adam declared, 'I'll pay you well.'

***

Armed with Sebastian's address, Adam knew Corrimony was still some way off and he sent up a prayer of thanks that the ostler had got his boy to set him in the right direction. He forced himself to ignore the pain that seared his injured knee and dug in his heels hard into the horse's flanks. The creature balked as he drove it forward but Adam's whole being was set on the urgency of finding Leonie. Crashing sounds echoed about in the undergrowth as animals raced in panic to escape. Adam forged ahead, almost demented in his concern.

Minutes or hours passed, he couldn't tell how long, when his heart missed a beat. The dust storm was coming.

It came abruptly; a sudden change in the atmosphere. First, an ominous silence, followed by a wind so violent it shook the ground and almost felled him. It screeched like a banshee, hurling tree branches and debris all around. A dense black cloud of dust descended as he gripped the reins and slid to the ground, not caring as his knee buckled. 'Come on, come on, you devil!' He tugged the terrified horse forward and struggled along on foot, scarcely able to pick out the track.

It seemed an age before a faint cry reached him from somewhere ahead. Hardly human in its fear, it sparked a deep response in his guts. 'Leonie!' His lungs were choked with dirt as he yelled into the screaming wind, 'I'm coming!'

***

Dense clouds of dust engulfed Leonie. 'Help!' Her frightened cry issued of its own accord. 'Help me!' she screamed. Using every muscle she dug her feet hard into the nag's flanks and twisted the bridle about. It seemed like a miracle. Clearly only used to responding to harsh treatment, the beast grew docile. It turned about to Leonie's shout and stumbled back through the dense undergrowth. Leonie rubbed her sore eyes, unable to shift the grit, but drew a deep breath of relief as they reached Clyde. She leapt down and cast the reins over a thorny bush. Desperately she reached into the pannier attached to Clyde's horse and grabbed the flask of water. His shivering beast reeked of sweat.

Crouching down beside Clyde she gathered a wad of her shift and soaked it with water. His face was ashen as she pressed the dampened cloth to his temple. The wind shrieked and howled and filled the air with flying debris. There was a loud buzzing noise in her head. 'Drink, drink it Clyde.' She pressed the flask to his mouth. Tree branches swayed and creaked above them and she squeezed her eyelids to shut out her fears. After what seemed like hours she gave a start as the sound of someone shouting in the distance swirled about like words in a dream. Instinctively she was up on her feet, grasping the tree trunk for protection as crashing noises grew near and warned of someone's approach. What if it was those ruffians that woman mentioned?

It was Clyde's horse who tried to bolt this time. Leonie gripped its reins with all her might but it dragged away from the branch and charged off, spooked by the noise of someone approaching. 'Stop, stop you brute!' she yelled. Her heart pounded her ribs. Clyde couldn't help her – he hadn't moved. Her heart rocketed behind her ribs as a scruffy-looking man emerged from the gloom, tugging his horse along. Her mind blank, she stared wildly at him.

'Dear Leonie, it's me, Adam!' he was half crying with relief as he shouted.

She saw a dishevelled man, his face streaked with dirt. Yet weren't these the words she'd longed to hear? Was she fantasising? It couldn't be Adam. It's shock, she told herself. Silly, how could Adam be there? But despite his rag-taggle look, Adam gradually seemed real enough as he stumbled towards her, leading his horse. She strained her eyes as if to peel away the layers of dust as he threw the reins over a branch and reached for her.

'I've been desperate, Leonie dearest, thinking I'd never find you.' His breath fanned her cheeks as he leaned forward, about to embrace her.

Leonie clutched Adam, planting hot kisses on his dirty neck. 'Oh Adam, dear Adam…'

Adam's fond expression faded as he saw Clyde on the ground. 'You're with Clyde then,' he stated abruptly.

Her voice was weak as she nodded and said, 'Clyde's taking me to Corrimony.'

Avoiding looking at her, Adam stared down at the other man, puzzled, and he seemed to have difficulty forming words. Finally he heaved a big sigh, as if he had no control over the situation, and asked, 'What happened?' He looked up at Leonie, his brows creased.

Leonie came to her senses as Adam's horse snorted and stamped the ground. 'Clyde was thrown off; his horse just bolted. His head took an awful knock on the tree.' All the while she was trying to believe Adam was there.

'But you, Leonie? I've really been so worried that you were safe.'

'I'm well.' Her voice sounded hysterical.

Adam touched the side of Clyde's head gently. 'Nasty bump there.' He was slowly getting to his feet.

She felt Adam's hand gently remove a twig from her hair. He was so close, waves of emotion chased through her veins. 'Oh Adam!' her feelings erupted and she clutched Adam again, but now sensed his reticence. So she knelt down and once more pressed the damp wad of fabric to Clyde's head.

'It'll soon be night time,' Adam muttered. 'I hadn't thought you'd be with Clyde.' He shot Leonie an odd glance. 'I'd better not stay here then. Are you both headed to Sebastian's? I'll head back to the city…' Adam was looking from Clyde to Leonie with a frown.

As Adam's words impinged on her consciousness, Leonie stared at the two men. All at once it struck her. Adam must think she and Clyde were more than friends. 'For God's sake,' she burst out. 'Clyde's a friend of Sebastian's. He's invited Clyde to stay with him! I'm frantic to see my aunt and Sebastian are safe and Clyde offered to take me to them!'

She gasped as Adam stumbled and all at once her resolve to hide her feelings vanished. 'Oh Adam,' she cried, standing up. 'I'm so very happy you are here, my love!' And without another thought, she flung herself into his surprised arms.

Adam relaxed and held her tight. 'I feel the same, dearest!' They both jumped as Clyde let out a groan and half opened his eyes. As they reluctantly broke apart, Clyde mumbled, 'What the…?'

Leonie bent down, picked up the flask and placed her hand on his shoulder. 'Clyde, Adam's here to help you. Here, drink this.' She waited while he took a few sips of water.

'Good sign, a surface bump most likely. He'll come right round soon, I'm certain.' Adam's tone was reassuring. Bending down to Clyde's ear he asked quietly, 'Do you think you can stand, Clyde? I'll help you up when you're ready.'

'See to the others. Take cover!' Clyde's shout came without warning.

Leonie flinched. She saw Adam grit his teeth.

'Take it easy; you're safe, Clyde. You're here with us in Australia now,' Adam murmured.

Clyde drew a deep breath and slowly opened his eyes. She saw how he clenched his fists as he struggled up onto his feet, shaking his head.

'Let me take the strain,' Adam insisted, taking hold of Clyde's arm.

Clyde twisted his head about, his eyes unseeing, and motioned Adam's hand away. 'Thanks my friend, I can manage by myself.' But his legs gave way and he slumped to the ground.

'Help me get him onto *my* horse, Leonie.' Adam's horse pawed the air as if keen to get moving.

Together they dragged Clyde up, but his weight defeated them. 'We can't lift him any higher.' As gently as possible, they lowered him back to the ground.

Leonie twitched as Adam's arm brushed hers.

'I'll give him a drop of brandy.' Adam reached for his flask.

It did the trick. Clyde gulped down the fiery liquid and shook his head fast from side to side. In two seconds he was up on his feet and had regained his wits. 'Adam Mallory! Where the devil have you sprung from?' His voice was brisk. 'Thank the Lord you and Leonie have found one another. I'll save questions till later. I guess we're all headed the same way – Sebastian's farm? Where's that horse of mine?'

'I'm afraid it bolted off.'

'It'll find its own way home,' Clyde said. 'So, how are we three to travel then?'

'Look, I'm so afraid for Aunt and Uncle – can't we hurry?' She caught the searching look which passed between the two men.

Clyde had gathered the doubt that still lingered in Adam's mind. 'Leonie's uncle and I have become friends. Mind you,' he remarked, giving Leonie a twisted grin, 'I hope Leonie is my friend too.' He was altering the stirrups on Adam's mount. 'He looks a strong fellow. Seems mine took off. Horses have a way of finding their own stable. How about you and Leonie on this fellow? I'll manage on old Flossie here.'

'You'll be all right now?'

'See, I'm right as rain, thanks to you both.' Clyde patted the lump on his head. 'Suffered worse in battle; nothing a dose of brandy won't clear.' Delving into the leather coat he pulled out his own silver flask and offered it to Adam. 'Now you have a sip of mine. No, your turn,' he insisted.

Adam's shoulders relaxed as he took the flask from Clyde. 'I'm afraid there's been a misunderstanding between Leonie and me. I've got some explaining to do.' He shifted the weight of his leg awkwardly and lifted his head to take a swig of brandy.

Until that moment she hadn't noticed Adam's limp. 'Your leg's hurt.' She frowned and pointed.

'Why ever do you think I had to stand you up? That night when we parted I was attacked by a bunch of ruffians and kidnapped; escaped the next day – just got back to the ship before I passed out. Found myself basking in the Southern Ocean weeks later!'

Relief almost had her speechless. 'Oh Adam, and I've been stabbing pins in your photograph.'

'Why are we standing about? Come on, let's go!' Clyde interrupted, putting away his flask.

Adam grinned at Leonie as he held her arm. 'One day this'll seem like another adventure, don't you think?' He put his good leg into the stirrup and swung the injured one over the horse.

Leonie raised her arms as Adam reached down to haul her up behind him.

It's only a dream, she told herself. That was until she felt the solidness of Adam as she gripped onto his back.

'Your hair's tickling my neck,' Adam said with a laugh as he half turned around, his breath fanning her cheeks.

She watched Clyde mount the old nag and grasp the reins.

'All present and correct,' he declared.

Mirth rose in her throat at the sight of Clyde, his long legs straddling the old mare, his feet in the stirrups barely above ground. 'Don Quixote!' she whispered to Adam, and heard him chuckle. They rode off behind Clyde through the clogging dusty atmosphere.

'Follow in my tracks,' Clyde instructed. 'Look, see up there, we must have caught the tail end of the storm.'

The wind had dropped to a breeze. It seemed like a miracle as Leonie saw a faint light filtering through the tree canopy. She stared upwards through it to see a yellowish moon shy clear of swirling clouds to cast a wavering light.

Clyde pointed out some stars. 'We're headed in the right direction. Now you two, keep your eyes peeled for those fallen telegraph wires.'

***

Ruth awoke from a horrible dream as her heart gave a sickening lurch. She couldn't see a thing, the room was in total darkness. Slipping off her bed she stared about and slowly some light entered her consciousness and she saw pale brightness through chinks in the blinds. Why were the windows covered up? A sense of doom overcame her and it took several agitated moments to heave on her canvas boots and button them up.

Gradually, her mind focussed. She remembered lying down on her bed fully dressed to take a few winks after lunch. Her heart beat fast. The house was ominously silent. 'Molly, Molly!' she called, her voice loud in her ears. There was no response.

A little tremor had her on tip toes running over to the door. She opened it a crack and gave a start, breathing in the reek of cinders. She saw dirt piled up along the skirting boards. Something awful must have occurred. Where was everyone? She caught sounds from outside; animal squeals and dogs barking. Her heart began to pound. Terrified the creaking above her head meant the roof was about to crash in, she flew out through the door onto the veranda. The sight which greeted her failed at first to register, till fear for her brother got her dashing down steps into the yard. All was devastation, worse than her bad dream.

She stared wildly about at the hens clucking and flapping amongst fallen timber, uprooted shrubs and twisted wire netting. The air choked with grit. 'Sebastian!' she called, her sharp cry echoing about the gloomy place. She took a ragged breath filled with the smell of burning as the sound of piglets screaming and squealing filled her ears.

Ruth never knew how she rallied. She would come to believe that dear Bertram sent the huge swell of strength to power her actions as she stumbled over debris to the pig pens. She clenched her mouth shut against rising nausea. The sow was dead, its head cleaved in two by a piece of corrugated tin. Swamped with blood, her piglets danced frantically about the sow's swollen body, screaming with fear. Tears flooded her eyes and without a thought save to comfort them she gathered her skirts, climbed over and squeezed into the pen.

Clutching two of the squealing piglets under each arm, she was standing with her arms bloody with gore and filth streaking her gown when Ned Bullen galloped in on horseback.

'My God!' he bellowed. 'Mrs Fox!' Leaping off his horse he scrambled over the debris to her side. 'My dear lady, are you all right?' he asked, his face stunned with dismay. 'Here, let me…' he removed the tiny creatures from her arms.

'The poor little mites,' she cried. 'Whatever can I do?' His forthright manner calmed her even as she noted his sweaty, grimy face and realized he'd had a hard ride.

'Don't fret now, we'll get them all into the kitchen. They'll soon recover.'

'Where's my brother? Oh, it's so dreadful!' Her voice was strained as she gazed about. Dusk was falling and darkness sudden.

'Yes, a bad dust storm all right. Mr Grant will be up on the hills with the workers, salvaging the harvest,' he reassured her. 'Now come along in, won't you? Where's that maid? We'll get her to make tea, Mrs Fox.'

***

Leonie's breath left her body. On arrival in moonlight at Sebastian's farm she was reminded of a Cornish tin mining community she'd once visited with Uncle Bertram. The same grittiness hung on the air as on that hot summer day in Cornwall where everything lay coated with thick dust. The Reverend had been anxious to assess the deprivation those folk suffered and to organise charitable relief.

Sitting up behind Adam on his horse all this flashed through her mind. She fastened onto the memory and tried to drive out the scene which lay before her. There was silence, unlike the Devon villages where life continued against a background of noise and activity. It was uncanny, the lack of familiar sounds; the ring on iron at the blacksmith's; the moo of cows and the lively exchange of banter as people went about their work.

It was impossible to blank out the present. Her stomach squeezed with fright. 'Where are they?' she cried. 'Where are my aunt and Sebastian?' She saw the barn roof sagged, buckled like a dented can; corrugated tin sheets and planks with broken bits of machinery and split bags of meal littered the yard. Her sight riveted on a stream of red liquid escaping a barn.

Adam was helping her down from the horse. There was a catch in his voice as he said, 'Don't imagine the worst. They'll be safely inside the house.'

Clyde looked at the red stream of liquid seeping from the barn as they tethered the horses to the veranda rail. 'Don't be afraid, Leonie. That's red wine spilled there. The vats must have split.' He shook his head. 'What a waste.'

Despite these reassuring words she shivered, the hairs prickling the back of her neck. Something was amiss. The farm looked deserted in the eerie light. As her sight adjusted she saw utter devastation. 'What's happened,' she cried. 'Where is Mr Grant?'

Suddenly Molly appeared on the veranda, her words incoherent.

Clyde quickly made his way to her. 'Tell me, where is Mr Grant? Is he here?'

'No, sir, he went off on his horse,' she said, mopping her face with a dirty apron. 'There's some strong tea on the hob…'

'Is my aunt safe?' Leonie demanded.

'Oh yes, miss. Mrs Fox is… Mrs Fox is a saint!' she burst out. 'She's asleep in her room.'

It was such a surprising outburst that even as relief swept in, Leonie's mind floundered to make sense of it.

'I'll rub down the horses and get them watered. The men will want help out here,' Adam said, nodding in the direction of the storage barn.

Clyde beckoned the maid to lead the way as, guided by the sound of men's voices, Leonie hurried after them towards the kitchen. Two men, one of them Ned Bullen, stood by a rough wooden table. The other had tied a rag around his head over pale, straggly hair. She watched Clyde hold out his hand.

'Clyde Ferguson, Highland Light Infantry,' he announced. 'I've escorted Miss Grant back from the city. What a dreadful business this is.'

'Honoured to meet you, sir. Ned Bullen, foreman here.' Ned clasped Clyde's hand and smiled at Leonie. 'This big fellow came for the harvest,' he explained, turning to the other man.

'Arni,' the worker introduced himself. His voice was guttural. 'Bad, very bad.' He pulled out chairs for them.

Leonie and Clyde remained standing. She saw Arni's red rimmed eyes; his face ingrained with dirt and, with a start, realized hers must look the same. 'But my aunt,' she pursued, a tic throbbing in her neck, 'is she really all right?'

'Mrs Fox is hunky dory, if you'll pardon the expression Leonie,' Ned replied, his mouth twitching.

What an odd thing to say. 'I'll have tea later,' she said, keen to go right away to see how her aunt was. As she crept up to her aunt's door and hesitantly turned the knob the men's voices faded. The little creak when she eased open the door got her heart pumping as she stepped into her aunt's darkened room.

***

Waiting until Leonie had left, Ned voiced his feelings. His lips were tight. 'Yes, it's disaster all right. The men have been working through the night. We won't need any extra barrels now.' He heaved a sigh and shook his head, 'Sebastian – Mr Grant, put his heart and soul into this place.'

Clyde noted Ned's familiarity with his boss and recalled there was no class differential in Australia; all men were equal. He guessed it harked back to a time when they had to rub along together or perish.

'What hope for saving any of the harvest now?' Clyde asked. His face was grim as he took two of the mugs of brown tea being passed around. 'I'll take one of these out to my friend,' he explained. 'Adam Mallory's with the horses. We met up by chance *en route*.' He shook his head. 'His knee's in bad shape, not helped by the ride. Best he stays on here at the farm for a while.'

Ned touched Clyde's arm. 'There's worse news,' he muttered. 'One of the Abo fellows rode in just now. Fire is spreading down from the north. We're taking a quick breather then going up to search for the boss.'

Arni shook his head and stood up, shuffling his feet, anxious to set off.

'I'll be back in a moment,' Clyde said. 'Just taking this tea outside to my friend.'

Arni was packing a saddle bag when he returned. Noting his square jaw and his neck thick as an ox's, his big rough hands, Clyde guessed this giant of a man was Prussian stock.

'How long has Mr Grant been gone?' Clyde's features were shadowed but his voice was firm.

Arni spoke up. 'Left about noon. Karl's ridden off to fetch the doctor from Hahndorf.'

So, they suspected the worst. His reply sent a spasm of pain through Clyde as he brooded that hard working, self-reliant Sebastian didn't deserve any of this. 'I'm riding with you to search for him,' he stated, 'no point in me getting scrubbed up.'

Ned grabbed his felt wide-awake hat off a peg. 'We could be in need of Arni's strength,' he muttered. He called to the maid who was somewhere out in the scullery. 'Where's Rita, Molly?'

The maid came to the doorway, wiping her hands on her apron. 'Gone walkabout,' she said with a frown. 'Rita's one of them Abo people. Lives in the shack behind the barn,' she explained for Clyde's benefit.

For a few moments Ned looked lost and then shaking his head said, 'Well I suggest you try and rustle up hot soup for everyone. We'll welcome that when we return with the boss.'

The alacrity with which Arni drew himself up smart would have done credit to the parade ground and Clyde nodded approvingly. 'Is there a fresh horse? Mine's fair whacked,' he said.

Soon, the three men on horseback were riding hard uphill. To anyone staring up from the farm they'd have looked like stiff card shapes etched against the dim skyline. An oily yellow moon cast a fractured light over them. The horses displayed trained skill on the hazardous trail, jumping over wreckage and felled trees. All three men had strips of cloth tied around their necks and mouths since the chilly night air swirled with heavy clouds of dust.

Anger filled Clyde's chest as he saw first hand the destruction of Sebastian's livelihood. Rows of uprooted vines staggered all over the place like old men on sticks. He trailed behind the other two riders as leaving the slopes they climbed higher to a grassy plain. A few eucalyptus trees dotted a wide expanse, some standing straight in defiance of the elements. A stony track wound around a hill, worn by grazing cattle. They rode on, gaining higher ground, and on either side lay areas of burnt scrub. The wind got up, sending grit and soil flying about them.

'Black fellas,' Ned shouted, coming alongside Clyde. 'Abos.' He wasted no words. 'Burn the bush, clear it regular then everything grows back fresh.'

'Interesting,' Clyde managed as they galloped fast along a track. He caught the smell of tobacco and tea on Ned's breath. Suddenly an acrid smell twitched his nostrils – burning vegetation. But, he sensed, not intentional this time!

'Sebastian would've gone up this way to check the horizon.' Ned pointed ahead.

They all scanned the surrounds, checking for signs of Sebastian. The track now narrowed and forced them single file. Up front, Arni suddenly reined in hard and the others shortened their reins, the horses' heads jerking up as they took the pull.

'Hear that?' Arni shouted back.

Straining his ears, Clyde heard a faint crackling sound coming and going as the wind swished about in gusts.

'B...!' Ned yelled. 'Bloody fire – coming this way!'

'Damn and blast!' Curses fell from Clyde's mouth. We've got to find him!' He clenched his teeth.

'Right on. Blow that whistle, Arni!'

Arni blew three sharp notes, followed by a three second break, then three more loud blows of the whistle, and kept up this routine as they all moved steadily on and peered about them. The crackling grew louder, accompanied by crashing noises. Showers of sparks exploded a hundred feet high to light up the sky. Ned reckoned the fire was less than a mile off and leaping fast towards them. Soon, red hot cinders blew about the scared horses, setting fire to the tinder-dry grass at their feet so the horses baulked and tossed their heads.

For a brief spell, a mental image of battle flew into Clyde's head: the three of them like Boer farmers, bravely fighting off the might of the advancing Red Coats. He was astonished when one of his dreaded 'episodes' failed to materialize and Ned's Aussie voice placed him firmly back in the present.

'Can't go no further,' Ned muttered, and leaning back he yelled for all his worth, 'Sebastian you dog! Where are you?'

A few yards ahead, Arni raised an arm.

'What's up, cobber?'

'Some'at over there.'

Their sight was keener than Clyde's in this terrain but a surge of fear swept into his belly. *Please God*, he prayed, *let Sebastian be alive*, aware that this unassuming man was terribly important to him. Leaping down from his saddle he walked his horse over to the others. Shocked to the core, he stared down.

Sebastian lay in a crumpled heap. Swiftly Clyde dragged the rug off his horse and knelt down to throw it over his friend's body. Ned was on the other side, his ear pressed to Sebastian's chest. Blood oozed from a huge gash which ran from Sebastian's temple to his chin. Quickly Clyde extracted a tin from his belt, forced it open and took out a roll of lint wrapped in brown paper. 'Emergency medical stuff, issued to us in South Africa,' he said, tearing off the paper. 'Shortage of medics in battle, have to deal with casualties oneself.' He knew Sebastian's chances were slim, lying out here first in the midday heat and now in the night chill which struck through your bones. The two men watched as Clyde dabbed his fingers with alcohol and pressed them gently to the gash before swiftly winding the bandage diagonally over his friend's head and fixing it securely.

'Well done, mate!'

They heard a low moan escape Sebastian's mouth. Clyde pulled his flask from an inside pocket and passed it to Ned. 'Try to get a few drops of brandy down his throat.'

But Sebastian's mouth was clamped shut.

'He's a fair bit crook.' Ned reflected the Aussie habit of keeping cool and playing down danger. 'Can't leave him here or he'll catch his death.'

Arni knelt and raised Sebastian's head in his large hands while Ned held the flask to his boss's cracked lips. They stayed firmly shut.

A desperate surge charged through Clyde. 'Come on Sebastian old man! Drink the bloody stuff! Remember that Chinese place, that fiery drink we downed?'

'B... me!' All three men exploded with oaths as Sebastian's lips parted and Ned tipped the brandy down the sick man's throat, making him cough and splutter.

'Good on you mate!' Ned grinned up at Clyde. 'Let's get him down home. Dante won't be far from his master; Arni'll catch him.' He unfastened a drag stretcher attached to straps on his horse. The animal stood stock still as Ned released some buckles and shook out what Clyde saw was a large piece of leather strung between two poles.

'Bullock hide; tough enough to carry a bull.'

Arni returned with Dante. Clyde watched with approval as with skilled hands the two men competently fixed the contraption between their two horses.

'Best if you ride back to the farm behind Dante,' Ned instructed Clyde. 'Arni and I will be slower with this slung between us. If the doctor's arrived warn him what's happened, eh?'

Another understatement, Clyde realized. These men from the outback were the very best and he prayed the fire wouldn't overtake them. It was a new experience, taking orders, and he listened attentively as Ned explained another task, his voice calm despite the noise of the fire raging within half a mile of them.

'Yes, I'll go fast,' Clyde agreed. A quiver of apprehension ran through him. Was this the last time he'd see his good friend alive? 'I'll ride back with the doctor fast as the clappers and meet you *en route*,' he told them firmly.

Arni gave Dante a big whack to set him going. 'Mind how you go, sir!'

'The name's Clyde; and God be with you!' Clyde shouted. He dug his heels into his horse's flanks and drove him hard, chasing back down the route they'd come, behind Dante's pounding hooves.

Chapter Twenty

The candle on her aunt's dressing table sent a wavering beam over the bed and Leonie gasped. Two tiny piglets nestled in the eiderdown beside her, their stomachs gently rising and falling as they snored contentedly.

Leonie's head swam. She ran softly from the room, closed the door and dashed along the passage to the scullery. It was well into the small hours of the morning but she could hear the maid still working. 'Molly!' she cried as she flew into the outhouse, 'My aunt's gone mad. Whatever's she doing?'

The sturdy girl was up to her armpits in suds, scrubbing clothes on the wash board. She stopped and cast Leonie a mischievous smile. 'Oh miss, what a lark! Mrs Fox been out there,' she nodded to the yard. 'She rescued some piglets. The poor old sow got her head cleaved in,' she said in a rush.

'She fetched pigs into her bedroom?' Leonie stared open-mouthed at Molly.

'True as the nose on my face! Mr Bullen, he came back from neighbours' and found her with them. Oh dear, such a gory mess. But your aunt wouldn't get changed till she'd sat and fed the blessed things. Mr Bullen got some bottles and teats they wean newborn lambs with,' she said with a giggle. She began to scrub the clothes again. 'I'm dashed if I'll get all the blood and pigswill out of Mrs Fox's clothes.'

Leonie tried to grasp what Molly said. Aunt Ruth was a stickler for cleanliness and always conducted herself in a proper fashion. What in the world had changed her? Her pulse throbbed as an idea took hold – something to do with Ned Bullen. That must be it! Things must have moved along swiftly without her niece's help. In dire need of a wash, Leonie slid a large pan under a tap in the wall. 'Cold will do,' she insisted as Molly turned to the hob for a kettle of hot water. 'You'll need that for the soup. I'll come and give you a hand to make it as soon as I've changed.'

Wearing a pair of green pantaloons topped by a thick cotton smock, Leonie hurried back to the kitchen. Her emotions were all jumbled up. What had happened to Sebastian? He'd become terribly important to her. She pressed her arms to her sides as fear opened a dark pit in her mind. What if he'd had a fatal accident? She thrust the thought away but unsettling images swirled in as she imagined the worst. A little chill caught her about the heart. How would she and Aunt survive here without him?

Taking deep breaths she fixed her mind upon Adam and instantly warm, comforting feelings chased away dark thoughts. She fought the urge to rush out and find him in the barn, knowing it was necessary for her to provide sustenance for the men. They'd be returning soon, exhausted. Hot soup would restore them all.

She stood for a moment, deciding what tasty things went into a soup. Reaching up to a shelf she pulled down a big copper pan and dragged it under a tap and then filled it half way up. 'Molly? Could you please come? I need help to carry it.' Padding into the scullery with a wicker basket, she peered into the vegetable bins and grabbed a pile of carrots, turnips, onions and potatoes. Hunting for salt and pepper, she dislodged a pile of wooden objects – little wooden blocks; a baby's first toys. Hastily, she shoved them out of sight as Molly appeared. They must belong to Rita.

'I've hung up Mrs Fox's clothes in the outhouse. Oh I do fancy those pantaloons,' Molly said cheekily. She saw Leonie busy working. 'I'll chop them veggies.' Molly's mouth opened in a huge yawn behind her hand.

'No. I'll manage. You go off to bed and snatch some sleep.'

'Are you sure?' Molly tried to hide another yawn. 'I'll carry the pan to the stove.'

'After that you go. You'll need to be awake again in a short while.'

Left alone, Leonie set to chopping and stirring and before long tantalizing aromas filled the kitchen.

She waited for it to simmer and then, exhausted, flung herself down in the large chair by the settle to await the men's return. She must have dropped off when the creak of the outside door opening shook her awake. Adam stood on the threshold, his eyes wide with surprise.

'Adam!' she cried. 'Oh, you do look done in. Come and have some soup.' She was up on her feet, running to the stove.

'I thought I'd strayed into a harem!' Adam exclaimed with a laugh as he glanced at Leonie's odd dress. 'Instead of which I find beautiful Cinderella dreaming by the stove. No, no thank you. I'll eat later, Leonie dear. I'm absolutely filthy – I've just come in to scrub myself down in the scullery.'

Leonie's heart flipped. Even looking a shambles, Adam's charm fetched heat coursing through her and her face, already warmed by the stove, felt fiery hot. 'There's a kettle of hot water out there.' She turned away, aware of being so near to him and on her own. As he disappeared to the outhouse she busied about the kitchen and the clatter of rummaging for bowls, forks and spoons helped ease her tension. It was as if a fragile cord linked her with Adam; a cord that might gently pull… She stiffened as sounds of a commotion outside reached her. Adam came quickly into the kitchen, his face clean, shirt buttons undone, rubbing his damp hair with a towel.

'It's the men,' she said urgently. 'They're back.'

They stood for a moment and gazed into one another's eyes, their unspoken thoughts heavy with emotion. To Leonie it seemed they were imprinting themselves, one onto the other, before they both turned and dashed outside. *Please let Sebastian be safe and well*, she prayed. Dawn had broken and shafts of sunlight stretched with yellow talons, picking out the wreckage in the yard. Her heart drummed in her ears and it took a moment before the group of men made sense. 'Sebastian!' she cried, stumbling towards the men. She saw them releasing straps which secured a primitive sled slung between two of the horses.

'Your uncle's all right,' Clyde called to her. 'He's just knocked out.'

'Easy does it then.' Clyde and Ned's arms strained as together with Arni they lowered the contraption gently to the ground.

How calm and competent Clyde was, Leonie decided. Just the person you need in an emergency. 'It's a miracle you've found Uncle and brought him home,' she said quietly.

'A blessing that bush fire changed course, or it might've been a bit ticklish,' Ned said wryly. He indicated Clyde. 'Clyde rode to meet the doctor and bring him back here.'

Adam touched her shoulder. She inhaled carbolic soap on his clean skin as he whispered reassuringly, 'He'll be in good hands, you know.'

An elderly man holding a Gladstone bag and wearing a dusty black frock coat bent down to check Sebastian's pulse as Leonie wobbled over a plank to get near. The doctor must be used to dealing with this kind of accident out on isolated farms, she comforted herself.

Fatigue slowed Clyde's voice. 'Sebastian's been hurt but don't be alarmed, Leonie. He'll recover, the doctor assures us.'

'Sorry circumstance to make your acquaintance, Miss Grant.' The doctor stood up and held out his hand.

'However can I thank you enough for riding out in this awful storm?' Her voice cracked. 'Is he very sick? He will recover, won't he?' Her words faded.

'Mr Grant's a strong man; kept himself fit by the look of him.' The doctor stroked his pointed beard and consulted his pocket watch.

She knelt in the dirt beside her uncle. The part of his face not bound by a bloodied bandage was grey as dust. 'Dear Sebastian, please hold on.' She leaned over and kissed the top of his head and smelled soot in his hair. 'Please everyone, go into the house and take a glass of brandy and some soup,' she insisted, getting to her feet. 'There's broth on the simmer in the kitchen.' She gave them a wan smile. 'I'm really so grateful to you all.' Seeing Clyde's taut face, his eyes sunk with tiredness, she murmured, 'Thank you; you've been wonderful, Clyde.' She caught Adam's glance as she touched Clyde's arm affectionately.

'I'll go and see to the horses,' Adam said.

Surely he couldn't still think she was more attached to Clyde? Leonie led the way as, carrying the improvised stretcher with the unconscious man, the troop entered the house and shuffled along the passage to Sebastian's bedroom.

***

Leonie perched on a chair beside Sebastian's bed and focussed her sight on the doctor as he wrote his notes. He took little slurps of the tea which Molly had brought on a tray, snapping the Bath Oliver biscuits into pieces and chomping them noisily. The doctor had assured her that Sebastian's injuries were not serious. She watched him place his old-fashioned black hat at his feet and the sight of a grass stalk sticking up in his wispy hair was Leonie's undoing. Bubbles of mirth overcame her.

'Happens with shock,' the doctor looked up, a stern expression furrowing his brows. 'People can't help grinning – unfortunately I see it often.' Rustling amongst his potions he produced a small packet. 'Take these, Miss Grant. They're to calm the nerves; you'll need to gather your strength to look after Mr Grant.'

She took a grip of herself. 'Thank you, Doctor. I'm most obliged. I'll go and take one straight away.'

Halting by her aunt's door, Leonie knocked and entered. Ruth was sitting up in bed. 'Thank God you've got here safely,' she cried. She mouthed the words, 'Was that Sebastian? Is he all right?' She slipped out of bed, throwing a wrap over her night gown. 'I must see him! Tell me he's not been...' The words choked.

Leonie rushed to her and flung her arms about the thin body. 'He's going to be well very soon. Just a nasty cut on his head knocked him out. The doctor's looking after him.'

Her aunt seemed to have taken for granted that she'd arrived back at Corrimony, Leonie thought with surprise. Maybe her whole life had been changed in some way.

As Ruth sank down on her bed, the piglets scrambled up and squealed. 'Aren't they adorable? The poor little orphans.' She turned and lifted one up. 'Back to the scullery, my young friends. A lady's boudoir is not for you!'

'Oh Aunt,' Leonie grinned and wrinkled her nose. 'Molly told me how you saved them.'

'Yes, yes. Now I think I'd better attend to my toilet and dress myself quickly, don't you? What's been happening? However did you get here?' Scarcely waiting for a reply, she added, 'Perhaps you'll get Molly to find a basket and blankets and put them near the stove.' She began to pour water into her wash basin.

Leonie hovered, trying to think how best to tell Ruth that Clyde Ferguson was here. Then, aware of the urgency, she said quickly, 'If it hadn't been for Captain Ferguson, I wouldn't be here.'

She saw her aunt give a start. Ruth turned around, her frightened expression sending shivers down Leonie's spine. 'Whatever is it, Aunt? Why does he scare you?'

With relief, she watched Ruth's face relax. A hint of a smile lifted her mouth as she murmured, 'So be it. The time has come.'

***

For some time Sebastian had been aware of a buzzing noise, like a swarm of locusts. The sound rose and fell, irritating, spoiling his dreams and dragging him unwillingly back to reality. A tremor ran through him. He tried to speak but nothing came and he clenched his teeth as that persistent noise echoed like the wind through a gulley. His arm lashed out and knocked the bedside table over and then clarity shot in.

'He's come around.' It was a stranger's voice.

'Thank heavens.' A female this time.

Scratchy, scuffling around his bed.

'I've picked it all up.'

Sebastian feigned sleep as he heard the table replaced. A rasping voice he couldn't place said authoritatively, 'He's over the worst; should heal with a good rest. I'll be on my way now.'

Next came an urgent, familiar, masculine voice.

Sebastian's heart beat against his ribs. Clyde? That was Clyde! How the dickens was he here? There were too many riddles. Where was Ruth? Why was he lying in bed? Cold sweat chilled his body, his mind a worried jumble.

The rasping-voiced fellow again. 'I don't foresee any complications. Perhaps better to get him away from seeing all this…'

'That's something been concerning me,' Clyde replied slowly.

Get him away? Unease swept through the sick man, prickling the hairs at the nape of his neck. Why couldn't he stay in his home with his sister?

Footsteps creaked from the room.

All kinds of fears flooded Sebastian's brain. Was his house in danger of collapsing? With a jolt, his brain cleared and he relived that violent dust storm hurtling down like all creation before oblivion blocked it out. The harvest! A picture of ripened grapes entered his head. For God's sake! Was he ruined? That was what those voices implied. He struggled, trying to push off the tight bedclothes to no avail. A huge, helpless sigh filled his chest as pain needled his head. Waiting for it to subside, he cautiously raised his hand to the bandage. Behind his closed eyelids he saw hills of heather and heard the pleasant trickle of a mountain stream as he drifted back into darkness.

***

Leaving the doctor's medicine in her room, Leonie scampered to the kitchen. Savoury smells made queasiness coil inside her. She saw a big hornet buzzing giddily about the stove. She hurried outside and the heat of day spread through her body as she scuffed her way through the debris, anxious to find Adam. A lizard's beady eyes fixed upon her before it slid under a broken barrel. She paid no notice to splinters or the nail which gouged her leg. Nor did she notice the stifling, dusty air which came with each breath. The stench of rancid straw and manure hit her as she entered through the heavy stable door. 'Adam. Adam, are you there?' Desperately afraid he might have left, her voice quavered in that lofty place.

'Yes, I'm over here, Leonie.'

Relief swept through her as she spotted Adam in a far corner tending a horse. Her head filled with delight at the sight of his familiar fair hair flopping over his brow. Then she saw him put one foot in the stirrup, ready to mount. Moving towards him she heard the shuffle of hooves, caught a whiff of dobbin and as her mind dizzied she lost her footing and tripped. Adam leapt down and, unable to stop, she fell against him. 'You were leaving without saying goodbye!' she said fiercely, pushing at his chest.

'Not by choice.' Adam spoke ruefully. 'Wish I could stay, but I've got to return this horse and report to the ship.' He nodded. 'Clyde has more right to be here than I. Tell me,' he hesitated, 'is he someone special to you, Leonie?'

'Clyde's a fine person and I have high regard for him; but he's not special in that particular way. Does that answer your question?'

Adam shook his head quickly from side to side. 'Damn it! I'm all churned up. What am I to think? I can't just leave you like this. Leonie, Leonie my dearest, don't you see?' He held out his hands diffidently. 'I love you so desperately. I'm terrified you don't return my feelings.'

Her heart felt fit to burst as she stepped forward and took his hands. Her voice shaky, she murmured, 'Please, hold me close, Adam. I love you back, truly I do! Oh, there's so little time.' There was a marvellous sense of belonging as he took her in his strong arms. She felt their heartbeats merge with a sharpening awareness of one another.

'Oh dear love, I knew this was meant to be. Will you wait till I come back to you? I'm determined to try my luck here in Australia.'

So Adam wasn't going to stay in England! He was returning! 'Only if you don't delay for years till I'm old and bent double over my camera,' Leonie exclaimed delightedly. She flung her head back to gaze into his eyes. 'Promise me you'll come back very soon.'

'What – delay and miss more adventures?' Adam's grin stretched from ear to ear. 'Leonie, my dear love, we'll make such a good pair of idiots!'

His mirth excited her far more than serious words could ever do. Leonie's happy laughter rang out as she raised her arms and, leaning her head against his neck, felt a pulse throb under the warm skin.

'Are you sure? You really do care the same as I, dearest?'

'Darling Adam – ever since we met at Port Said.' She saw the quirky smile that first thrilled her in what seemed a lifetime away, as he tightened his arms about her waist. He ran a finger around her mouth and then very gently, lowered his lips to hers. She was vaguely aware that the horse neighed and stamped its hooves as a delightful sensation swooped in. Breathless, Leonie couldn't resist a quip. 'Oh, didn't I say?' She turned bright eyes to his face. 'There is some connection I should mention about Clyde.' She put on as straight a face as she could manage. She felt Adam flinch and hastened to add, 'Not in any romantic way. It's just an extraordinary coincidence: Clyde's father was my grandparents' landlord in Scotland.'

Adam's shoulders relaxed. 'Now that's quite astounding, isn't it? A strange thing indeed. Does your uncle know?' He smoothed back hair from her damp forehead.

'Oh yes. He and Clyde got to know each other in Sydney. That's why Clyde came here.'

'I didn't understand all that back during the storm. I was so concerned to protect you.' Changing the subject, he remarked, 'My father expects me to go into the city when I return home – join a banking firm. Ugh! I'd rather be here with you even if it means swilling out pig sties!'

'Oh Adam, dear Adam. Many a light-hearted word spoken in jest…'

And with that, they both burst out laughing.

'You won't ride off while I go and check on Sebastian? There's still some broth left. How is your leg? I'm very concerned you're not fit to ride yet,' Leonie gabbled.

'Leg's not bad. A bowl of your broth will sort it out. I'll wait in the kitchen for you. Please convey my good wishes to your uncle.' He reached out as she turned to leave and pulled her back. 'Just a moment; take my hand will you, and remember this vow.' He looked at her solemnly. 'You'll always be near me, however far the oceans part us.'

***

Clyde was in a small back room, kept prepared for those whose business meant an overnight stay.

There were matters to deal with before he could relax and take a nap. He'd ask Ned to get one of the men to ride down to Adelaide. The Andersons must be anxious about Leonie and to know how things were at Corrimony.

Quickly stripping to the waist, he picked up an urn of cold water and, ignoring the surface grime, poured it into the china bowl and dunked his head. His worries for Sebastian refused to go away. His friend had two broken ribs and extensive bruising. He'd find it hard to leave here until Sebastian recovered. Raising his head he shook it, spraying cold water about his body. For a few seconds he staggered about, feeling for the towel as water dripped down his bare chest. *Not much different to camping rough out in the Transvaal*, he thought with a wry grin; except there his orderly would be on hand to assist. He rubbed his short hair dry then lathered his chest with the bar of carbolic soap. Rinsed and refreshed, his mind focussed again on Sebastian. Thank God that old doctor proved nimble on horseback. He'd already ridden twenty-odd miles from Hahndorf. If they hadn't raced here Sebastian might have been a goner. Ned and Arni deserved a medal. They'd shifted obstacles by brute force to clear a way for the drag sled.

He shook his dusty shirt and then dressed again. Sipping the brandy Molly had provided, he smoothed his moustache. Mrs Fox and Leonie would have to care for a sick man. He frowned, knowing he must soon return to the *Britannic*.

Opening the wooden slats on the window he peered through. The wind had abated but the shadowy sun failed to lift the clouds of dust. Anxiety for Sebastian again pressed on Clyde's mind as he focussed his thoughts. He'd see Ned and discuss the most urgent job he could help with.

There was a tapping on the bedroom door. Thrusting it open, fearing Sebastian had taken a turn for the worst, he uttered a curt, 'Yes?' before he realized who it was. 'Oh, I beg your pardon, Leonie.'

Leonie took a step back. 'Clyde, it's me. My aunt asks would you please join us in Sebastian's room? She wishes to talk to us.'

Chapter Twenty One

The actual sequence of events that night remained confused. Leonie smelled the distinctive taint of Sal-volatile and iodine around Sebastian which would forever be connected with the amazing revelations she was still trying hard to absorb. The chemical smells of chlorine and bromide transported her back to the past, to memories of working beside Uncle Bertram in their old dairy in Devon, developing their photographs.

Clyde drew up three chairs beside Sebastian's bed; one for Ruth, another for Leonie and one for himself. Ruth acknowledged Clyde with a nod. Why had Aunt requested the three of them here? Leonie waited as she passed on Adam's good wishes but received no response.

Ruth sat clutching her journal, her face a blank slate. Leonie's heart thumped in her breast. The air seemed to quiver about them with portent. She heard Clyde speaking to her uncle, explaining his accident. 'You were caught out in the dust storm; a nasty kick from your horse. A few days' rest, the doctor says, and you'll be right as rain. Ned Bullen's a fine man, by the way,' he added. 'Just the sort I could do with in my battalion.'

Ruth interjected and her comment caught Leonie by surprise. 'Yes, I find Ned a wonderful support,' she said, her cheeks growing pink.

'What about the vines?' Sebastian asked hoarsely.

'Not all lost. Ned reports there's still quite a fair crop. No sense fretting now. Here, drink this, my friend, it'll do you good.'

Sebastian pushed away the water glass. 'The outbuildings – are my workers all safe?'

'No one's reported a mishap.'

'Dante? He's not been put down?' Sebastian's voice cracked.

'No, certainly not. The fine fellow led me all the way back here to fetch the doctor.'

With a deep sigh, Sebastian sank back on his pillows.

Ruth suddenly stuttered. 'I've got things to say… awful things to tell.' Her mouth trembled as emotion got the better of her. 'Can you bear to listen? I can't keep silent any longer.'

They all stared at her.

Leonie saw her aunt's eyes flicker like a scared cat and she placed an arm around her shoulder. 'It can't be that bad, Aunt. Whatever it is, it's better to tell us; never good to bottle things up.' She spoke gently and felt Ruth's slight frame shudder.

'Thank you, Leonie. Oh, my dear child; I pray you'll not reject me!' Tears filled her eyes as she turned to Sebastian. 'I shall need your forbearance and understanding, dear brother.'

Her pleading words speared Leonie's brain. 'There's nothing you say that will ever make you lose our love.'

Clyde had propped Sebastian up with pillows.

'Get on with it then, sister,' Sebastian urged. A half smile of encouragement leaked from the bandage which half concealed his face. 'Come now, a dose of something strong will help us all. The glasses are in that cupboard. Would you please pour the brandy Clyde?'

'But the doctor said…'

'Confound the doctor's good intentions. I say a brandy is called for!'

They waited until each of them held a brimming glass.

Leonie's gaze fixed upon Ruth and for a fleeting moment she saw an outline of a stranger, a kind of double image quivering about the familiar person. She shook her head and it dissolved. Ruth looked aged; her face sagged. But her eyes were soft with love as she turned to Leonie. 'You, dear, deserve to hear this first.'

A twist of apprehension tightened Leonie's throat. What more could there be?

Startled, she watched Ruth down her brandy in one gulp; so she barely took in the stuttered words which followed. 'I shall have to bear your condemnation. Oh, it's been such a long, cruel time.' Ruth's knuckles glowed alabaster white as she gripped her journal.

No one spoke; just the faint clink of glass as they all placed their empty brandy glasses on the marble-topped table.

Ruth gave a nervous cough.

A pulse ticked in Leonie's neck; fearful but unable to guess what was coming. The air in the room was suddenly heavy, weighing her down.

Ruth fumbled with her journal; then suddenly, with a catch in her voice, her words tumbled out. 'Beloved Leonie, I beg your forgiveness.' She stopped and stared wildly about. 'It was me the laird raped… Oh, Leonie dear. You are my natural child,' she cried. 'It's out at last.'

It felt as if every fibre ripped from Leonie's body. Noises shrilled in her head. How could it be? Aunt was… her mother? A hundred tiny incidents fought for space and burst with insight. She fought to control her mind and was aware of pressure around her shoulders as Clyde put his arms about them.

Ruth sat motionless. 'I must finish,' she croaked as though she dare not stop; 'explain why I tried to distance myself from you, my dear child, unwilling to accept you as part of my flesh and blood. Born out of shame, you see.' She choked back the words. 'But I could never deny a mother's natural love.'

It was Sebastian whose firm words diffused the moment. 'My dear, dear, Ruthie,' his voice broke in. 'Why ever didn't you share your secret with me? God! If I'd known I'd have come back and strung the brute up!' He reached out for Leonie's and Ruth's hands. 'Please don't fret. I'm overjoyed Leonie is your daughter. My God! We're the same loving family as we were.'

While Leonie took comfort from his words, anxiety curled inside her, still fearing the stigma of her birth might alter Adam's feelings.

'There's more,' Ruth whispered. 'Shall I go on?'

Leonie's world seemed to shrink into a tiny hard nugget. Bewildered, she murmured, 'Yes... do.' Deep down, her heart began to ache for the suffering of that frightened young girl who'd been raped.

Clyde's words of support came quickly. 'I'm here for you all when needed, but I'll leave the family to talk of these private disclosures.'

'No, please stay!' Ruth raised her voice. She reached out and touched Clyde's arm. 'You will soon know why.' She turned to her brother. 'Are you strong enough for this, my dear?'

Sebastian nodded, his face scarlet, but whether with fever or shock, she couldn't tell. 'Yes of course, Ruthie. Come on, get it all out.' He took another gulp of brandy.

'I want you to try and understand my dilemma. How was I to resolve my feelings for a child born to me of savage rape? Oh my dearest Leonie, I beg your forgiveness. From the bottom of my heart I'm ashamed of all the sham and deceit. But would you have been happier had you known the truth?' She didn't wait for a reply but hurriedly went on. 'Be prepared, please, for another horrible shock, all of you.' She hesitated. 'You see, I was just fifteen years old when the laird Osmond MacLeod, my parents' landlord, took advantage of me. So, you know who sired you Leonie… under circumstances too painful to relate.'

For a few seconds the room stilled.

Then a deep groan filled the space. 'Monster, I damn you to hell!' Clyde's curse broke the spell. 'Osmond MacLeod was my father, but in name only. Given half a chance I'd have killed the loathsome beast that tormented my own mother with my bare hands.' Turning to Ruth, his face distraught, he pronounced, 'Dear Mrs Fox. I'm so terribly sorry. He was an evil brute.'

'Come here,' Sebastian pulled his sister towards him. Ruth dropped her head on his chest.

Leonie's mind hurtled back down the years. She found she could now make sense of all Ruth's unpleasant snips. She grasped Ruth's fear that her child had inherited that odious man's traits. Leonie's breathing was tight.

'My dear one,' Ruth whispered, sitting up and reaching for Leonie. It was as though she read Leonie's mind. 'You have none of that man in you, I promise. Neither has Clyde. You are a Grant through and through, and I love you dearly.' The two females clasped one another.

Leonie felt Clyde's attention fix upon her and eased away. They stared at one another. Images shuffled in her head like a shutter which opened and clicked. Revelation hit them both. Her heart did a bolt. By nature's law, she was related to Clyde – his sister, then. Clyde was first to utter the words aloud. Eyebrows raised, he cried, 'Brother and sister, Leonie? Incredible! Wonderful!' His face radiated love as he held out his arms and Leonie fell into his embrace.

'It's unbelievable. I can't take it all in.' Leonie's mind danced away and she suddenly realized the pull of affection she felt for him. 'Thank God, Clyde, you weren't romantically inclined toward me, because I might have made a play for you!'

Their laughter eased the tension.

Clyde gathered Ruth and Leonie to him. 'Dear Mrs Fox…' he started to say.

Ruth interrupted him. 'My husband Bertram knew of this and he supported me. He came to stay with our parents in Scotland to do some fishing. My father, the ghillie, and Bertram became friends. Bertram was a saint. When the true facts of my child's birth were put before him, it made no difference to him wanting me for his wife. "I'm too old to start my own family," the Reverend Bertram Fox declared. "What a lucky man I am to find one ready made."'

At this revelation of how her life started in Devon, a great joy swept through Leonie. 'Oh, that's so wonderful,' she murmured.

'Another glass of brandy all round please, Clyde!' Sebastian instructed.

None of them declined.

With a heightened pitch, Ruth exclaimed, 'I'd like you both to call me Ruth in future. You are adults and I think "Mother" doesn't seem suitable after all these years.' She sank down on a wicker chair, the journal on her lap. 'Can you now appreciate my anguish when I discovered who Clyde was at dinner on board ship? Beside the fright that all this might come out, I was terrified that brother and sister might be attracted. When I saw you two together on Milson's Island I feared the worst. My distress at meeting Osmond MacLeod's son – I almost hoped to die. I believed God was paying me back for what I'd done.'

'What *you'd* done!' Their cry was unanimous. 'You weren't the guilty one!'

'Oh, but I'm afraid that's not so.' Ruth stared into the three faces which gazed fondly at her. 'I must now finish the story. I beg your forbearance.' She took a handkerchief from the sleeve of her blouse and blew her nose. 'It'll be easier for me to read from my journal,' she said quietly.

Deep down in Leonie's subconscious, blurred images struggled to the surface. She stared at Ruth as she slowly turned back the pages of her journal.

'I wrote this in a terrible state. You were already big inside me, Leonie dear.' She snuffled into her handkerchief. 'So you must understand it's a garbled entry. I was barely sixteen years of age when you were born.' Her lips trembled. 'Written from the heart, you might say.' She took a quivery breath and slowly began to read.

June, 1879.

I called out to the ravens, please, oh please help me! But they went on circling high above the elms and ignored my terror. The blue sky looked diluted – as if Cook had mixed it with milk. My heart thumped wildly as I tore along the edge of a field, my skirts catching the long grasses left by the reaper sending up clouds of pollen. He was almost upon me! My swollen belly jerked painfully up and down. How prettily the little birds sang in the hedgerows. In my terror I saw them flit between light and dark as I dashed by. But they can't save me, I sobbed. My heart lurched. The brute was close behind, his heat hot as the sun on my back. My face burned like a red hot poker as I reached the darkened forest, weak with fright. I raced to the place I'd marked; stopped short; felt the swish of hot air as he lunged for me with a lustful growl. Quick as greased lightning I stepped aside. My God! That horrible grinding clunk of metal jaws! Hellish shrieks... I couldn't move. Icy shivers slid down my spine. Oh, those ghastly bulging eyes! His flabby neck; raised blue veins. 'Save me!' he choked, before a fountain of blood spurted from his mouth.

Shock silenced them all. Leonie shuddered. A dense black shadow dropped over her brain. She watched Ruth's face and gleaned courage and defiance.

'I murdered your father, Clyde. You see, I remembered that old trap my father had set years before and forgotten – I thought it would just trap his leg...' She broke down and huge sobs racked her thin frame.

Leonie's cheeks were wet. She leaned down and gathered Ruth in her arms. 'How you've suffered!' And for the first time in her life she said, 'My poor, dearest mother.'

'You're a marvel, sister.' Sebastian kicked back the bedclothes and struggled from the bed. 'My dear, wonderful sister, that evil man blighted our parents' lives. I'm humbled by what you did for our family.' He joined them all in a clumsy hug, so they formed a close, loving ring. 'Something more,' he announced. 'Has it passed you all by? Ruth and I have gained a close member of the family – our nephew, Clyde, eh?' He fell back onto his bed. 'Come, let's clink to that!'

Leonie tried to anticipate how Adam would react. This would be like those sordid tales in *News of the World*. What if he couldn't ignore the urge to gain merit by reporting it…? What if he wanted nothing more to do with her! Then the sight of Ruth, more animated than she'd been for years, forced her to quell such thoughts.

'Now all of you pay attention,' Clyde said with mock severity. 'I've decided to buy myself out of the army and return to Australia. I'm not short of a penny. I've not only inherited the Scottish estate, but also a fair sum from my Devon guardians. I intend to transfer my inheritance from the Blair Athol estate and invest it here in Corrimony. No, hear me out,' he shook his head fiercely as Sebastian raised his hand in protest. 'I consider the Blair Athol estate belongs to your family by right. My parent treated yours abominably.' He turned to Ruth and said gently, 'You, more than anyone, are owed this at the very least.' He raised his glass again. 'To you, Ruth.' His smile was warm. He turned to Sebastian. 'Perhaps I'll start up in competition with you Sebastian,' he added with a chuckle.

Their exclamations, laughter and tears must have alerted Molly, for she appeared at the door. 'That young man of yours is beating his head waiting in the kitchen, miss.'

'Oh, I must go!' Leonie exclaimed, desperate to confide the revelations.

'What young man?' Ruth's utter relief at their response to her secrets lit up her face and fetched back a semblance of her youth.

Leonie's reply was impulsive. 'Don't be upset, Ruth dear. He's that reporter, Adam Mallory…'

'My goodness, child! However does he come to be here? Well now, you'd better not keep him waiting. Oh, do bring him in, won't you? We must renew our acquaintance.' She looked happier than anyone had seen her for years.

Sebastian grinned. Nothing must spoil this extraordinary moment.

***

'Molly said she heard laughter coming from your uncle's room. I hope that means he's recovering?'

'Quite over the worst, thank the Lord. Oh Adam, there's incredible revelations. Good and bad,' she added trying to keep calm, determined to be honest and not hold anything back. Adam raised his eyebrows.

'Stop teasing!' He placed an arm about her waist to draw her close as she slowly began to recount everything. When he tightened his embrace and displayed no adverse reaction to the nature of her birth, Leonie relaxed.

'What an amazing story; how ghastly for poor Mrs Fox having to conceal her terrible secret all these years.' He frowned. 'And for you, Leonie dearest, not to know she is your mother.' He shook his head in bewilderment before giving her a cheeky grin. 'Of course I'm more than pleased Clyde's turned out to be your brother. Got the wind up, thinking you and he might be more than good friends.' He placed a finger under her chin. 'You couldn't wish for a finer person as a *brother* than Clyde Ferguson,' he declared solemnly, 'especially as I long for you to be my wife.'

His proposal came without warning. She felt his lips press the top of her head and a joy so intense it swept away any doubt. Adam waited, an anxious smile hovering about his mouth.

'I accept with all my heart. But it's not that simple. What about your father? You said he refused your sister marrying because her fiancé was illegitimate.'

Adam broke in, 'It's a cliché and unfair, but men are treated differently. Besides, I've no qualms about resisting his authority.'

They stood close together in the kitchen. Domestic noises reached Leonie; voices in the yard; the clatter of horses' hooves and a cart brought in to clear the debris. She could scarcely breathe. 'It's all happening at once. I must be stupid, never to have guessed Ruth is my mother.'

'We sometimes blank out the truth, you know,' Adam said gently. 'Like you not suspecting how deeply I care for you.' He squeezed her hand.

'When I spotted you with your pretty cousin I jumped to conclusions; thought you were just flirting with me. Oh, Adam! It's much too soon to say goodbye. I don't know how I'll bear not seeing you for months.' Her forehead creased.

'You will be busy planning our wedding for my return. Perhaps you'll also take up Mr Kershaw's invitation for that short trip as well?'

Leonie's face brightened. 'You're right; I've lots of exciting things to do. I think I shall take up Mr Kershaw's offer. It will only be for a week or so and will really test my photography knowhow.'

'By the way,' Adam's tone was serious. 'I made up my mind about something when I was in Sick Bay aboard the *Britannic*.'

Leonie waited on tenterhooks, wondering what could possibly be coming.

Adam continued, 'I'll return the horse and take a train to Sydney – sort things out with my aunt, Lady Stratton. She'll be able to assist me in forwarding my resignation to *News of the World* in London. I'll also write to my father.' He straightened his back. 'I intend to set up as a publisher, here in Australia.' He paused as Leonie gasped with joy. 'My knowledge as a journalist persuades me there is a niche for a…' he drew his brows together in concentration, 'a lifestyle magazine. Expensive houses are shooting up all over Australian cities – people will need advice, be competing with one another with modern interiors.'

Leonie pressed her arms to her body as she strove to take this in. Her heart beat like the clappers, shortening her breath, firing her cheeks. He must have talked some more and she came back to earth to hear him say, 'I'll be in need of a professional photographer…' He reached for her willing hands. 'Will you consider my offer of the job, my love?'

Lost for words, Leonie clasped her arms about his waist.

'You'll write to me, won't you?' Adam's blue eyes reflected the love she felt for him. His finger entwined a tendril of chestnut hair as he pulled her into the pantry.

There, with only the shelves of cold glass jars, canned bully beef and sacks of dried pulses for witness, they clutched one another in a last, desperate embrace. When their lips met it seemed myriad flashing stars danced in Leonie's head. How could she bear to be parted? She buried her face in Adam's rough jacket and breathed in the essence of him. 'I will wait for you, my love.'

Adam held her gently away. 'I think I should speak to your family before I leave, don't you? I must ask for your hand.'

'Yes. My... mother, Ruth, asked to see you,' she said happily. 'I'll fetch my camera; take a picture of us all – a whole new happy family!'

***

Later, Leonie sat on a bale of straw in the yard and watched as Adam and Clyde prepared to leave. This time she took no snap but recorded every small detail to memory. She smiled. Adam had been welcomed by everyone into the family. Sebastian had said, 'Let us all hold hands and pray together; send up our thanks to the Lord.'

Leonie's smile was radiant, boosted by the plans they'd all made for their future in Australia together. She stayed close to Adam as he mounted his horse and leaned down to bid her farewell.

'We'll both return – sooner than you know!' Clyde called back.

An ache churned Leonie's stomach as Adam trotted out of the yard. When both men gained the track, Adam turned one last time then blew a kiss and waved before driving his horse into a canter to catch up with Clyde.

Leonie's heart drummed against her ribs and she continued to stare long, long after their tiny specks dissolved into the murky distance.

THE END

Acknowledgements

Thank you to my wonderful family for your endless patience and on-going support.

I owe a big thank you to Brixham Writers, whose professionalism and clear insight has been of enormous help to bring this book to completion.

And I am grateful to Endeavour Press for taking me on board.

This fictional story is based on an actual happening at the time of the Boer War. The idea came when I had sight of a *Military Gazette*, an account of the *Britannic*'s historic mission to Australasia which was written on board by the newspaper correspondent who travelled with the troops. On their return to Britain a copy of the *Gazette* was given as a memento to each of the troops who'd taken part.

The father of the elderly man who showed me the *Gazette* was one of the soldiers on board the *Britannic*.

Printed in Great Britain
by Amazon